Dear Grandma and Grandpa Janeiro,

Thank you for the shorts set and hat you sent for my birthday. I'll wear them when I visit Daddy in June.

I wish Mom could come with me, too, but I guess divorced people can't spend their vacations together. Daddy always makes me laugh, though, and Mom hasn't taken a vacation or laughed in a long time. I think she would have fun.

Please say hi to Uncle Manny and Aunt Michelle, and Uncle Mike and Aunt Augie and all the cousins. I hope I get to see you this summer.

Love,

Cara

Please address questions and book requests to: Harlequin Reader Service
U.S.: 3010 Walden Ave., P.O. Box 1325, Buffalo, NY 14269
CAN.: P.O. Box 609, Fort Erie, Ont. L2A 5X3

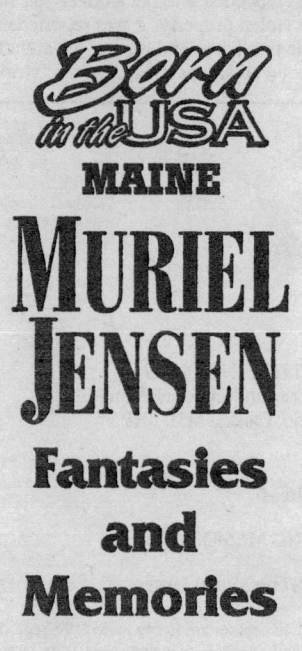

Born in the USA

MAINE

MURIEL JENSEN

Fantasies and Memories

Harlequin Books

TORONTO • NEW YORK • LONDON
AMSTERDAM • PARIS • SYDNEY • HAMBURG
STOCKHOLM • ATHENS • TOKYO • MILAN
MADRID • WARSAW • BUDAPEST • AUCKLAND

HARLEQUIN BOOKS
225 Duncan Mill Road, Don Mills,
Ontario, Canada M3B 3K9

ISBN 0-373-47169-6

FANTASIES AND MEMORIES

Copyright © 1987 by Muriel Jensen

Printed in U.S.A.

Dear Reader,

I'm so happy to see the reissue of *Fantasies and Memories*. This book is from very early in my career and is dear to me because it is composed of my own fantasies and memories.

I've always longed to visit Maine with its rocky coast, solitary lighthouses, snug harbors and homes and churches from another time. I was sure it was the perfect environment for love and romance.

Life has taken me to thirty other states, but never Maine. So I took it upon myself to indulge my fantasies and visit by gathering books from the library and setting a story there.

I tapped into my memories for the Portuguese background because my father, like Rafe, was the descendant of immigrants from the Azores. The *linguiça* and *malassadas* that Destiny is so fond of are sent to me regularly in Oregon by my sister, who still lives in New Bedford, Mass., where we were born. I think I enjoy the Portuguese food so much because the aroma and the taste bring back the love and warmth of my childhood.

I hope this story brings love and warmth to you.

Best!

Muriel Jensen

P.O. Box 1168
Astoria, Oregon 97103

To Albert E. Audette,
a New Bedford fisherman
who looks like a romance hero.
Thanks, Albie.

Chapter One

Rafe Janeiro lay stretched out on a chaise lounge, every muscle in his six-foot body relaxed. The early summer sun beat down on his bare chest and limbs, its hot rays producing a languor that bound him to the chaise. He felt the strain of running a multimillion-dollar corporation drain from him as his body began to realize it was on vacation.

Strange patterns danced across his closed eyelids, and the only thing that kept him from dozing off was the awareness of a growing thirst.

"You guys want a beer?" he asked lazily of his two brothers.

"Sounds good." The response came from Manny, who was lying on his back on the chaise at Rafe's right, a cigar clenched in the corner of his mouth.

"Mmm. Yeah," Mike agreed. He was partially reclined in a third chaise, a baseball cap over his face.

"Good," Rafe replied without opening his eyes. "It's on the third shelf in the fridge. Bring me one, too."

There was a moment's silence; then Mike, the youngest of the three, protested in an injured tone, "But you're our host. Getting the beer is your responsibility."

"I made breakfast."

"You opened a box of Grapenut Flakes."

"Still..."

Stretching, Mike arrived upon a solution. "Manny will get it. Won't you, Manny?"

"Surely you jest," Manny replied.

"No. I'm serious."

"Couldn't we send Joe?" At the mention of his name, the black Labrador retriever resting at the side of Rafe's chaise raised his head expectantly.

Rafe dropped a hand and ruffled the dog's ears. Then Rafe sat up with a dramatic groan and swung his legs over the side. "Did you ever see such malingering, Joe?" he asked of the dog. "Did you ever see such lazy, buckpassing...?"

"Hey, hey!" Manny objected, shading his eyes to look up at his brother. "What would you be doing now without your two slavey siblings who freeze their butts off in the winter catching fish on George's Bank while you're in some warm and comfortable boardroom turning the fish into profits?"

"I'd be enjoying the first week of my vacation alone," Rafe replied heartlessly.

"Aw!" Mike sat up, placing the baseball cap on his head. "I thought you liked our company. I thought having us around sort of lent color to your humdrum single existence.

"You were mistaken," Rafe said.

"But you're miles from nowhere!" Manny, too, sat up. "Here you are in the boonies of Digby Head, Maine, where you have to strain to hear a car buzz by on the interstate half a mile away, and the only other sound is birds."

"There's a lot to be said for quiet," Rafe pointed out dryly. Then he laughed as he studied his cigar-munching brother, who was two years younger than himself. Manny would never understand the need for quiet. He required noise, activity, excitement. An eight-year-old daughter, three sons under the age of seven and a wife who was a verbal and physical whirlwind were Manny's idea of paradise.

"You have your precious quiet eleven months out of the year," Mike said. "The first week of your vacation, you know you're deeply thrilled to have our company while our wives are relaxing at a spa and our children are farmed out to various grandparents." Mike gave his brother a coaxing smile. "Aren't you?"

"Deeply." Rafe replied without expression.

"I knew it." Mike got to his feet. "I'll get the beer. After all, I am the youngest. I keep forgetting that you're pushing forty. Why, you're probably suffering from arthritic pain, fighting against shortness of breath and other physical infirmities I'm far too sensitive to mention."

Rafe squinted at his brother. "You're going to be far too dead to mention them in a minute."

Mike shook his head in apparent dismay. "Age has certainly taken its toll on your disposition, as well as your body."

As Mike loped off toward the house, Manny and Rafe lay back. Joe squirmed under Rafe's chair, dozing off in its shade.

"We should have let the kid drown that summer at Horseneck Beach," Rafe said. To Rafe and Manny, who had fished together while their brother was still in grade school, Mike would always be 'the kid.'

"You're the one who went in after him," Manny corrected. "All I did was help you haul him onto the sand."

"If only I had known how he'd grow up."

"Mmm. I swear he's got more persistence than the North Atlantic itself. He's the best hand I've ever worked with, next to you. And the damn kid can put in four more hours after I'm worn to a frazzle."

"I told you to let me know when you're ready for a desk job," Rafe admonished.

Manny laughed. "I'll never be ready. I want to go to my grave on a scalloper. Even though your genius in the boardroom has fixed it so that Mike and I could retire now, I'd rather keep fishing. You used to feel that way once, before…'' Manny paused one awkward moment, then went on lightly. "Before you met Destiny. Remember when we used to say we'd fish together until we got too old to haul the cage up?"

When Rafe did not respond Manny went on. "Of course, little did we know that Janeiro and Sons would grow under your guidance to become the biggest fleet in the fishing business in New England and then acquire Atlantic Canners, as well, 'The pick,'" he quoted their current advertising, "'of every discerning housewife in America'."

"Life takes some interesting side roads," was all Rafe would admit.

"Doesn't it? Are you going to have Cara this summer?"

There was a frown line on Rafe's forehead, though his eyes were still closed. "I'm not sure. Des is on tour, and she thought she might have a couple of weeks off this summer. If so, she'll want to have Cara with her. Des is supposed to call me when the tour's over and let me know."

Manny asked casually, "Why don't you invite them both here for Destiny's vacation?" Then he braced himself for Rafe's reaction.

"Now, that would be absurd, wouldn't it?" Rafe replied dispassionately.

Disappointed, Manny mentally shook his head. He should have known. Rafe did not have one dispassionate bone in his body. Every ounce of energy and enthusiasm he possessed went into everything he did. He was intensely loyal, unwaveringly honest and loved selflessly. He treated no other subject in his life with the careful politeness with which he handled his ex-wife. Michelle, Manny's wife, astutely theorized that Rafe still cared for Destiny and that he had put a distance between them to spare himself the risk of sharing his feelings with her.

"I don't see why?" Manny persisted. "It's far from over between you two."

"It's been over for five years."

Manny snickered. "The hell is has! Why haven't either

of you remarried? You haven't had a serious relationship since Destiny.''

"Who's got time for serious relationships?''

"And she works like a demon, hopscotching all over the globe like she's on a spring.''

"It's her job, Manny. The studio keeps her moving.'' Rafe opened his eyes and slanted his brother a grin. "Relax. Just because you thrive on family life, it doesn't mean we're all cut of the same cloth.''

"You loved having Des and Cara around. You were always showing them off, taking them—''

Rafe's expression sobered, and though his voice maintained a jocular note, Manny knew his brother well enough to know that he'd had enough. "Do you want me to throw you out? I could call Mom and Dad and tell them you've decided to go home early. They'll return your kids, and you'll have to play chauffeur like Michelle does and keep the house clean until she comes home—sometime next week.''

Manny considered that alternative, bit down on his cigar and closed his eyes, leaning back again. "You've got a mean streak, Janeiro.''

"Hey, Rafe!'' Mike shouted from the back door of the house.

Rafe groaned at the prospect of having to move. "What?'' he demanded.

"Destiny's on television!'' Mike called. "I was trying to find the score of the Boston/Chicago game and there she was! She's going to be interviewed in a minute! Hurry up!''

With his eyes still closed, Rafe heard Manny scramble off the chaise lounge. Rafe was just deciding that he didn't want to see her. Talking to her on the phone when they planned Cara's summer visits was hard enough on him without having to look at the face that had haunted his fantasies and his memories for the past five years. The pain of losing her hadn't abated, but he had learned to control it, to function, even to perform with skill and precision despite the throb of loneliness that lived inside him like an abcess.

"She's coming on right now!" Mike reported, obviously watching the television over the breakfast bar from his position at the door. "God!" he said feelingly. "She looks like hell!"

Despite himself, Rafe was up and sprinting for the house with a quiet oath. Mike pushed a beer into Rafe's hand, and Rafe, coming in from the glare of the afternoon sun, squinted while his eyes adjusted to the dimness of the room. His eyes closed in on the TV screen, and he leaned a leg against a bar stool.

David Gambel, one of daytime television's most popular talk-show hosts, turned to a blond woman in a sequined blue dress seated in a deep chair opposite him.

"What are your plans now that everyone's talking about your costumes for *Stormwind*?" Gambel went on to explain to the audience that Destiny Black's costumes for the Victorian period film were so accurate to the last detail that the Council of Costume Designers had awarded her its highest honor. The council and Olympus Films were co-sponsoring Destiny's tour.

Rafe took a sip of beer, fighting a convulsive movement in his throat to get it down. His first thought was that his brother was crazy; Destiny was even more beautiful than the last time he'd seen her, waving at him from behind the window of the VW Beetle as she drove out of his life. Her golden hair was swept up in a formal style, which left a fringe of curls framing her face. On the screen, the swell of breast at the neckline of her dress, the glimpse of knee and thigh at the side slit made his heart lurch uncomfortably, and he took another sip of beer. Then the camera closed in on her and Rafe saw what Mike meant. She did look terrible.

The once-soft contours of her face were now all dark shadows and harsh angles. Eyes that he remembered as bright green shaded toward gray and betrayed a very deep weariness. He leaned a little closer to the screen. His youthful wife had been slender but lively. This woman had a look of fragility about her that appeared ominously unhealthy.

At that moment the sturdy shield that protected him from photos of Destiny in the newspaper, the sound of her voice on the telephone and the damnable clarity of his own memories, shattered and fell around him. He felt naked and completely vulnerable.

"It's probably the lights and the makeup," Manny said. He was positioned behind Rafe, leaning around his brother to watch the screen. Mike's forearm rested on Rafe's shoulder as he pointed his beer at the television.

"But she's so skinny!"

"I understand you're considering a contract from another studio," Gambel went on. "And there are whispers of a juicy offer from the fashion industry. Will you share your plans with us?"

Destiny smiled at the camera, but it seemed to require effort. And before the gesture had completely formed on her lips Rafe saw fear in her eyes, uncertainty, confusion and just a trace of panic.

She looked straight at Rafe, and his heart began to hammer. Of course she had no idea he was watching; he knew that. But she seemed to be searching her unseen audience, looking for rescue. In her eyes was a plea for help.

"I'm still undecided," Destiny replied, her voice softer, lower-pitched than he remembered. "I feel a certain loyalty to Olympus Films, and there are six months to go on my contract with them. I'll…" She sighed, a gesture that seemed filled with helplessness despite her smile for the camera. "I'll be too busy until then to even consider the other offers."

"Do you begin work on another film as soon as your tour is over?"

"I have a final stop on the tour in Portland on Friday,

then I'll have a few weeks off with my daughter before the crew leaves for Morocco.''

"Morocco?" With alacrity Gambel leaped at the mention of the exotic site and used the opportunity to relate his own experiences in Africa. Then Destiny introduced the models who would be showing her award-winning costumes.

While Destiny's voice described the period gowns, Rafe paced to the end of the bar and back again. He took a swig of beer, walked to the patio doors and looked out over the expanse of lush lawn and the soft summer green of the forest across the road.

Then he swung back to the screen as Gambel thanked Destiny and wished her luck. The camera panned over the audience, the theme music rose and Gambel began to list his guests for the following afternoon's show.

Rafe crossed to the television and snapped it off. Manny and Mike exchanged looks of concern. Rafe stood stock-still, hands loosely on his hips, his head turned to the side as he studied the now-blank screen. Manny had seen him like this on the boat, deciding whether to ride out heavy weather or run for a sheltered harbor. He was assimilating data, shuffling alternatives, reaching a decision. Manny prayed that he'd put that damned dispassion aside.

"So," Rafe asked finally, walking toward the stairs. "Who's going to help me pack, and who's going to call my secretary and have her scope out Des's flight number?"

BY THE TIME Rafe had fought his way through the usual airport crowds and found the arrival gate, he decided that Los Angeles International Airport posed a more serious threat to one's health and sanity than did the North Atlantic in February. Or maybe it was just that he was nervous. He wasn't sure what he was doing here anyway. So what if Destiny had looked as though she was on the brink of collapse? What did he think he could do about it? What would she let him do about it? His managing of her life had been the reason she'd left him in the first place. He hadn't understood the problem then, but he'd come a long way emotionally in the last five years. Still, he wasn't hoping to reestablish their relationship or try to make Destiny see things from his point of view. He just wanted to know what had happened to her to reduce her to a shadow of the woman he had known, and he wanted to do whatever he could to help her.

The public address system announced, "Flight 219 from Portland arriving at gate 11." Rafe put his hands in the pockets of his light cotton jacket and stood back among the anxious families that gathered at the gate.

DESTINY SHUFFLED ALONG with the long line of disembarking passengers as it moved through the narrow aisles between the seats. Her carry-on case was a burdensome appendage to her right hand. God, she was tired. But her weariness wouldn't keep her from lying awake for hours tonight. The insomnia had become a pattern. After a year of it, she could feel it coming on—the intense weariness with the slowly building undercurrent of tension, the strange sensation of feeling everything at work in her body: brain, blood and an inner tremor, on which she could not quite focus.

And it was still at least a half-hour drive to Beverly Hills and home. She wanted to cry. She was feeling queasy from the flight, nervous because of the two fussy small children and their oblivious mother who had occupied the seats beside her since Denver, and too exhausted to drive. But Destiny hadn't wanted anyone to meet her at the airport because she couldn't have taken Frances's solicitous reprimands about the state of health she'd let herself fall into, and there was no one else who could have come for her.

That had been a sobering thought this morning in her plush but lonely hotel room. Because of the praise and fame and adulation of the past several months, the world was full

of people who cared about her abilities as a costume designer. Yet only two people in the vast universe cared about
Destiny Black, the person: her nine-year-old daughter,
Cara, and her housekeeper, Frances Brophy. There was her
mother, of course, but Destiny was never quite sure how
they felt about each other.

A smiling steward held Destiny's arm as she stepped
from the plane onto the boarding ramp leading to the ter-
minal.

Taking a stronger grip on her case and anchoring her
purse on her shoulder, she started the long trudge. The line
of passengers who preceded her peeled off to the left and
right as families and friends greeted them. Then Destiny
cleared the gate and kept walking. She didn't see Rafe until
she nearly collided with him when he stepped out of the
rows of stationary seats to intercept her. The world seemed
to freeze in time as she looked into his face. She heard
cries and greetings all around them, but nothing and no one
seemed to move. It was a long moment before she could
force a sound from her throat.

"Rafe!" she whispered in complete surprise.

"Hello, Des." His smile was faint, his voice as low as
hers.

Her mind was distracted from the shock of his presence
for a moment as her eyes took in his appearance. Physically, he looked very much the same as he had five years
ago, but everything else about him, all the subtle little
things that gave a man appeal—impact—were different.
And she saw that in an instant. Oddly, she recalled that in
the past she'd been struck by his good looks, his energy,
his sexuality. But now she got an impression of control, of
calm. Or was it just that it had been so long since she'd
last seen him?

"Hello, Rafe," she replied. "Why…?" Then the most
obvious reason for his presence here to meet her plane oc-
curred to her, and she paled. Her shadowy eyes opened

wide in fear, and her sorely tried nervous system reacted violently.

"No," Rafe said firmly, reading her eyes. "Nothing is wrong with Cara. I'm here because…"

But Destiny didn't hear him. There was a loud buzz in her ears, and she had the strangest feeling that messages from her brain center weren't reaching her legs. She remained conscious long enough to register relief that Cara was all right, then fainted dead away in Rafe's arms with an apologetic little shrug.

THERE WAS A BRIGHT LIGHT on her face, excited conversation, then pain in her hip. She slipped into a dark mist, and when it cleared, time had been miraculously rolled back and it was November of her freshman year at Wellesley. As though she were standing behind a camera and watching a drama unfold, she saw herself walking along a river front. Gulls swooped and the wind blew, and fishing boats bobbed at anchor under a muddy sky. She knew just what was on her mind as she pulled her collar up against the wind. All her classmates had gone home for Thanksgiving, and she was thinking how lucky she was to be able to explore the old whaling port of New Bedford, Massachusetts, on her own. There were advantages to having no father and a mother who was always jetting somewhere—particularly if one didn't mind one's own company.

Next door to the old New Bedford Glass Company was a small diner. She went in, took a place at the counter and ordered clam chowder and coffee. When it was served she asked the waitress for crackers.

"A New Englander," the man seated beside her said, "puts popcorn in clam chowder." He indicated the small bowl of puffy kernels with which he'd been served his thick white brew.

She looked up, startled, into a swarthy face with black eyes, a proud, beaky nose and a stubborn chin softened by a cleft. His hair was black and a little long, and it lay around his face in tight waves. He wore old jeans and a denim jacket and a go-to-hell air, which both appealed to Destiny and made her nervous.

He looked older than she by nine or ten years, and she wondered if he was some layabout who hoped to spice up a dull afternoon by picking up a girl.

"In Beverly Hills," she replied with what was supposed to be a quelling hauteur, "we eat our chowder with crackers."

"If you're going to name-drop," he countered good-naturedly, "John Kennedy ate his chowder with popcorn."

"In Beverly Hills," she repeated, "we're Republicans."

He smiled with an indulgence that annoyed her. "Wellesley, right?" he guessed.

She stirred her chowder without looking up. "Yes. And you? You got your education on the docks, right?"

He laughed aloud. "How'd you guess? M.I.T. first, of course. But now, the docks."

That brought her eyes level with his. Wellesley had a cross-registration program with M.I.T., and she had learned respect for the students with whom she'd come in contact from that highly regarded institution.

"What field?" she asked, noting the teasing sparkle in the depths of his eyes for the first time.

"Management." His lips quirked.

She sighed, resigned now to the fact that she'd been tricked into behaving like a snob. "All right. What do you manage?"

"A 105-foot scalloper."

She closed her eyes for a moment. A fisherman. A member of one of Massachusetts's most noble professions, significant both historically and to the contemporary economy.

"Rafe Janeiro," he said with a smile, extending a large, calloused hand. "I've had a good year and am, therefore, better than solvent. My parents are good church-going stock whose parents came from San Miguel in the Azores Islands.

I have two brothers and no children that I know of. Is that enough background information to satisfy Beverly Hills?''

Destiny took his hand with a self-deprecating grimace. ''It would be better if you could claim relatives on the Mayflower.''

''I can.''

She frowned. ''Via the Azores?''

''That's the name of my boat—the Mayflower.'' He shook her hand, then retained it, his eyes growing serious as they looked deeply into hers. ''I've always felt like a pilgrim on the sea of life...'' He smiled over his fanciful statement, then continued with a theatrical wave of his hand, ''On a quest toward destiny.''

She gasped, a heartbeat suspended as a pleasant little chill ran up her backbone. ''That's me!'' she said.

''Who?''

''Destiny...'' she whispered. ''I'm Destiny Black.''

DESTINY AWOKE to a familiar white-bearded face.

''Dr. Pointer!'' she croaked in surprise. Her throat was dry, and she swallowed to lubricate it. ''What are you doing here?'' Then she looked around herself at the small area visible in the puddle of light cast by her bedside lamp. The bedspread was her own, as was the sprigged sheet and the small oak table on which stood the ginger-jar lamp. ''Oh,'' she said, confused. ''I'm home.''

She put a hand to her head, recalling snatches of a dream that had combined the present with the past in a strange pattern of events. ''How...?''

''You collapsed at the airport,'' the doctor said, answering her unfinished question. ''Your husband took you to the hospital, and they released you in my care. I met the two of you here.''

''My husband?'' she asked, the hand falling to her lap.

Rafe stepped out of the shadows. He had shed his jacket, and his shirt sleeves were rolled up, the harsh lamplight glinting off the dark hair on his forearms.

"You are here," she said in amazement, putting her hand to her head again, closing her eyes once more. "I thought I had dreamed you. We were at Suprenant's Diner near the glass museum, and we were talking about college..."

He arched an eyebrow in question. "Suprenant's?" And she knew immediately that that part had been a dream. Of course. Their first meeting had taken place almost ten years ago.

"I'm confused," Destiny admitted. She opened her eyes, thinking perhaps Rafe would disappear. When he didn't, she put her hand out and connected with a broadclothed arm through which she felt tensile muscle and a well-remembered warmth. Cuddling up to him had always been like wrapping oneself in a warm quilt. "Why are you here?" she asked.

He smiled, taking the hand she had placed on his arm. "I'll explain that in a minute. Will you just say hello to Cara to reassure her that you're all right? She got quite a scare when I carried you in here."

"Sure. Of course." With the doctor's help Destiny sat up. She patted her hair, knowing it was in disarray but hoping her smile was still intact.

Rafe pulled her bedroom door open and reached out into the hall. "Come on in, Cara. Mom wants to see you."

For a long moment the child stood on the threshold of the room, her amber eyes wide behind her glasses. Her honey-brown ponytails were disheveled and part of the long cotton nightgown she wore was crushed in her right hand.

Destiny felt a rush of love for her daughter and a stab of sympathy. Cara was tall for her age, large-boned and inclined to chubbiness. Her sudden growth confused her coordination and made her appear awkward. Destiny knew it was a stage she would outgrow, but Cara, who compared herself with her mother and all the beautiful women she dressed, wanted more than anything to be invisible. But she appeared to have grown another inch or two while Destiny was gone.

Destiny smiled widely and stretched out her arms. "Hi, sweetie!" she said, trying to make her voice strong and even. Cara ran the small distance that separated them and flung herself into her mother's arms. "I missed you, Mom!" Cara cried, then pulling away, looked solemnly into Destiny's eyes. "You've been sick, and if you don't eat better and get some rest there's no telling what could happen."

Destiny pulled her back for a hug, laughing. "Yes, Doctor," she said, suspecting her daughter was repeating something she had heard adults discussing.

"Every word she said is true," the doctor confirmed grimly.

Cara smiled at her mother. "But Dr. Pointer's got everything fixed up."

Destiny smiled back, innocently unsuspecting. "He has?"

"Yes," Cara announced. "We're going home with Dad!"

Chapter Two

Destiny prayed that the fainting spell had caused her to imagine what she was hearing.

"What did you say?" she whispered.

"We're going home with Daddy," Cara repeated, her face suddenly free of anxiety and animated at the prospect. "Dr. Pointer thinks it's a great idea. We're gonna—"

"Cara." Rafe interrupted by pulling Cara gently off the bed, and she leaned against him happily as he put an arm around her. "You'd better say good-night to Mom now, so she can get some rest. We'll make our plans in the morning over breakfast, okay?"

"Okay. 'Night, Mom. I'm glad you're feeling better." Cara went to kiss Destiny, then reached up for her father's hug. "'Night, Daddy." She smiled broadly. "I'm glad you came."

He tugged a ponytail. "So am I, baby. Good night."

When the door closed behind the child, Destiny gave her pillow a punch that belied her weakness. Then she cast a suspicious glance from the doctor to her ex-husband. "Will someone," she demanded quietly, "explain to me what is going on?"

Dr. Pointer pulled a small cherry-wood chair to the side of the bed and fixed paternal blue eyes on her. "Destiny, I've warned you more than once that this would happen, but you refused to listen."

"I have a job..." she began.

"You are not indispensable. When you are dead they will find someone to replace you, and they won't stop to think for a minute that you gave your all for the studio." He removed his wire-rimmed glasses and spoke firmly. "Your body has given you a relatively mild warning, and so far, there's nothing wrong with you that we can't reverse, but you're not a very healthy woman. Your body is exhausted. You're anemic, your blood sugar is low, your blood pressure is too high for a woman your age and you're a good fifteen pounds underweight. Now..." he paused to assure himself of her attention. "You need complete rest and some serious attention to your diet. Starting now."

"I have two weeks before—"

"Two months," the doctor interrupted, "is closer to what you need, and I'm telling you in all honesty that, if you go off to another remote location in your state of health, I won't be responsible for the condition in which you come home...if you do come home."

Destiny rolled her eyes. "Really, Donald..."

"Destiny, I'm serious!" the doctor said loudly.

Destiny subsided against her pillows. "Then I'll ask to be excused from the Morocco trip and just stay home for a month."

"I'm afraid that won't do." The doctor scribbled something on a prescription pad, then tore the top sheet off and handed it to Rafe, who leaned against the post at the foot of the bed. "In the hour I've been in this house you've gotten a call from the studio you work for, a call from the studio who would like to win you away from the studio you work for, a fabric manufacturer and a dry cleaner wanting to endorse their services in an ad campaign. I doubt that two months in this house would be very restful."

Destiny sighed then cast an accusing glance at Rafe. "So, in your omniscience you've stepped in to manage everything."

"No," he replied mildly. "I just came to see if there

was anything I could do. Cara suggested that since she was supposed to spend the summer with me, and since you're supposed to get away from your hectic life-style, we could kill two birds with one stone, so to speak. You can just think of my house in Maine as a sort of convalescent home.''

When Destiny glared, Rafe went on briskly. ''If that's not acceptable to you, then we'll make other arrangements, of course. In fact your mother called.'' There was the barest movement of his bottom lip, challenging his briskness. ''She wanted to welcome you home, but when she heard about your collapse, she offered to have you spend the summer with her in Newport.''

Destiny's eyes widened in horror. ''What did you tell her?''

''I promised to pass on the message and have you call her as soon as you're able.''

Destiny sank into her pillows with a groan. The doctor cleared his throat.

''Normally, a little maternal attention would be just what you need right now, but...'' He shook his head and shuddered, recalling the time he had treated Serena Fleming for a sprained ankle when she was visiting Destiny. ''Your mother's life is even more frantic than yours. For your sake, Destiny, I'd seek an alternative. Well...'' He smiled at Destiny and shook Rafe's hand. ''Nice to meet you, Mr. Janeiro. Have the prescription filled first thing in the morning and see that she follows that diet I left.''

''Thanks, Doctor. I'll walk you out.'' Rafe smiled an ''excuse us'' and closed the door behind them.

Destiny turned into her pillow with a moan of distress.

''Are you going to live?'' Destiny's moment of solitude was shattered by the presence of her housekeeper. Frances was short and round and full of opinions and advice. She'd been with Destiny for two years and bullied and pampered both her charges with equal enthusiasm.

As Destiny turned over to face her, Frances nodded approvingly. "You do look a little more alive than you did when Mr. Janeiro brought you home. What did the doctor say?"

Destiny sighed. "That I need rest. As if that were possible."

"Of course it is." Frances took the cherry-wood chair and patted Destiny's hand. "You and Cara can go to Maine with your husband."

"He's my ex-husband," Destiny said, looking closely at Frances. Had the whole world gone mad? "I can't go to Maine with him."

Frances frowned. "You're not going to your mother's?"

"Lord, no!" Destiny clutched the sides of her pillow and pulled them over her face as if some primitive survival instinct prompted her to hide.

"Your husband's gorgeous," Frances insisted. "I think you should go."

Destiny sat up, agitated. "I lived with him for five years. He's gorgeous, but he's bossy."

"So? Bossy is a masculine trait. Men often back off when you fight back." When Destiny didn't reply, Frances tried another tack. "He seems very good with Cara and was very attentive to you. Cara was looking forward to the trip."

"She can still spend the summer with him. I've no objection to that."

"But you've been gone a lot this year. She was anxious to have time with you, too."

"Then we'll go somewhere." Destiny fell back against the pillow. "Arizona, maybe."

Frances looked at her employer consideringly, then stood and pulled the blankets up to her chin. "Do you think taking her away from her father is a good idea? You should have seen Cara when Mr. Janeiro walked in with you," she said, fluffing pillows and straightening the bedspread. "She didn't know whether to be upset about you or thrilled that her father was here. Those two have quite a close relationship considering the circumstances." Then Frances abruptly changed the subject. "Can I bring you a glass of milk or a cup of tea?"

Annoyed by her housekeeper's gentle application of guilt, Destiny glared at her. "I'd rather have a Pepsi."

"Sorry. The doctor said milk or tea. Your stomach, you know."

Destiny sighed. "Forget it, Frances. Go on to bed; I'll be fine. Good night."

As Frances turned the light off and left the room Destiny rolled onto her stomach and considered her predicament. She could spend several months with her mother, who never had anything in the refrigerator but pâté and champagne, who wore mink to the supermarket and had had three husbands. Or she could go to Maine with her ex-husband whom she had left five years ago after a fight that had all their tenement neighbors gathered in the hallway. On the one hand she didn't want to deprive Cara of her yearly trip to Maine, yet sending her alone would mean another separation, and Frances was right. They'd had too little time together this year as it was.

But what was Rafe doing here anyway? She tried to recall what he had said when she'd asked him. "I came to see if there was anything I could do," he'd said. But why? She hadn't collapsed until after she saw him at the airport.

A knock at her door interrupted the maze of her thoughts. "Who is it?" she demanded crossly.

"Rafe," was the swift answer.

"What do you want?"

"I've got the milk you asked for."

"Go away!" she shouted. "I asked for Pepsi."

The door opened, and she watched his shadow move toward her. He turned on the bedside light and put the glass on the small table. "Sorry. Doctor's orders. You have to settle for milk. Want me to help you sit up?"

"I can..." she began, but before she could finish he had slipped his hands under her arms and pulled her to a sitting position, fluffing a pillow behind her back. The heel of his hand brushed her breast on the right side, and the air in her lungs left her in a rush. She took a sip of the milk to hide the sudden flood of color to her face.

Rafe frowned at her and put the back of his hand to her forehead, then the warm palm of his hand to her cheek. "How're you doing? You look feverish to me."

Her heart began to thump erratically, and she drew away from him, studying him with suspicion. "You never did tell me why you met me at the airport," she said. "Why did you want to help me? I didn't faint until after I saw you."

"I caught your appearance on the David Gambel show," he explained, sitting in the small bedside chair. He leaned his elbows on his knees and watched her evenly. "You looked like hell. I thought I'd better see what was wrong."

She met his eyes over the glass of milk. "A woman is bound to change in five years."

"True," he conceded, "but she shouldn't look ten years older."

"Thanks," Destiny said dryly. "I'm so glad you came to help. It makes me feel so much better to know I look matronly."

"I didn't say you looked matronly," he corrected quietly. "But you did look like something was wrong. It's obvious that you haven't been eating, and Doctor Pointer suspects that you haven't been sleeping, either. What is it, Des? What's wrong?"

How could she explain to him the sudden dissatisfaction with her life, with work, with success, with traveling constantly? Every interview she'd given in the past two months had been meant to show the viewing audience that she had the world by the tail. So why did she feel constantly irritable and deeply unhappy?

She made a helpless gesture, raising a knee under the blanket and slamming it down. "I don't know. Burnout. The ravages of time." She studied him doubtfully. "I'm supposed to believe you flew across the country to find out what was troubling the woman from whom you've been divorced for five years?''

"Is that so difficult?" he asked calmly. "The woman from whom I've been divorced for five years has custody of my daughter. What would happen to Cara if you were ill?"

She angled her chin, resenting the implication that she might not see to her daughter's care. "Frances is excellent."

He nodded. "She certainly seems to be. But she's not Cara's mother. Anyway..." He sat back in the chair and rested the ankle of one leg on the knee of the other. "The camera did a close-up of you, and I saw a distress signal in your eyes."

"Oh?" she said lightly. "Well, maybe it wasn't directed at you."

"But it has to be," he responded as lightly. "You're my destiny, remember?"

Her expression became grim, and she put the glass on the bedside table. "We believed that once—and look at where it got us. It's just a whimsical name given me by a woman who thought destiny was a handsome young actor who got her pregnant, then left her, never to be heard from again."

"Sometimes we're not very logical about who we pin our dreams on."

She agreed instantly. "Tell me."

"Anyway..." He sighed, flicking at a piece of lint on his impeccable slacks. "It would never have worked between us then. You were still young enough to believe in happily ever after, and I was cocky enough to think I could give it to you."

"You were the stereotypical chauvinist," she accused. "You made all the decisions. You resented it when my career began to move. You wanted some sweet little stay-at-home wife, who was totally dependent on you for physical and emotional support.

"No, I resented the fact that your career meant more to you than I did," he said. "And as far as making all the decisions, and trying to run our marriage, you're right; and I regret that. I was handling my family the way my father took care of his—in the tradition of the Latin male. He is always responsible and in control. It just took me a while to realize that we've crossed into a different world from the one my parents know."

Destiny eyed him in surprise, feeling some of the fight go out of her at his admission that there were things he regretted about the past.

"I was unfair to you," he went on, "and I'm sorry. But it was out of youthful ignorance and not because I wanted to hurt or deprive you. I was wildly in love with you, you know, but a little insecure within myself."

"Insecure?" she repeated in dry disbelief. "You?"

He smiled thinly. "My father is tough and strong. He was the best fisherman in New Bedford. Then along I came with a head full of ideas and numbers. When I finally took over for him, I know he thought he was going to lose the boat and the business he'd worked so hard for. He never really believed in my ability to take over, because my approach was different. Even today he doesn't understand why I'm successful."

Destiny was surprised again by that admission of vulnerability. As well as she could remember, Rafe had never seemed to get upset by his father's subtle needling, his reference to him as a "college man." It gave her pause now to know that those remarks had hurt him and that he'd never confided in her, or worse, that she hadn't seen it.

She took refuge in their old problems. "You were gone so much," she said. "And when you were home, you were such a despot."

"You confused me." He offered the one excuse Destiny would have never thought responsible for his attitude. "I always felt like you were waiting for me to make a mistake. Oh, you were warm and loving and fun." He smiled reminiscently and added with a wistful grin. "You were a hell of a lot of fun. But I often got the impression that you were keeping score of all my inadequacies and that they were outdistancing whatever good qualities I had. You wanted me to be as perfect as all those tiny little stitches you labored over."

"All I wanted—" she strained away from her pillow in emphasis "—was for you to understand what I needed."

He nodded regretfully. "I thought I was trying to do that. I concluded that it was my low social status and income, comparing unfavorably to the wealth you'd grown up with, that made you unhappy. So I decided that my boat would be the one with the biggest catch on every run, that I'd buy more boats and get rich. I had to work hard to do that. I had to be gone. And I was tyrannical when I came home because what I was working so hard for didn't seem to be happening. Oh, I was making money and the future was looking good, but you were still miserable with me. Then you finally just drifted away from me like a dory in the fog."

"You never tried to stop me." She said the words quietly, but even her own ears heard the bitterness and pain in her voice. It had hurt so much then that he had let her go with little effort to stop her.

He studied her closely as though he, too, heard the hurt and bitterness and was confused by it. "I sincerely thought you wanted to go. I thought you'd find some tennis-playing fifth-generation Southern Californian out of the Blue Book. I kept expecting to get a note in a birthday card from Cara saying you'd gotten married. Then I saw you on television..." A frown blurred his forehead. "Your sparkle's gone, Des. What's happened? You're not happy?"

"Are you?" she countered quickly, a little aggressively. "Are you happy?"

For a moment he looked discomfited, then he said decisively, "No. I'm successful, somewhat fulfilled; I have caring family and friends, but...no. I'm not happy."

She leaned wearily against her pillow. "Maybe some of us aren't supposed to be happy. Or maybe you only get one chance at it. If you blow it, that's it."

"No, I think it's out there for everyone." Rafe smiled at Destiny and got to his feet. He urged her to slide down in the bed and cradled her head gently in one hand while readjusting the pillow with the other. "We just didn't try hard enough. I think it's a lot like the panic you feel when you're out there on the vast ocean in this small boat and there's a storm brewing. Your instinct is to run before it, to try to race it to land, when the safest course usually is to turn into it and ride it out."

She snickered. "Had we 'ridden out' our marriage, we'd have killed each other."

"Or maybe," he suggested, "we'd have made it through to sunshine and fair weather."

Destiny looked up at him candidly as he reached for the light switch. "Would you have liked that?"

He smiled down at her quizzically. "Would you?"

She thought about that a moment. "Sometimes I think I would," she said finally.

He smiled and turned out the light. "Sometimes," he acknowledged, his words floating out to her in the darkness, "so do I. Good night, Des."

There was no way her eyes would even close tonight, Destiny thought as Rafe left the room. Her heart was beating triple time, and a million little nerve endings that had lain dormant for five years were up and rioting. She could not spend the summer with Rafe. Period. Cara would just have to understand. Cara could spend a month with her father then join Destiny somewhere and spend the rest of the summer with her. Yes. That was an excellent solution. She would spend the long hours of the night planning the speech she would deliver to her daughter and her ex-husband in the morning. She turned onto her side to get a little more comfortable—and promptly fell asleep.

DESTINY AWOKE feeling confused and inexplicably anxious. She tried to focus her fuzzy mind on why she should be worried, when a shout of male laughter sounded from somewhere in the house. She fell back against the pillow, remembering where the anxiety had come from. A bleary glance at the clock told her it was after ten. She hadn't slept that late in a year. She began to suspect that Rafe had put something in her milk.

Testing her equilibrium, Destiny got slowly to her feet and reached to the foot of the bed for her lavender silk robe. She went cautiously to the door and opened it. Sounds of conversation filtered toward her from the kitchen. Pausing a moment to steady herself, she padded down the corridor toward the sound of her daughter's voice.

"And Jenny still lives there?" Cara asked.

"Yep," Rafe's voice replied.

"They moved in next door to Daddy last summer when I was there," the child was explaining to Frances as Destiny reached the kitchen. "We had so much fun! Her mom was gonna have a baby."

"She had it," Rafe informed his daughter, who was perched on the counter against which he leaned, her arm hooked in his. "A boy. His name is Andrew James."

Cara squealed delightedly. "I can't wait to see Jenny again and to play with the baby. Mom!" Cara leaped off the counter, overbalancing as she hit the floor. As she flailed to save herself, Rafe reached out to pull her upright.

"Ever consider a parachute?" he teased.

She grimaced. "Funny, Dad." Then she turned back to join her mother at the kitchen table. She had apparently done her own toilet this morning, Destiny noted. Both ponytails were askew. "Remember I told you about Jenny? Well, her mom had her baby, and it's a boy and his name is Andrew James. You'll like Jenny's mom. She sews, too.

Oh, not as good as you, of course. She doesn't do it for the movies or anything. But she makes Jenny dresses and stuff." Continuing on without pausing for a breath, she said, "You're supposed to have an egg and toast for breakfast." Then, as though to explain the order she added, "Dad said."

"Dr. Pointer said," Rafe corrected, pulling a chair out for Destiny. "How do you feel this morning?"

"Better. But a little rubbery."

"One soft-boiled egg and one piece of toast coming right up," Frances said from the stove. "Milk or tea?"

"Pepsi."

"Milk or tea?" The question was mercilessly repeated.

Destiny sighed. "I guess tea," she said, casting Rafe a wry look. "I think somebody messed with the milk I drank last night."

He arched an eyebrow in question.

"I slept," she explained.

"Ah." He nodded. "Doctor Pointer gave you a shot."

She had a vague recollection of a pinch of pain in her hip while she was dreaming. Had Rafe been present when she was given the shot? Her wide eyes questioned his, then slitted in annoyance when he nodded, a small grin shaping his mouth.

"The ravages of time," he said quietly as the ring of the telephone covered his words from their companions, "have left your fanny remarkably unblemished. I'll get your tea."

"Hi, Grandma," Cara said into the telephone. "No, she's up. She's right here." The child held out the phone to Destiny, who shuffled over to take it from her, glaring at Rafe's back over her shoulder.

Destiny drew a deep breath and prayed for patience. "Hello, Mother," she said.

"Darling!" Serena Fleming's center-stage voice gasped over the transcontinental telephone line. Destiny could imagine her in an untouchably elegant negligee, looking ready for the cameras though there wasn't one for miles.

Her mother played the role of star to the hilt. "How awful that you fainted! I'd have come to you, of course, but Rafe said there was no cause to upset myself and that you would be fine. But you didn't call, and you know how I worry."

"I'm fine, Mother," Destiny said as sincerely as she could manage. "The doctor says I need a little rest."

"Well, darling! You're welcome to join us. Brandon says he'd be only too pleased to have you."

Destiny tried hard to think, but she could not remember a Brandon. Husband number three had been Roland, and he'd been dispensed with several years before. "Brandon?" she asked.

"Yes, dear. We're getting married at Christmas. You'll just love him. Do come and stay with us. I'll fly out to meet you…"

Husband number four? Destiny replied quickly, "No, Mother…"

"Or we can send the Lear for you."

Panic rose in Destiny at the thought of long evenings playing mah-jongg while she and her mother pretended to be happy in each other's company and her lecherous new love looked on. "Mother…"

"Yes, that would be best," Serena went on. "The food on those commercial airlines is dreadful!"

Serena had three poodles who ate toast and drank coffee for breakfast and slept together on a Chippendale chair. "No, Mother."

"But, darling! Celestine is getting a room ready for you right now."

"That's kind of you, Mother, but I can't come," Destiny insisted firmly.

"But, why?"

Because you and I will never have anything in common. Because you chose a man to be my father who was worthless and shallow and didn't stay around long enough to find out if I was boy or girl. Because you run from man to man as though it were a race and that disgusts me. Unable to voice either of those reasons aloud, Destiny sighed, defeated. "Because I'm going to Maine with Rafe and Cara," she said.

Keep cool, Janeiro, Rafe told himself as he poured boiling water over a tea bag in a china cup. *Don't react. Don't even look at her.*

Actually, his heart had jolted, and he kept the kettle steady with difficulty. He was more than pleased at Destiny's decision, despite the reluctance with which she made it.

Though he had left Digby Head and presented himself at the airport solely for the purpose of discovering what was wrong with Des and what he could do to help, his intention to be merely politely distant, wavered at first sight of her. Last night, as he sat beside her bed, waiting for the doctor to arrive, it had been completely overcome. The fragile beauty that had so attracted him almost ten years ago had matured into the indefinable essence that made her a woman. It was obvious that she had worked hard, suffered and prevailed. Even ill, she had a look of strength she'd never had before.

He had lifted the fingers twitching at her side as she slept and felt the calloused fingertips. He remembered them from the last two years of their marriage when her career had begun to blossom and she was creating costumes for many of New England's little theater productions. Holding a pencil, plying a needle, working on rough fabrics and under difficult conditions had made the pads of her fingers as rough as any workman's. But their touch against his flesh had been erotic.

"Rafe." She had called his name softly in her unconsciousness. He had held her hand firmly, trying to give her a link to reality. "That's me," she said softly out of her dream. "Destiny...your destiny."

He had finally realized in that moment why he had come to her side, but there was much of the past to be mended before he could share his reason with her.

DESTINY HUNG UP the telephone and shuffled back to the table. Cara was jumping up and down, lopsided ponytails bobbing. She threw her arms around her mother as Destiny sank into a chair.

"Mom, you're gonna love Digby Head! And you're gonna love Joe! There's the ocean and the forest, and there's a place in town that has the most wonderful ice cream! We can—"

"Hey, hey..." Rafe interrupted gently, placing Destiny's tea in front of her. He extricated Cara from her lap. "You're going to wear Mom out before she gets there. Why don't you start packing while she has breakfast."

With a parting hug and a squeal of excitement, Cara skipped away.

"I should have my head examined," Destiny mumbled as Frances put her breakfast of a soft-boiled egg and toast in front of her.

"Doctor Pointer did that," Rafe said, sitting across from her with a cup of coffee and a broad grin. "He said there was nothing he could do for your head. Too far gone. So he decided to concentrate on restoring your body instead. He said to eat slowly so you can get it all down."

She picked up her fork and looked at him in annoyance; he winked and turned his attention to the housekeeper.

"Are you coming with us, Frances?"

She turned away from the dishwasher, looking a little flustered. "Well...I haven't been asked."

He looked at Destiny over his cup. "We'll need her, don't you think?"

"Cara and I would perish without her."

"That settles it, Frances," he said. "Will that work out for you?"

She smiled and dipped her head toward Rafe with a deferential look Destiny didn't recall ever getting from her. "It will. I'd love to come. Thank you."

"Good." Rafe turned back to Destiny. "Can you be ready to go in the morning?"

She paused to think. "I don't know. I'll have to notify the utilities, the newspaper, the..." Her eyes widened in horror. "My producer! He's expecting me—"

Rafe halted her effort to stand with a hand on her forearm, pushing her back down in her chair. "I called him this morning."

"Rafe!" Destiny slammed a small fist on the table, her irritation rising. "It's my career at stake here. You don't know what Clay Kennedy is like! Producers are—"

"I know. He didn't like it, but he said they'll try to carry on without you."

Her irritation was momentarily diluted by admiration for his efficiency. It was just after ten o'clock. "How did you know whom to call?"

"I called Olympus Films and explained the problem, and they put me in touch with Kennedy."

"I should have done that!" Destiny protested, angry again.

Rafe sipped his coffee. "Maybe. But I was afraid you'd let him talk you into going to Morocco after all."

"See!" she said, color flushing her pale cheeks as she gesticulated wildly. "It's starting already. We're still in my house, and you're already handling things."

He put his cup down calmly in its saucer. "I thought you'd want him notified as soon as possible so a replacement could be found for you. Still, there's nothing to prevent you from calling him, too, after breakfast, is there? But Doctor Pointer has entrusted me to carry out his orders. You are not to go to Morocco and you know damn well Kennedy will try to talk you into it whether you're ill or not."

"Rafe—" she began to protest further, but he cut her off exasperatedly with, "Eat your breakfast, *cara linda*."

It had been five years since Destiny had heard that Portuguese term of endearment, and it had the most curious effect on her. She melted inside, all her irritation and righteous indignation evaporated in the soft sound of the words.

During their courtship and the first few years of their marriage he had called her *cara linda* when teasing her or making love to her. In Portuguese it translated to pretty face. When Cara was born and they were still undecided on a name, it struck Destiny that "Cara Linda" was the perfect label to identify the product of their love.

Destiny looked across the table at Rafe, feeling the draw of forces beyond her control. But he was gathering their dirty dishes, excusing himself to make a few phone calls.

"I'll take care of packing for you and closing up the house," Frances said. "You curl up on the sofa with a blanket, and Mr. Janeiro and I will handle everything."

Exhausted by the simple act of eating breakfast, Destiny frowned at Frances. "How come you're on his side already?"

"Because he's gorgeous," Frances replied candidly, then added on a more serious note, "and because he's on your side."

Chapter Three

In the red Mercedes Rafe had left in long-term parking at the Portland Airport, Destiny, her housekeeper and her temporarily reunited family swept along the highway, which bordered the Atlantic Ocean. The air through the open windows smelled sweetly of the warm fragrance of early summer and the tantalizing, mysterious scent of the sea.

They drove through the small coastal town of Digby Head with its many picturesque remnants of colonial days and its small but busy harbor. As they proceeded out of town the road began to climb, and soon it paralleled a rocky headland covered in yellow wildflowers. Where the coastline jogged far out into the water on a slim pencil of land, a lighthouse stood against the clear blue sky.

Leaning her head back against the upholstered rest, Destiny let her hair fly about her face and closed her eyes to inhale the sweetness from the open window. She pushed away all thoughts of where she should be and tried to absorb the atmosphere of where she was. The countryside, all green grass and tall trees, was wonderfully quiet; and each farm or church or simple structure looked like a subject for which one of the Wyeths would have set up an easel. Despite her annoyance with Rafe, she drew a deep, even breath and thought wryly that this might not be a bad place to spend a couple of months.

"What are you thinking?" Rafe's voice penetrated her

thoughts over Cara and Frances's conversation in the back. She smiled without opening her eyes. "That if I have to be under house arrest for a few months, this isn't the worst place to be."

"Who said anything about confining you?" he asked.

"So far you've behaved like an abductor," she accused quietly.

He smiled at the road. "You could have gone to your mother's."

A glare told him what she thought of that alternative.

Rafe shot her a grinning glance, then turned back to the road. "Do you find this…kidnap exciting?"

"I find it annoying, demeaning and inconvenient." But the indignation sounded a little fragile even to her own ear.

He glanced at her again, his dark eyes quickly taking in her flush of color, the dancing of her wild hair around her face and the sparkling of her green eyes lively with annoyance.

"Liar," he said softly.

He was right, she thought, though she gave him an exasperated look and turned to study the ocean. She had been so sure for so long that no one cared about Destiny Black except Cara and Frances. It was stimulating to be ensnared by his forceful attention, but it was frightening also. After all, this had happened to her once before with rather painful results.

"There it is!" Cara exclaimed, pointing to a blue colonial standing about thirty feet back from the cliff, its simple shape making a pleasing picture against the sky. "That color is called Williamsburg blue. I helped Dad touch up the porch last year. Didn't I Dad?"

"You sure did," he agreed, then added in a loud aside to Destiny, "It took me three weeks to get the paint out of my hair."

Cara laughingly slapped his shoulder. "It did not! Anyway, that was Joe's fault. He knocked the brush out of my hand when he ran by 'cause you said you were gonna *walk* around the house and check for bare spots.''

Destiny was able to laugh with them, knowing from Cara's tales of her summer visits that Joe was Rafe's black Labrador and that one must never say the word "walk" or jangle car keys for fear of being trampled by the dog in his eagerness to join any expedition, be it on foot or on wheels.

"Who took care of Joe while you were with us in Los Angeles?" Cara asked in sudden concern.

"Jenny came over to feed him and take him for walks."

Cara leaned up against Rafe's shoulders and pleaded, "Can I call her right away when we get home? Please?"

Destiny felt a vague uneasiness about this unusual situation. She had sent Cara to Rafe every summer for the past five years with complete confidence in his ability to care for her, both emotionally and physically, to discipline her if necessary and to make her feel loved. Cara always came home when the summer was over, full of stories about what they had done, what her father had said, jokes and bits of wisdom he had shared with her. She knew Cara had enjoyed her summers with her father and that she could barely wait for the next one to roll around. But, somehow, Destiny had never quite seen father and daughter together in her mind—how Cara eagerly took his hand, teased with him, leaned against him. She had never quite imagined the bond Rafe was building with Cara, but she discovered it now in his eyes. For a father and daughter who saw each other only a half-dozen weeks out of the year, they were very close. And that made her present position uncomfortable.

She didn't want Cara to begin thinking that this was a reconciliation. She had just referred to Rafe's house as "home." Was that just a matter of semantics because it was their destination, or did she really consider this more home than the house she shared with her mother and Frances in Beverly Hills?

Jealousy intruded upon Destiny's budding sense of well-being. She felt ashamed of it instantly and pushed it away.

"Why do I have to wait until after dinner?" Cara was asking. "I'm not very hungry."

"But Jenny and her parents probably are, and it wouldn't be polite to interrupt them until they're finished. You can call her at seven-thirty, okay?"

The thought of more food made Destiny lean back, a hand to her already protesting stomach.

"I'm still stuffed from the plane," she told Rafe.

He gave her a falsely sober side-glance. "You shouldn't have eaten it," he said. "Those jets'll give you heartburn every time."

Cara and Frances collapsed into giggles and Destiny groaned, unable to halt the bubble of laughter when he winked at her.

"Here we are." Rafe pulled onto an unpaved road that deposited them in the driveway of the blue house. Even before the motor died, a large black dog danced around the driver's side door. The moment Rafe stepped out, the Lab launched itself at him, welcoming his master home with much whining and bouncing and tail wagging.

Cara received a welcome that was almost as enthusiastic, and Frances was approved, as well.

"You open up, Cara," Rafe directed, handing his daughter a ring of keys, careful that they didn't jangle. "Do you remember which one it is?"

"Of course," Cara replied with a grin. "I live here, too, you know. Sometimes."

"Right. Go on in, Frances. I'll bring your things in."

Cara ran up to the house, trailed by the housekeeper, as Destiny stepped out of the car. Joe immediately came to offer his friendship.

"He certainly is big!" Destiny declared, dropping her purse and makeup case on the walkway to stop and pet the huge head.

"Down, Joe," Rafe commanded quietly as the dog responded excitedly to Destiny's overtures. "Watch your slacks, Des. He doesn't mean any harm, but he's got a paw like a cleaver."

Destiny scratched behind Joe's ears, having no objection to the enormous, licking tongue. "I take it he isn't a guard dog," she teased.

"He's a friend," Rafe said, picking up her things with a grin, "But if you look at me cross-eyed, he'll take your arm off."

"Goodness," she grimaced. "Then I wouldn't be able to wear anything but togas."

"Or be nice to me," he suggested, leading the way to the house, "and you can wear whatever you like."

Destiny returned his grin and marched past him to the porch. "I'll weigh my decision carefully. Right now I'd sell my soul—I'd even be nice to you—for a Pepsi."

"You still don't drink coffee?" he asked, reaching an arm beyond her to push the front door open.

"No. I know it's un-American of me, but I don't understand how something could smell so wonderful brewing and taste so revoltingly bitter."

"That's a very philosophical observation," he said with quiet cynicism. "Sounds a lot like our relationship. It had such promise and left us both..."

Without stopping to consider, she denied instantly, "I'm not bitter."

They faced each other on the porch, her green eyes darkening as a sudden somberness crept into her mood. Rafe looked considering and a little surprised. "I was going to say that it left us both changed."

"Changed," she repeated, embarrassed by her unnecessary admission. She tried to make her manner offhand. "Yes. I think you could say we've changed. We've come a long way from Belleville Avenue in New Bedford, Massachusetts."

"One of my packing plants is still in New Bedford," Rafe said, studying Destiny's eyes. "But my administrative offices are now in Portland, about forty miles from here."

"You don't still rent the tenement?"

"No." He shook his head. "I let it go after you left."

She saw it clearly in her mind's eye suddenly, the brown frame, three-story tenement house in which they had rented four small rooms. In New Bedford the tenements were kept in good repair, and they housed a large percentage of the city's middle-income population. She and Rafe could hear other tenants' arguments, the television upstairs, the children downstairs, yet when they closed the bedroom door they were locked in a velvet cocoon of tender love and flammable passion. Memories of those nights, memories that had become the fantasies of the last lonely years, now swept over her with debilitating clarity.

They were preparing dinner in the small corridor kitchen, bumping into each other and laughing. They were sitting in a corner of the sofa watching television, arms and legs all entangled, feeling languid and replete. They were walking arm in arm into the bedroom, pausing by the bed in the darkness as Rafe's warm hands reached with gentle possession under her shirt.

"Des?"

Destiny refocused on the present with a start, the pulse in her throat ticking madly. She swayed a little in reaction. Rafe put her case down and swung her up into his arms.

"I'm all right," she insisted, but she was too late. He was already striding through the doorway and into the house with her. He deposited her on a chair in the living room and looked down at her in concern. "Do you want to lie down?"

"I'm fine. I didn't feel ill, I just got..." She stopped herself, unwilling to tell him that memories of their tenement on Belleville Avenue had taken her over for a moment. "I've been so inactive the past few days I just got a little woozy. Oh, I remember those!" The chair in which Rafe had placed her faced a stone fireplace. On the mantel were familiar pictures of his brothers and his father aboard the Mayflower, and on rough wooden shelves on both sides of the fireplace was Rafe's collection of fishing memorabilia, some pieces of which she recognized from the tenement. There were other objects that were not familiar to her. "What are those?"

"Parts of old cannery equipment," he replied, sitting on the arm of the sofa near her. "None of it is valuable. I just found the shapes and their obvious age pleasing."

Destiny looked around herself at the room, absorbing its cozy warmth. The chair in which she sat, along with its mate and the long sofa, was upholstered in a blue, beige and brown plaid fabric with a wide weave; there were two sturdy oak end tables on which stood tall brass lamps, and a coffee table that she was sure had been fashioned from a hatch cover. The overall environment was comfortable and conducive to conversation.

"This is a wonderful room," Destiny said. "Did you decorate it yourself?"

Rafe laughed. "I rarely get to do anything of a domestic nature by myself. Michelle and Augie feel obliged to lend their expertise to their lonely brother-in-law. They're anxious to come to my rescue at the drop of a hat."

"Augie?" Destiny asked, puzzled.

"Mike's wife," Rafe explained. "I forgot that you've never met her."

"Of course. Cara has talked about her, but she calls her Aunt Augusta." Destiny tried to appear casual. "So they consider you helpless and lonely?"

He laughed again. "I think I'm a pathetic figure in their eyes. They're always giving me long matchmaking looks and forcing their assistance on me if I have to decorate or go Christmas shopping or do something that they feel requires a woman's supervision."

"Why did you never get any?"

"Any what?"

"Feminine supervision," she clarified, forcing herself to look him in the eye. She had often wondered why he had never remarried.

He gave her question a moment's smiling consideration. "I suppose because I've already had it once."

"Ah." She nodded, trying not to betray the hurt she felt at that answer. "And you didn't like it."

"No," he corrected gently. "I did like it but didn't know how to handle it. It seemed foolish to try again and risk the same outcome."

Destiny swallowed, feeling his hurt as well as her own. "Well," she said briskly, getting to her feet. "I'd like to clean up and put my things away. Where will I..." Her cheeks reddened suddenly, and she couldn't believe she was stumbling over the simple question. She braced herself and began again, not faltering, this time. "Where will I sleep?"

Mercifully he ignored her discomfort. "Come on. I'll show you."

They climbed into the warm shadows of the upstairs to a bedroom in cool shades of oyster, gray and blue. Rafe crossed the room to throw open a window, and the room was instantly filled with the scent of roses and the smell of the sea. As Destiny moved to place her purse on the bed, she paused, staring at the piece of furniture in surprise. It was maple with four turned posts, one of them still bearing the scar from a figurine she had aimed at Rafe's head during an argument.

"Our bed," she said aloud, surprised by the sound of her voice.

He came toward her, helping her off with her light jacket. "Yes. It's still a good piece of furniture."

She nodded. "Your parents bought it when they first got married and...and gave it to us."

"When I bought modern furniture for my condo in Portland, I furnished this place with some stuff I already had from the old days." He parted the wardrobe doors to hang up her jacket, and she noticed two things simultaneously. One was the complete lack of sentimentality in him for the bed that held so many memories for her; the other was that the closet was half filled with his clothes. She chose to concentrate on the matter she thought she could deal with. "This is your room?" she asked.

"Yes." He turned to her, apparently speculating on the meaning of her slightly aggressive tone of voice. "But, relax. I won't be in it."

"That wasn't why I asked," she said in a tone that scolded. "I was merely going to point out that you don't have to forgo your comfort for me. That sofa downstairs looked perfectly comfortable."

"It's no problem," he insisted. "My office is at the other end of the hall, and it has a Hide-a-Bed. I'll be fine, as long as you don't mind my leaving my clothes in here. You should still have plenty of room for yours."

"I don't mind."

"Good." He threw a door open in a corner of the room. "Bath's in here. Cara is next door to you, and Frances is across the hall. Go ahead and freshen up, and I'll call you when dinner's ready."

She halted his exit from the room with a light hand on his arm. She withdrew it instantly when she felt a sudden tension between them.

"Heartburn from the jets notwithstanding, Rafe, I'm really not very hungry."

Hands in his pockets, he faced her, his expression sympathetic but insistent. "I know. But Doctor Pointer said you have to reestablish a regular eating pattern, even if you only eat a little, so your stomach gets used to receiving food." His brow furrowed and his eyes darkened. "You're not in very good health, Des. But we'll eat lightly—sandwiches or something. Mike and Manny were staying with me, so I could feed an army on what's in the kitchen. Take your time. It'll be ready when you are."

When Rafe disappeared into the hallway, closing the door, Destiny wandered to the window. It looked out over the wide expanse of ocean, and she watched the water darken as the sun went down. Birds swooped, preparing to settle down for the evening, and following their graceful flight, Destiny spotted the distant lighthouse. She smiled. This was a far cry from the view out of her bedroom window in Beverly Hills. After the hectic pace of the past five years of her life, this quiet, uncluttered landscape felt strange, though pleasant. She leaned against the window frame and sighed.

She found Rafe unsettling. One moment she felt relaxed and at ease with him because he was very much the man she remembered: handsome, energetic, dispatching directions with the confidence of a seasoned skipper. Then he would be carefully considerate, sensitive to her in ways he had never been before, and he became suddenly someone else—physically familiar but emotionally different—a man she didn't know. Glimpses of that sensitivity in Rafe made her feel a little panicky because she had taken control of her life after their divorce, and she liked that feeling of independence. But when he seemed to understand her needs, she felt forces at work she couldn't control. She felt drawn to him, felt herself wanting to know this new Rafe, felt herself wondering what it would be like to share everything with him.

Destiny found the bathroom stocked with fresh towels and soap and spent a delicious ten minutes under the shower. When she emerged into the bedroom, her two suitcases were on the bed and two empty drawers in the wardrobe stood open, inviting her to place her lingerie and sweaters inside. Another thoughtful gesture from Rafe.

When Destiny got down to the kitchen in a denim skirt and sweater, she found Rafe and Frances at work on sandwiches, Cara supervising from her perch on the counter beside Rafe. The table was set, a teapot and a carafe of coffee in the middle of the table.

Then Rafe swung Cara to the floor and handed her the plate of sandwiches. She put it on the table, then pulled out a chair and sat down as the rest of the group joined her.

"You've got a little color back in your cheeks," Frances

noted as she filled Destiny's teapot with boiling water. "In fact, you're looking a little like your old self already."

Rafe studied Destiny across the table, his eyes evaluating the look in hers. He smiled. "Try to get half a sandwich down. There's crab salad or sliced turkey."

Destiny helped herself from the plate he offered and smiled a thank-you, her heart beating a little too swiftly.

"I can hardly wait to see Jenny's little brother!" Cara said excitedly, munching on crab salad. "I wish we could have a baby, too."

When Rafe and Destiny's eyes met across the table, hers in panic and his in amusement, a silent, mutual agreement was reached to let the comment pass.

Never one to skirt an issue, however, Cara pressed insistently, "Couldn't we have one this summer? Now that we're all here, I mean."

"It takes longer than a summer," Destiny replied calmly, carefully avoiding Rafe's eyes. "And your father and I aren't married anymore."

"I know. It takes nine months and one week," Cara spouted knowledgeably. "So we could have it in..." She closed her eyes to calculate. Then she looked at her father. "In March, right?"

He nodded seriously. "Right."

"Right," Cara repeated. "So we could get one started, though, couldn't we?"

"Cara," Rafe said gently, but in a tone meant to capture the child's attention. "You missed what Mom said. We're not married anymore."

"But she's here with you," Cara pointed out.

"That's because she needed a place to rest away from her work, and this house is perfect for that. Even though I'm no longer her husband," he explained, "I can still be her friend."

Cara looked puzzled. "But isn't that how marriages happen? Friends want to be together always?"

Destiny closed her eyes, dryly thanking the fates that had

given her such an astute child. "Marriage is a step beyond friendship," she said. "An important step. But sometimes friends don't know whether they love each other or not. It's just not a good idea to…to start a baby when the climate's uncertain."

"Climate." Cara said the word over, turning to her father. "Doesn't climate mean weather?"

"Yes," he said, smiling. "But a lot of things have a climate—meaning that they have sunny days and stormy ones, too. And you don't want to bring babies into a situation when you're not certain which it'll be."

Cara studied her father gravely. "That's what happened to me, isn't it? I came into a storm."

Destiny felt the question like a blow. Cara had never expressed distress over her position in their divided family before. Even Rafe looked unsettled for a moment, but then he replied evenly, "No. You were born when the days were bright and sunny." He covered her hand with his own and squeezed. "But the weather can change. That's why you try to be careful."

Her throat tight, Destiny reached out to cover Cara's other hand. "We both love you, and the change had nothing to do with you."

In an adult gesture of independence and determination that reminded Destiny alarmingly of Rafe, Cara pulled her hands gently away and picked up her sandwich with a toss of her dusty blond ponytails.

"It seems to me that after a storm, it gets sunny again," she said. "And maybe you could go from friends back to being married. You did it before."

Rafe and Destiny's eyes met again, his amusedly considering this time and hers filled with a cautious curiosity. What would it be like to have a baby with him again, she wondered. He had been an attentive expectant father, reminding her not to overdo, providing the back rubs that became more precious than gold, helping her on with her shoes toward the end of her pregnancy, holding her close to him as they negotiated the tenement steps.

He had still been a little inclined to order rather than ask and speak as though there would be no question about what he said, but he had been loving and kind and made her feel secure. Following her mother from husband to husband, Destiny had known precious little of that security. Rafe had been a strong, warm haven to her in those days, until she grew up and discovered that the woman inside required more freedom to move, more scope in which to express herself. And that was when the trouble started.

Destiny came back to awareness of the present in the soft, dark web of Rafe's gaze. She looked back at him with a kind of sadness, still trapped in her happy memories of her pregnancy.

Then Rafe was distracted by Cara. "Please can I call Jenny now?"

Rafe pulled his eyes away from Destiny to glance at his watch. "All right. If she wants you to go over, I'll walk down to pick you up at nine o'clock."

As Cara skipped away and Frances began clearing the table, Rafe turned to Destiny with a curious expression. "I watched you go from a smile to a frown in the space of about thirty seconds. What were you thinking about?"

She leaned her chin on the heel of her hand and studied him consideringly. He enjoyed teasing her; it would be interesting to see how he took it.

"I was thinking about having babies," she admitted.

One eyebrow lifted in mild surprise, but deep in his eyes she saw a small flare. "Cara got you thinking."

She nodded. "Yes. I was remembering how attentive and sweet you were when I was carrying her."

He smiled, folding his arms on the table and leaning toward her. "That's because you were so beautiful—even more so than usual. And who could be unkind to a woman who constantly craved grape soda and peanut butter cups?"

Destiny laughed. "Well, Cara doesn't seem to have suffered for it," she said. "Unless you consider a tendency to be a little too candid cause for concern."

He got to his feet and pulled out her chair. "She feels sure she can tell us what she's thinking. That can't be bad."

"That's true," Destiny agreed. "Only embarrassing."

"Step into my parlor," he said, his hand at her back, pushing her gently toward the living room. "I think we should come to an agreement about that."

She stopped at the chair on which she had sat earlier and turned to him as he sank onto the sofa, propping his feet up on the coffee table. "Agreement about what?"

"About our being embarrassed with each other."

"Oh." She sat, leaning with deceptive calm into a corner of the chair and crossed her legs. Rafe watched the movement, and when the skirt slid back against her slip, revealing too much thigh, she pushed it over her knee with a gesture that expressed more composure than she felt. "That's a little difficult to avoid, isn't it, considering the circumstances?"

"Apparently," he said, his eyes going in merriment from her skirt to her eyes. When she frowned at him, he smiled. "There's no reason we should be uncomfortable with each other. Just because we were once intimate, it doesn't mean that we can't conduct a platonic relationship for the sake of your health and my enjoyment of my daughter. The fact that we'll be sharing the same house for a few months doesn't mean that we're gasping to get into bed again." He grinned. "Or into the shower, or in front of the coal stove, or in the rocker, or any of the other places we used to find so delightful."

If that statement was supposed to put her at ease, it backfired, Destiny thought dryly as her face pinked and her heart began to pump like a steam engine. They had been rather resourceful in their lovemaking, and she suddenly saw them in vivid detail in her mind's eye on the braided rug in front of the stove. They used to joke about how the stove in their apartment lacked the romance of a fireplace, but it had warmed their bodies deliciously while their lovemaking fused a bond between them it had seemed nothing could ever dissolve.

"You're wearing that look again," Rafe said, bringing her out of her thoughts. "A moment ago you were smiling, and now you look as though you've lost your last friend. What are you thinking?"

She gave a little mirthless laugh. "I'm sorry. I know it's completely at odds with how comfortable you're trying to make me feel, but I was thinking about how much in love we were." She shook her head helplessly. "I don't know what's gotten into me. Frankly, I haven't thought about 'us' at all in three years. The first year after I left was pretty rough; the second year was a little easier to cope with because I got the job with the studio and got so busy that there was little time to think. The memories would only come back to me at odd moments when I would look into Cara's eyes and see you, or when I would be the recipient of that exasperated look she sometimes gives me that's so like one of your expressions...." Destiny shook herself out of the sadness that tried to take over once more. "But I worked hard, became head designer, and was so proud of myself, so...so..."

"Satisfied?" he suggested.

She sighed. "No. At least not lately."

"Mmm. Burnout, you said."

"I think that's part of it. I guess I'm just ready for a change." Destiny looked up to smile at Frances as the housekeeper walked into the room. "What have you got, Frances?"

The woman bustled over to the coffee table with a tray bearing two steaming mugs. She put the tray down and handed a mug to Destiny. "It's a toddy. The doctor said you could have a little liquor to help you sleep." She fixed Rafe with a pointed look as he reached for his mug. "And after the past few days you've put in, sleeping hardly at all,

I'd like to see you drink all of that, too. You don't mind me using your brandy?''

Rafe took a cautious sip and toasted his approval. "The kitchen is yours, Frances. Thank you."

As Frances disappeared into her domain, Rafe leaned against the sofa cushions, resting the cup against the upholstered arm. "So tell me about the life of a costume designer for a major studio," he said. "Is it as exciting as it sounds?"

"It's very exciting," she replied, but her tone was colored with a jaded weariness. "You mingle with some of the world's most outrageous personalities, observe some of the world's finest creative minds at work and dress some of the world's most beautiful bodies." She smiled, trying hard to convey how she felt about her career. "I've grown and learned so much. I'm sure with all you've accomplished, you know there's little else more rewarding than the realization that you've done something you once thought you couldn't do."

Rafe nodded, his relaxed manner encouraging her to go on.

Destiny's eyes clouded. "But...many of those mercurial personalities are pushed and tested to their limits; twenty-hour days, endless retakes, sometimes unspeakable discomfort in the interest of the film's authenticity. They come close to breaking, but they have careers at stake, families to feed, or simply lives that must go on." She shook her head, feeling sad for the brilliance she had seen compromised in the interest of remaining on top. "Drugs are passed around like chewing gum, alcohol fills the lonely hours and somebody else's wife or girlfriend is fair game because none of it is real anyway."

Rafe watched her quietly.

"All the crews aren't like that, of course, and not everyone is a druggie or an alcoholic, but the last film I worked on before I did the tour had more than its share of them, and the tension wore me out. We shot part of the film in a small town in Mexico where we were warned to stick to studio food, but I was never free when it was available. I think I lost fifteen pounds during those five weeks. The rest of the time my stomach was too knotted up with tension to receive food."

Destiny balanced her cup on the arm of her chair and tucked her feet under her, smiling at Rafe. "It isn't all horror, and I don't mean to imply that it is, but sometimes I feel like a stranger in a madhouse; everyone is caught up in the fiction, and I'm trying to dress them to look real." She shook her head. "Weird thought, I know. But during this last film there were a couple of times when I felt like I was slipping over onto the side of unreality, and it frightened me. I decided to find a way out."

Rafe frowned. "Yet you were ready to head off to Morocco next week."

"I was contracted for that film," she explained, then fixed him with a look of censure, remembering his management of that detail. The fact that Clay had tried to talk her into going to Morocco anyway when she called, as Rafe had predicted, didn't help.

"During the television interview I saw the other day, Gambel mentioned an offer from a clothing manufacturer." Rafe neatly sidestepped a possible argument.

Recognizing the maneuver, Destiny decided she was too tired to do anything other than comply. "It's the perfect solution to my dilemma, just the break I've been hoping for. I'd still be in the field I love, but I could spend more time with Cara and, for most of the year anyway, live where I want to live." Despite her enthusiasm for the opportunity, her expression was troubled.

"But?" Rafe prompted over the rim of his cup.

"But..." Destiny admitted with a grimace, "I'm terrified."

"When you've just won one of the highest honors in your field?"

"Costuming and fashion are very different. In the past

I've always had a script to follow and very specific standards to meet. But fashion..." She paused to shake her head doubtfully. "Fashion is understanding women...their needs and the image they'd like to project. I'm not sure I know myself that well. I'd really be breaking free of all I've done in the past and striking out into new territory." She shook her head to admit, "I'm not sure I can do it."

Rafe smiled as though her uncertainty amused him. "Des, where's the courage that made you pack up your portfolio full of all your little theater work and show it to a studio? As a single woman on her own with the responsibility of a child, you broke into costume design for films and topped that by winning a very prestigious award and in such a short time. I'm sure after Wellesley and the apartment on Belleville Avenue, Hollywood was a blind step into new territory, and now you're standing on top of their mountain. All the things you're afraid of attempting, you've already mastered."

"But this is different."

"If you did it then, you can do it now. You're older and wiser and that much more experienced. Did you respond to the offer?"

"I told them I'd try to have some sketches in their hands by the end of August." Destiny sighed and looked around herself at the quiet living room. "I thought I'd have to do them in my spare time in Morocco. Maybe there is a chance."

"There's more than a chance," he said, sounding completely convinced. "This is where your innate cussedness pays off. You can do it, Des."

"I appreciate your confidence in me," she said, laughing. "If not the reason for it." She smothered a yawn and opened her eyes wide as she felt them trying to close.

Rafe got to his feet and reached down to pull her to hers. "Come on. I'll help you upstairs. I've got to get a few things out of the closet."

While Destiny pretended to fidget with her suitcase, Rafe

went to the built-in drawers in the wardrobe and pulled out pajamas, underwear and socks. He balanced the pile between his two hands and fixed her with an inquiring look.

"Got everything you'll need?"

She nodded. "I think so. Are you sure about the room?"

"Positive. If you need me…" He paused but there was no wicked smile, no suggestive intonation. "I'm at the far end of the hall." He held the stack of clothes carefully and glanced at his watch. "I'm going to walk down to pick up Cara in a few minutes, but it's just down the slope. I won't be long."

"All right," she said evenly. "Thank you, Rafe. Good night."

"Good night, Des."

Destiny closed the door behind him and took her time about changing into pale green silk pajamas she had designed and made herself. She was sleepy but not relaxed, she realized as she paced to the window. Would she ever be able to relax around Rafe, she wondered. Despite his assurances that there was no reason they should feel uncomfortable with each other, her mind kept playing tricks on her, calling incidents out of her memory and reeling them out for her so that she remembered in detail everything about Rafe that she had loved.

She had to get hold of herself, she thought, as she felt tension beginning to build. She was a capable, intelligent woman. She could turn those memories off if she wanted to and remember that she was here to rest. Had she chosen to go anywhere else, her daughter would have been bitterly disappointed. She and Rafe could be friends now, and that was all either of them wanted. There. Feeling she had things in perspective, Destiny turned out the light and pushed the covers back, got into bed and was immediately set upon by every ghost she thought she had just so intelligently thrust aside. This had been their bed; she suddenly remembered her first night in it and Rafe's loving care and patience. Then her body seemed to find just the place toward the middle that was molded with the contour of her body. She felt Rafe move on the other side, pulling her into his arms. Then his lips were on hers, sliding to her ear. Her stomach contracted and shivers rippled down her spine. He was nipping at the cords of her neck, raining kisses down to the scooped neck of her nightgown, pushing it aside and capturing a breast with a warm, calloused hand. Her nipples pursed and hardened.

Destiny sat bolt upright, her heart pounding, her eyes searching the darkness for reality. Was she awake or asleep? Her chest was heaving, her pulse racing, her skin tingling as though it had been touched.

She fell back against the headboard, beginning to wonder if she should have gone to her mother's. She would have been driven crazy within two days, but she'd have been heart whole. Already, after only two days in Rafe's presence and one day in his house, she felt she would never leave here with that claim.

When she'd been flying to L.A. from Portland, thinking about the lonely drudgery her life had become, she recalled the changes that had taken place within herself during the past five years—the designer in her was making great strides and looking for new worlds to conquer; the mother in her was learning and loving every moment; the daughter in her was trying desperately to be tolerant and understanding and toss aside old grievances; but the woman...the woman was dying.

Yet now—and as Destiny slipped under the covers and lay still in the darkness she could feel it—something was stirring in that dark little corner of her. The movement was cautious, just an exploratory stretch, but the woman in Destiny Black was coming alive. She pulled the blankets up to her chin, afraid.

At the other end of the hall, Rafe lay fully clothed in the darkness of his office on the sofa bed he had yet to open. Cara was home and in bed, and the house was still.

You really are full of it, Janeiro, he told himself, remem-

bering what he had said to Destiny in the living room.
*"Just because we were once intimate, it doesn't mean we
can't conduct a platonic relationship for the sake of your
health and my enjoyment of my daughter."* She had looked
a little relieved to hear him say that, so he had nobly added,
*"The fact that we'll be sharing the same house for a few
months doesn't mean that we're gasping to get into bed
again."*

She might not be, but he sure as hell was. He ran a hand
over the tense knot in his gut, reminding himself that he
didn't want to make the same mistake again. The loneliness
of the past five years had been hell, but it had done a lot
for his potential as the second party in a relationship.

At sixteen he had physically looked like a man. He had
worked the boat with his father during the summers, pulled
his weight like a man and drank with the crew at Mallo-
ney's, where they never checked ID's. Though Rafe had
loved fishing, he had suspected that his real strength lay
elsewhere. His father hadn't understood. Rafe had had to
fight to go to college, and when he graduated and went
back to the boat, he'd had to tolerate the condescending
nickname of "college man." By then he'd had ideas about
what could be done with the business his father had built
with hard work and unfailing integrity. But it wasn't until
the old man broke his hip on an icy deck that Rafe was
given the opportunity to try. As the *Mayflower*'s skipper,
he studied new equipment and techniques and more effi-
cient ways to market their fish.

And that was the man Destiny had met and married, a
man in fighting trim shape and king of the mountain. He
could get anything he wanted in life, and he wanted her to
love him with the same fire that burned inside him. She
had loved him, he knew she had, but he never felt that her
love matched the deep intensity of his.

He had thought he could force the feeling from her, like
he wrested scallops from the sea—and she had finally run
from him. In the intervening years he had learned a lot from

boardroom politics. He had watched men wheel and deal, force an outcome through cunning and power; and he had known that he could never live with that kind of success. What came to him had to come because his honesty and skill earned it—and one day it had dawned on him that that same principle applied to his marriage. He could not force from Destiny what she was unwilling to give. He recognized that he had not truly been a man until the moment he understood that.

He sighed heavily and swung his legs over the side of the sofa, fighting the teasing discomfort of unfulfillment in his groin. So he was now a man—and his woman was sleeping at the other end of the hall. Coming to terms with himself had afforded little gain. He stared into the darkness as longing washed over him and reminded himself that one day patience on his part would change that.

Chapter Four

The ringing of the telephone woke Destiny the following morning. Fighting for full awareness, she sat up, clutching the sheet to her breasts. She looked up into Rafe's dark eyes as he put down a glass of orange juice and picked up the phone beside the bed.

"Hello," he said. Then he smiled and pushed her blanket-clad legs aside to sit beside her. "Hi, Mom."

He wore jeans and nothing else, his broad back and well-shaped feet were bare. His black hair was a wet mass of tiny ringlets hugging his head, and he smelled of a spicy cologne. Destiny tried to appear unaffected by his sexy proximity.

What sounded like a long and excited monologue was coming from the receiver held to Rafe's ear.

"No, Mike wasn't teasing you, Mom," he said gently, glancing over his shoulder at Destiny. "She's here with me." He listened another moment. "No, not exactly. The three of us needed a little R and R and decided to spend it together."

Destiny mouthed a "Ha! Ha!" at his interpretation of his collusion with Doctor Pointer. He narrowed his eyes in mock severity.

"Yes, she's right here. Want to say hello?"

Destiny shook her head at him, panic bunching like a fist in her stomach. She hadn't contacted Rafe's parents in five years, and only received news through Cara. Although his mother had always treated her with kindness and affection, she and Rafe's father had never gotten along.

Rafe held the phone out to her with a smile that was gentle but merciless.

She glowered at him. Then, drawing a deep breath, she said with what she hoped was unself-conscious affection, "Hello, Mom."

"Destiny, *querida*!" Josephina Janeiro replied. Her greeting forced a pleased smile from Destiny despite her apprehensions. There were no recriminations in that voice.

A first generation American, Josephina had been raised in a strict, old-world Portuguese family and looked as though she might have just arrived from the old country. She was built on the same rotund lines as Frances and had graying black hair tied in a tight bun. She had bright black eyes with which she had blessed all three of her sons.

The two women small-talked for several moments, each carefully avoiding discussion of the divorce and the fact that Destiny was staying at Rafe's house.

"How is Cara?" Josephina asked.

"She's fine," Destiny assured her, adding with a grudging glance at Rafe, "She looks more and more like her father every day."

That seemed to please Josephina enormously, and Destiny heard her speaking softly in Portuguese to someone with whom she was sharing the phone.

"You'll come and see us, won't you," a masculine voice asked, "while you're on the east coast?" The deep baritone with the broad Massachusetts vowels belonged to Rafe's father, Toby.

"Hello, Toby," Destiny replied. "I...don't know if that'll be possible." She looked at Rafe again, her green eyes anxious.

But Toby was talking, telling her how eager the Janeiros were to see Cara again. It had been a whole year since Rafe had brought her home to visit. "And what's this about R and R?'' Toby asked in the blustery, teasing manner that had always been the only way he could deal with her. "That's for soldiers. Married people live together forever. None of this divorce and R and R business."

Josephina's groan was audible, and there was another sound that might have been a small fist striking a hard shoulder.

"I'm sure you'd like to talk to your son," Destiny said with barely concealed irritation. Glaring at Rafe and slapping the receiver into his hand, she scrambled out of bed and into the bathroom.

Just why her dismay at Toby's remarks had turned to anger at Rafe she wasn't sure, but Rafe and anger formed a familiar pattern, which she seemed to slip into with relative ease—even after their mellow discussion of last night.

Under the hot, pounding spray of the shower Destiny cursed herself for her present position and for the way in which she had allowed the next few months of her life to be managed.

She shouldn't have listened to anyone; she should have done what she wanted. She should have ignored the doctor, ignored Rafe... But what had she wanted to do? She couldn't remember that any of her options had been particularly appealing. She hadn't been enthusiastic about going to Morocco, that was certain. And she had been tired of everything about her work.

Destiny turned off the shower and pushed her wet hair back out of her eyes. Hadn't she been just a little...interested in observing Rafe's life-style? In seeing the house in Maine that Cara talked about incessantly? In seeing if there was anything left alive of the five years they had spent together?

No, of course not. Briskly she wrapped a towel around her body and another around her hair. She had wanted to spend time with her daughter, and she felt it prudent to follow the doctor's advice. That was all.

It annoyed her to come face-to-face with Toby's attitude

again; she found herself less tolerant of it now than ever. Five years on her own had tested her resources and her flexibility to the limit and helped her find wells of ingenuity she didn't know she possessed. Her considerable inherited wealth aside, she would never have to depend on a man for financial or emotional support.

But it wasn't fair to take her anger at Toby out on Rafe. In the old days she used to think Rafe would mature to become just like his father—a swaggering, one-dimensional throwback to the Stone Age. She had to admit she'd been wrong about that. What she'd seen of him in the past two days showed Rafe turned in quite another direction.

Destiny pulled the door open and marched into the bedroom.

Rafe, still bare-chested and barefoot, reclined on the trunk at the foot of the bed. His eyes ran over Destiny's shoulders and legs, visible to him above and beneath the towel, then settled on the complex expression in her green eyes.

"Don't take it so hard," he said softly as he rose to his feet. "Dad didn't mean to hurt your feelings. He lives in another world."

"I'm sorry I was rude," she admitted grudgingly. She pushed the closet doors open to reach for her jeans and threw the denims on the bed. "But I don't know how or why your mother puts up with him."

"She loves him."

Destiny snatched a pink sweater out of a drawer and tossed it after the jeans. Her eyes flashed at him. "How can you love someone who dedicates himself to managing everyone else's life?"

"It's the old world way." Rafe picked up her sweater, which had missed the bed and landed instead on the floor. "Why do you love your mother when she's on her fourth husband and neither of you has ever understood the other?"

"I don't..." She had begun to deny that she loved Serena Fleming but found that she couldn't. The words lodged in her throat. "The old world is an ocean away from us," she said instead, "and many years gone. This is late twentieth-century America." She carried panties, socks and tennis shoes to the bed.

"My father's attitude is more than a time and a place," Rafe tried to explain. "It's born in the bone in a Portuguese man, in a fisherman. A man against the sea lives life with all the layers of civilization stripped away. If he isn't strong and tough and in control of himself and his crew and his boat—they're all going to the bottom." He lifted a brawny shoulder. "That's hard to turn off just because you're suddenly standing on the dock. He loves us all, my mother and my brothers and me, and he'd die in a minute for any one of us."

"Well, I don't want anybody to die for me," Destiny said angrily, pulling the towel off her hair. "I just want them to let me be who I am without having to listen to their condemnations and strictures." She gave him a feeble glower, the anger dying inside her replaced by depression. She sank onto the edge of the bed. "I should never have come."

"Look." Rafe knelt on one knee in front of her, balancing himself lightly with a hand on her bare knee. Every drop of blood in her body seemed to race to the spot. "I'm sorry he upset you before you even put your feet on the floor this morning," he apologized gently. "But he's two hundred miles away in New Bedford, and you don't have to see him if you don't want to. You're going to concentrate on eating and relaxing and, when you feel up to it, working on your sketches."

She nodded, not entirely convinced. "Sure."

His attention was suddenly caught by the pile of clothes beside her and the absence of a garment his young bride used to resent. "Do you still go braless in the summer?" he asked. His smile was blandly innocuous but his eyes were teasing.

She looked down at the things beside her and noted the omission. She smiled thinly. "No. I just forgot it."

"You used to be so adamant about how uncomfortable it made you."

She shrugged a delicate, naked shoulder. "That was before maturity and a little less muscle tone than I had all those years ago forced me to be practical."

Rafe studied the wispy tendrils of golden hair beginning to dry at her temples and the wide eyes full of mysterious complexities. His eyes wandered to the delicate slope of her shoulder, the perfect line of her collarbone above the small swell of ivory skin that disappeared into the towel. "Everything about you seems even more perfect than it was then," he said softly.

He felt the quiver of her thigh muscle under his hand and saw her lips part as though to register a protest. He wanted to reach up and take them, remembering their silky touch against his mouth. Looking up into her eyes, he found them frightened but fascinated, unfocused as though she, too, were trapped in memory.

His hand explored a little higher, the action almost beyond his power to stop it. He heard her draw a breath and hold it, time and air suspended as his hand moved higher still and encountered towel.

Then her fingers closed over his, and the breath left her in a gasping little rush. Rafe's heart was pounding, and he pushed himself to his feet before he followed every clamoring instinct that demand he rip the towel away and push her back on the bed to remind her of how it used to be.

"Jenny's father called this morning." He took a deep breath and was surprised to find a normal tone of voice. "He's taking Jenny to the high school for the Digby Day's play tryouts, and she wants Cara to go along. Is that all right with you?"

Destiny swallowed and cleared her throat. "Of course. If Cara wants to go."

He nodded. "He promised to have her home by dinner.

If you quit fiddling around and get dressed, I'll start breakfast. Drink your juice. Frances has gone to town for a few things.''

"I'm not..." Destiny began to protest.

"Fifteen minutes," he called back without breaking his stride down the hall. And her last word, "hungry," fell with no one to hear it.

Fifteen minutes later Destiny was drawn to the kitchen by a tantalizing smell that was spicy and vaguely familiar. Something about the aroma and the quiet kitchen filled with early morning sunlight began to lift her depression. Rafe was at work at the stove, and she peered around his shoulder to see him stirring crumbled sausage in an iron skillet.

"*Linguica!*" she exclaimed. She had developed a love for the fat, spicy Portuguese sausage while married to Rafe. She leaned over to sniff the contents of the pan.

"Oh!" she groaned blissfully. "Oh, Rafe, can I have a bite?"

He frowned down at her. "Doctor Pointer said you were to be on a bland diet, remember?"

"I know." She looked at him imploringly. "Just one small bite? I haven't had *linguica* in five years. Please?"

With an exasperated sound that told her he was conceding against his better judgment, Rafe took the fork with which he stirred the sausage and speared a piece, holding it out for her.

"Blow on it. It's hot."

She complied, then snapped it daintily from the fork. She closed her eyes to savor the flavor. When she opened them Rafe was smiling softly at her.

"Good?" he asked.

She rolled her eyes in gustatory ecstasy. "Delicious! Can I have one more bite?"

"You said just one."

"I'm greedy."

He gave her an apologetic smile. "Sorry. That's it or you'll be sick. Eggs up or over?"

"Over, please." Destiny fixed him with a carefully posed look of disappointment, but he failed to notice. "Where's Cara? Did I miss Jenny's father?"

Rafe broke three eggs into another skillet. "No. Jenny came over to play until her father's ready to leave. She and Cara are in the backyard. With Cara occupied today, that leaves us free and clear to do some shopping. Get the butter, will you, please?"

"Shopping?" Destiny looked at him over the refrigerator door. "For what?"

He put a pot of tea in the middle of the table. "A drafting table, a sewing machine. Whatever else a designer requires."

She carried the butter dish to the table, surprised by his suggestion. "Thank you, Rafe, but that isn't necessary."

"Of course it is." He smiled at her over his shoulder. "I can remember you working on costumes on a Sunday afternoon, running from the dining room table where you were sketching to the sewing machine to see if this or that would work."

She sat at the table and smiled dreamily at him. She had loved those Sunday afternoons because he had been there, within reach of her hand, instead of God knew where in some storm, making her crazy with worry and missing him.

"The sunshine will be good for you; you'll get to see a little of Digby Head; and you'll have what you need when you're ready to go to work on the sketches." He brought her plate to the table and gave her a diagnostic look. "Think you're up to walking around?"

"Of course I am. But you don't have to entertain me if you have better things to do."

"I'm on vacation," he said, sitting across from her with his own plate. "I left orders that I wasn't to be called unless something burns down. Pass the salt, please."

She looked at her plate with its single egg and one slice of decrusted toast, then at his plate with its two eggs, three pieces of toast and a fat link of *linguica*.

He held a hand out for the salt, then arched an eyebrow when he looked over to find her clutching the large stoneware shaker possessively.

"I'll trade you for another piece of sausage," she bargained.

He looked into her level gaze, unmoved. "Destiny…"

"Just one." When he didn't react, she tilted her head, widened her eyes and made them look doleful. "Please?"

He put a hand over his eyes, unable to withstand her plea. "Don't do that!"

"Then give me a piece," she insisted. "Now."

Grudgingly he complied with a small sliver of sausage. She handed the salt over with a triumphant smile.

"You must be fun to deal with when it comes time to negotiate your contracts," he observed.

"I have an agent for that," she replied, laughing. "And that kind of ploy usually only works in matters of a personal nature and only against a man."

"So you've become worldly and wily?"

She laughed again, at herself this time. "No. But I've watched some of the finest actresses at work. I was bound to pick up a thing or two."

He looked up from a sip of coffee. "Who do you use it on?" The question and his manner were casual, but there was something very serious in his eyes. Did he really care, she wondered.

"Actors who are arguing about their costumes, lighting men who aren't doing their best for the actor, and therefore my clothes, directors who want to cut a scene that has my best costume in it."

"Are they all pushovers like me," he asked, "or do you sometimes lose?"

"I often lose," she admitted. "There's a lot of ego out there. It makes one ruthless and able to resist the most powerful persuasion."

"Good," he said grinning. "I'd hate to have you get overconfident."

They continued eating in silence and were almost finished when a flushed Cara appeared at the back door to announce breathlessly, "Jenny's father's here!"

Jeff Morrison was a short, round man with a wide smile and a crippling handshake. After being introduced to him, Destiny tried inconspicuously to pry her fingers apart. She also tried hard to hold back the explanation for her presence that she felt gushing from a core of confusion within her.

Jeff seemed very well acquainted with Rafe, and Destiny was sure he was wondering why his neighbor had suddenly shown up with a wife and his once-a-year child. The scene was all so domestic, somehow, parents smiling over their daughters, exchanging pleasantries.

But Jenny's father gave her no strange looks—only an open smile and a sincere invitation to come by one evening and meet his wife and their new baby. Perhaps Rafe had explained her presence. She wished she knew what he had said.

Cara and Jenny, a small, dark-featured child, tossed a ball back and forth, and Joe ran crazily between them.

"Okay, girls, let's go!" Morrison called, moving toward his station wagon. "I'll have Cara back for dinner," he promised Rafe and Destiny as he got into his car and the girls climbed in on the passenger side.

"Bye, Mom." Cara waved through the open window as they headed down the driveway. "Bye, Daddy."

Rafe and Destiny waved back, then turned toward the house. "Cara's a ham," she said. "She'll love watching them try out."

"She may do more than watch. There's a role for her if she wants it, according to Jeff. Come on. Before we go I'll show you the room I was talking about."

Standing in the middle of a large, square room with a wide window looking out onto the ocean, Destiny had to admit that it was perfect. There was a deep wardrobe closet with built-in drawers, which would be ideal for storing files and supplies. She knew she could happily work on her sketches in this room.

She looked around at its current furnishings of a small sofa and chair. "Don't you use this room for anything?"

"Just as a guest room when the family visits."

She paced off the area under the window. "A large worktable would fit comfortably right here," she said absently, her mind already organizing the room for her purposes. "It's so light in here. There's not a bad place to put anything."

Then practical matters claimed her attention. "I'm not sure I have that much cash with me. Surely credit cards are welcome in Digby Head?"

"I'll take care of whatever you need," Rafe said simply.

"No." She folded her arms, looking firm. "I don't want you to do that."

He pulled the door open and gestured her out into the hall. "Let's not argue about it. I'll take care of what you need. You might want your cash and your credit cards for something else later. When you get around to it, you can open a bank account here for the summer."

"Rafe..." she began to protest.

"Let's go," he was saying as he headed toward the stairs. "We can..."

"Stop!" The commanding note in her voice surprised both of them. Rafe turned slowly to face her in the quiet hallway. The patch of carpet on which she stood was spotlighted by the sunlight from the room they had just inspected. He looked at her steadily, not quite annoyed but definitely not pleased, either. She drew a deep breath, and the front of her pink sweater rose and fell with an undulation he found distracting. He forced himself to focus on her eyes as he walked slowly back to her. "Yes?" he asked quietly.

"If we're going to coexist," she said, refusing to be intimidated by a sudden awareness of his size and controlled energy in the confined space, "we have to be honest. Correct?"

His expression became wryly reluctant. "As I remember, with you being honest usually preceded being critical, but do go ahead."

She drew another breath to damp down temper and said evenly, "Fine. Old habits are exactly what I want to discuss. When you didn't want to hear my side of things while we were married, you'd find an excuse to walk away and I had to either chase you, explaining, or forget it. I don't intend to run after you for an entire summer."

"Des, all I did was offer to pay for what you need," he said patiently, "and you insist on being stubborn."

"I will not have you buying what I need," she insisted. She saw anger flare in his eyes though he was careful to keep his features calm. "I will not be managed, and I will not be walked away from."

He studied her one long, tense moment, then he shrugged. "Fine." He turned away from her and started to walk toward the stairs, then stopped. He raised a mocking eyebrow and asked, "Can I go now?"

Destiny walked up to Rafe, arms folded, and stood toe to toe with him, trying hard through square shoulders and tilted chin to make up for the ten-inch disparity in their statures. "I'll let you buy me lunch," she offered.

He, too, stood tall, not giving up a centimeter of his height advantage. He closed his eyes, groaning. "Destiny…"

"Those are my terms." She remained firm, a slight smile quirking her lip. "We can stand here and argue or we can get out into that beautiful sunshiny day, visit Digby Head—" she looked at her well-trimmed row of fingernails "—buy those furnishings you're so anxious for me to have…maybe a Pepsi…"

"No Pepsi."

"Tea, then."

He shook his head in exasperation and put an arm around

her shoulders, drawing her with him toward the stairs. "Let's go."

In the kitchen, on the way out the back door, Rafe patted his side pocket, checking for keys, and frowned. "I must have left them upstairs," he said, giving Destiny a gentle shove toward the door. "Go on out. I'll be right back."

As he started to leave the room Destiny spotted his ring of keys on the edge of the counter. Forgetting what everyone who lived with Joe knew so well, she hooked the keys on one finger and shook them, trying to get Rafe's attention before he started upstairs. "I found them. Don't…ah!" She screamed as a black streak leaped out at her from under the table. Destiny and Joe went down to the floor in a flurry of fur and feet, the dog pinning her there with two paws on her chest and a velvety tongue working over her face with whining enthusiasm.

As Destiny groaned, bracing herself on her elbows, she looked up into Rafe's half-concerned, half-laughing face. He knelt over her and pulled her gently to a sitting position.

"Are you all right?" he asked. Joe turned his attentions to his master's left ear. "Joe, sit!"

Ears back, whine deepening, the black dog took a position beside Destiny, his shoulders still tense and ready for the run to the truck and the promised ride.

"I forgot the rule." Destiny accepted Rafe's hand up and winced as she dusted off her bottom.

"Nothing broken?"

"No." She reached down to pet the dog who was immediately beside himself at her forgiveness.

"Now we have to take him with us." Rafe broke the news while smoothing her hair back.

"I don't mind."

He laughed. "He has to have the window seat. He gets carsick. You'll have to sit close to me."

"Horrors!" she exclaimed, picking up the purse that had

landed near a table leg. "The price one has to pay for one mistake." She gave him a theatrical smile and turned to the door. "I'll try to bear up."

Chapter Five

Had Destiny conjured up Digby Head out of all her notions of what a two-hundred-year-old town on the coast of Maine would look like, the reality could not have been more perfect. Globed streetlights marked every corner of a downtown that Captain Ahab might have walked. Destiny had wandered several sets constructed to convey the maritime flavor of the old east coast, but this was real and honest, and for a moment she felt herself transported back in time. She heard the clop of horses' hooves, the peal of a church bell and saw children rolling hoops down a cobbled street. She wore a long muslin dress and a bonnet and had come to town for buttons and thread. Her companion wore leather breeches and a calico shirt and a small-billed black cap. He had a hand lightly on her shoulder so that the ruffians in front of the tavern knew that she was protected.

"Des?" Rafe passed a hand in front of her unfocused eyes, wondering where she had gone. She had done this to him on occasion when she was working on a particular costume, which had finally come out the way she wanted it. It was as though the garment, now perfect, had transported her and she was wearing it, assuming grand airs or some quality of tragedy, whatever it required.

He smiled at this look. She seemed so soft, so demure, the Destiny he had thought he wanted as a young man. He realized with sudden clarity that, though she now seemed lost in the role, the fragility wasn't there. It surprised him that he didn't mind.

At a well-equipped art shop on the waterfront, Destiny purchased a drafting table, then Rafe took her to a small shopping center, where she bought a quality sewing machine.

"You said something about a worktable," Rafe said as they stood out in the sunlight, shoppers bustling by them. "What did you have in mind?"

"Nothing fancy. Just a large slab, really, but it has to be something with a smooth top that won't run the fabric." She looked thoughtfully up and down the street. "Is there a secondhand shop in town?"

"Yes. The sheriff's wife owns a fun place called the Trading Post. Want to check it out?"

At her nod, he led her down a side street to a renovated old house with rooms full of antiques and collectibles and a basement filled with what the owner termed "good junk."

Faye Eastman, an attractive woman with a Southern accent and flawless plantation manners listened to Destiny's needs and took her under the stairs, where a splintered picnic table awaited repair.

"I can put a Formica top and sides on it to give you the smooth surface you need." Rafe got down on his haunches to study its structure. A push against the legs proved it steady. Faye named a ridiculously low price.

"Then it's perfect," Destiny said with a smile, pleased. "Will it fit in the truck?"

"Easily."

While Rafe and Faye's son loaded the table into the back of the truck, Faye invited Destiny into the back room for a cup of tea. On counters around the room were soft toys in various stages of construction. A large, scruffy bear in a corner caught Destiny's attention and then her heart. He wore a silly smile and had an enormous, huggable stomach. She knew Cara would love it. Destiny made the purchase and placed the bear on her lap while she and Faye got acquainted.

Coming into the back room to find Destiny, Rafe rounded the corner and came face-to-face with a furry gray beast leaning against Des's small, firm breast. She stroked its stomach absently while sipping her tea and studying a pattern Faye was showing her, acting as though it was not at all unusual for a national celebrity to be found in the back room of a secondhand store clutching a teddy bear.

"I suppose you're going to try to convince me that's for Cara?" Rafe came closer to inspect the toy.

"Don't you think she'll love it?" Destiny's green eyes sparkled with laughter and enthusiasm. As she hugged the animal to her, Rafe suggested with a gentle smile, "Maybe we should buy two."

"Oh, Cara will let me share." She got to her feet and smiled at the woman who had quickly become a friend. "I'll be back," she promised. "I'm working on some designs, and it'll be nice to have someone to talk to who understands the problems."

"Anytime, gal." Faye walked them to the door and gave Rafe and Destiny a parting wave. "I'm here every day but Monday. Call first and I'll put on the tea."

"I will. Bye."

"She's brilliant," Destiny was telling Rafe as they walked to the truck, totally oblivious to the stares she and the bear were drawing. "She's designed some wonderful stuffed animals and dolls. I'd love to work on something with her."

He smiled down at her, trying to keep the pleased surprise out of his eyes and voice. He knew it was too much to hope for already, but that did sound like a long-range plan. "She's a lovely lady. I'm sure you'd both enjoy the experience."

As Rafe opened the door to the truck, Joe barked excitedly and wagged his tail—until Destiny put the bear inside the cab. With a terrified yip he moved to the far side of the seat and alternately barked and growled at the fuzzy, gray object.

Destiny pulled the bear back out and clutched it protectively. "He won't eat it will he?" she asked Rafe.

"No, he just has to get better acquainted with it." He put the bear back in the cab, and when the dog drew away, barking, Rafe stroked the bear. "It's a nice bear, Joe. It's not going to hurt you. Come here."

As Joe's watchful brown eyes observed his master's petting of the doubtful beast, jealousy urged him forward. With his large snout he nosed Rafe's hand off the bear and sniffed the poorly groomed and obviously inferior competition. A further butt with his nose proved that it was softer than it looked and apparently friendly. He stopped barking and growling but continued to analyze as Rafe quietly closed the door and turned Destiny toward the Moby Dick Inn.

Destiny studied the inn's colonial decor while picking at a shrimp salad. Rafe had long since finished a plate of fish and chips and was working on a cup of coffee.

Destiny pushed her plate away, groaning. "I'm stuffed! I haven't eaten two meals in a row in months."

"You're looking perkier," he noted. "How do you feel? Besides stuffed."

She considered her reply for a moment. "Fine, actually," she said in some surprise.

"It'll probably take some time for you to learn to relax again."

She looked at him over her iced tea. "I thought I was doing fine."

"You're shredding your napkin."

She looked down at the paper in her hands. She had twisted it into a long irregular rope and was now tearing strips off it. She tossed it on the table. "Sorry."

"Don't apologize. I have a tendency to snap pencils in half when the price of scallops goes down too far."

Destiny leaned her elbows on the table and smiled at

him, realizing for the first time since he'd surprised her at the airport that his life for the past five years had probably been as difficult as hers. "Success leaves a lot to be desired, doesn't it?" she asked.

She hadn't expected to voice the question, just to ponder it as she had done so many times. Five years ago, though there had been love between them, their backgrounds and experiences had been so different that they'd had difficulty understanding each other. But she sensed that in the intervening time their lives had led them down many of the same lonely roads. Suddenly there were things she could understand about him.

"Absolutely," he agreed feelingly. "It does nothing for you in the middle of the night when there's no one to turn to."

She wondered for a moment if all he felt was sexual loneliness. Then he added, "Or in the morning, when you're reading the paper and you find something shocking or funny or sad. You can't say, 'Hey, listen to this!' to someone who really cares how you feel about it."

She was able to nod, sure now that he understood. She had Frances and Cara to share thoughts with at home, but so often one wanted to share intimate things that had nothing to do with sex but were something only a lover would understand.

They studied each other soberly.

"But you've done very well on your own," he said. "Splendidly, in fact."

She leaned back in her chair, angling him a slightly hurt look over her glass of tea. "You sound surprised." He nodded reluctantly. "When people first started talking about you and your name appeared in the newspapers, I was surprised. I knew you had the talent. But, until we got married, you'd always had everything you wanted. I wasn't sure you'd have the tenacity." His voice quieted and became more pensive. "But now that I see you, I'm no longer surprised."

Destiny put her glass down, not sure how to interpret that remark. "Now that you've seen the tough old bird?"

Rafe looked across at her softly sculpted face in the glow from the sun beyond the window and laughed quietly. "No, you haven't toughened, you've simply matured." He shook his head, thinking back. "Five years ago you had your sights so aimed at the top that you'd have never stopped to plan a project with a woman who works in the back room of a secondhand shop."

She thought of Faye and her brilliant designs. "Genius isn't diminished by where it lives," Destiny said judiciously.

His eyes sharpened on hers. "Just like love is no less genuine or intense because it's shared in a tenement rather than in a mansion."

She frowned at him, straightening up in her chair. "I never thought it was. What we had was very special and I knew that." Her shoulders slumped. "I think my money had a lot to do with it. If you hadn't been so stubborn about it…"

"I told you I didn't care if you used it for yourself," he reminder her. "But I wanted to take care of us as far as household bills went." He laughed softly at himself. "I had a lot to prove in those days. Looking back, I can't believe I thought that would work."

Destiny, too, looked back, able to laugh at herself. "And to think I agreed to it. It has seemed like the perfect way to defy my mother. Marrying you hadn't done it. She liked you and approved of you. But turning my back on all her money seemed like such a noble gesture. Until I had to live with it. It's too bad." She sighed wistfully. "We had a good thing going. It just couldn't survive the pull in two directions."

She stared silently at the fingers in her lap, then Rafe asked quietly, "Are you sure it hasn't?"

Her eyes focused on him in surprise, Rafe's dark gaze trapping her, unsettling her. Her heart seemed to catch in her throat, and she looked away. "That's too heavy a question for the state of my nerves right now."

"Getting tired?"

She looked up again to find the tension of a moment ago gone from him. He was now all solicitous concern.

"I suppose it's the big meal, but..." She blinked as her eyelids seemed to droop. "Suddenly I'm exhausted."

"Okay. We'll get you home." Rafe signaled for the waitress.

Within minutes they were on the way home, Destiny snugly ensconced between Rafe and Joe, the bear cuddled on her lap. Rafe was telling her about a farm they passed that had been in the same family for five generations, and she fell asleep to the sound of his voice.

In the driveway of the house, Rafe looked down at the sleep-flushed face leaning against his shoulder and felt a stab of emotion that was part tenderness and part naked hunger. How many times had he awakened in the morning years ago to find her just like this, snuggled contentedly against him, all the sass and spirit that seemed to plague his pursuit of a secure home life quietly asleep in her? For an instant he longed for those days because he could have awakened her and, angry at him or not, she would have responded hotly to his lovemaking. Then he sighed, knowing that both of them had changed, and those days could never be recaptured. But something new could grow; he was sure of it.

Careful not to wake her, he pulled Destiny gently with him as he backed out of the truck, then lifted her in his arms, smiling to himself as he had to crane his neck to see over the bear she still clutched. Joe ran ahead to announce their arrival to Frances.

LONG STREAMS of late-afternoon sunshine patterned Destiny's bedspread when she awoke. She was instantly aware of feeling fresh and a little excited. Why was that? Oh, yes, she thought, getting out of bed and putting her jeans and a fresh white sweater on, she had bought a sewing machine and a drafting table. She was going to start working on her sketches for Havilland House.

With the bear tucked under her arm Destiny raced down the stairs to the kitchen, where she heard conversation. Her heart was tripping briskly. It wasn't the exercise, she knew, or her work for Havilland House. It was the sound of the male voice now laughing with the two feminine ones. She tried not to analyze her feeling because it had dangerous implications. For now she was just enjoying the new experience of awakening to a light and carefree mood.

Cara had apparently just come in and was telling Rafe and Frances about her day at the "theater."

"Jenny and I are going to be Mr. Forrester's daughters, Charity and Mattie. I'm Mattie," she was saying as Rafe lounged at the kitchen table over a soft drink. He was wearing worn jeans and an old T-shirt and smiled up at Destiny as she took a seat opposite him. "They needed..." Cara's eyes narrowed on the bear, and she was instantly distracted. "Hi, Mom." She gave Destiny a coyly hopeful look. "What's that?"

"It's a bear."

Cara rolled her eyes. "I know it's a bear, Mom. I mean..."

Destiny held the bear out, unable to tease in the face of Cara's covetous expression. "It's a bear for you. A woman in town made it."

Hugging it to her, Cara exclaimed over its softness, then held it away to look at it. She giggled at its lopsided grin. "Thank you. I love it!" Cara gave Destiny a one-armed hug, her other arm holding fast to the bear.

"I picked it out." Destiny turned the child toward Rafe. "But your father bought it."

"Thanks, Daddy." Rafe became the instant recipient of a grateful hug; then Cara, perched on his knee, the bear on hers, grew thoughtful. "You guys did something like married people."

Destiny's eyebrow rose in puzzlement, and Rafe looked at his daughter curiously. "What do you mean?"

Cara helped herself to his can of Coke. "You bought something together for your kid. Jenny's parents do that all the time. But...well, you buy me stuff when I'm here or you send stuff to California. And Mom brings me presents from everywhere. But this is the first time...that I can remember, anyway...that you bought me something together." She hugged the bear a little harder and smiled broadly. "It's neat!"

Destiny's gaze met Rafe's and found it dark with challenge. Everything inside her fluttered. Then he turned his attention to Cara. "When you were talking about the play you started to say... 'they needed'...something."

"Oh, yeah!" Cara tossed her disheveled ponytails and got back to business. "They needed somebody to do costumes, Mom, so I told them you would."

"Oh, Cara!" Destiny moaned, her exasperation somewhat softened by her buoyant mood, the silly bear and that expression on Rafe's face. "We've had this argument before. You mustn't promise I'll do things without asking me first."

"But, Mom, this is just your thing!" Cara came to put her free arm around her mother's neck, her eyes behind their glasses wide in excitement. "Mrs. Barnes, that's our director, says they do a pageant every year, but this time, somebody—I think it's a high school teacher—wrote this play about a relative of the man who built the first ship in Maine. That's who Digby Head is named after. Anyway, the relative, his nephew, started building ships and built this special feet that—"

"Fleet," Rafe corrected, ennunciating the *l.*

"Fleet," Cara repeated, hardly pausing for breath, "that carried fur and codfish along the coast. Anyway—that man's the reason Digby Head is here today. And the best ship of the...the fleet was named the *Matilda*, after me, or after the character I play."

"When does this take place?" Destiny asked, praying that it was a period she had tackled before.

"The middle of the sixteen hundreds."

Destiny felt a slight relief. She had worked on two movies of that period; a trip to the library would refresh her memory.

"How big is the cast?"

"Eight and..." Cara finished a little lamely. "And one more." She turned to Rafe. "They need a navigator."

"Navigator?" Rafe asked.

"Yeah. You know. Someone who stands to the side of the stage and tells the audience what's happening."

"Ah. A narrator."

"That's it."

Father and daughter measured each other. Rafe folded his arms and asked mildly. "And you volunteered me?"

Cara paused barely a moment, placing the bear strategically in front of her. "Yeah."

He looked at Destiny, who was grinning at him. He turned to his daughter.

"They asked Mr. Morrison," she explained hurriedly, "since he's working on the play and all, but he said he'd be afraid to stand up in front of a bunch of people. But you...wouldn't be scared."

"How do you know?"

She shrugged as though it were obvious. "You're not afraid of anything."

Looking into Cara's eyes and finding sincerity there instead of flattery, he shook his head in resignation. "Did you bring me a script?"

She took the bound pages from the side table, where she had deposited two copies of the play and her jacket.

"We have until the end of August to learn all this stuff, but Mrs. Barnes says we should start right away so we can really get into our roles."

"Can we have dinner first?" Rafe asked seriously.

Cara considered that request. "If you don't dawdle, like

Frances says I do. We all have a lot of work to do, you know.''

''Yes,'' Rafe said, giving her a falsely stern look. ''Thanks to you.''

With a sweetly feminine expression that hinted at formidable wiles somewhere in the future, Cara kissed Rafe's cheek. ''Thanks to you for the bear.''

Defeated, he swatted her gently and pushed her toward the door. ''Go wash your hands.''

After dinner Cara retired to her room to study her lines, and Rafe and Destiny took Joe for a walk. Outdoors the tang of woodsmoke hung in the air and mingled with the scents of grass and pine and roses to make an intoxicating perfume. The first whiff in Destiny's nostrils stopped her in her tracks. Closing her eyes, she tilted her head back and inhaled. She felt her body absorb the sweet air and send its healing out to her extremities in a shivery rush.

Rafe hooked an arm in hers and pulled her along with him. ''Think you can walk and breathe at the same time?'' he teased.

''I was just marveling at the fact that there are no exhaust fumes in the air. This year, besides Mexico, I've worked in London, Tokyo, New York and Burbank.''

''Mmm. Places where the air has texture. I don't think Morocco would have been any better. No industry and probably not too many cars, but lots of camels.''

That made her laugh. In a rush of well-being she admitted rashly, ''This is a lovely place in which to relax.''

He unwound their arms, put his hand in his pocket and slid her arm through his. ''I'm glad you think so,'' he said.

They walked quietly down a corridor of tall poplars, and Joe ran on ahead, chasing some mysterious prey. An evening breeze was whipping up and clouds scudded along overhead, darkening to a threatening purple at the horizon.

Rafe looked down at her corn-silk hair flying about her face and stopped her, raising his hands to brush it out of her eyes and hold it still. "We should have brought you a hat. Do you feel cold?"

"No," she replied, her voice a whisper as the pulse in her throat reacted to the gentle work of his thumbs. "My...my hair keeps me warm."

Rafe's open, easy expression sobered, and he looked deeply into her eyes. "I remember," he said, "when it kept me warm, too."

Destiny felt trapped in his dark eyes, in the memories she saw there, reflections of her own. The wind made a frantic flutter of the curls at her forehead and whipped at her light blue windbreaker.

Rafe reached down to pull the sides of the jacket together and worked the snaps, retaining the ends of her collar in his hands. She pulled against the slight pressure he applied to bring her closer.

"Don't..." she whispered, her heart rocketing out of control. One move on his part that was more than friendship, and she knew she would be lost. But her traitorous body felt hot and was beginning to throb with a pulse that had nothing to do with the beat of her heart.

He smiled, applying the added pressure needed to bring her jacketed body in contact with his. "To quote an ancient song: 'There's yes, yes in your eyes.'"

Even through all their clothing she felt the toughness of him, the fitness, the stamina and that curious tenderness, which restrained all that muscle while still making it impossible for her to move.

She put her hands up between herself and Rafe, trying to wedge a small distance, but he moved his hands to her back and her efforts became futile.

"My...my head is in control here," she said. Her voice sounded pompous and not at all convincing.

His smile broadened as his head came down to blot out the treetops and the dramatic sky. "Good," he murmured. "Let's see what your lips can do."

His lips hovered over hers for just a moment, but when

she looked up at him he saw all he needed to know. Despite her protests her mouth became soft and yielding as it awaited his, and her attention was concentrated on him in a way that brought back sharply focused pictures of their lovemaking. For an instant he could neither breathe, nor hear, nor see, caught in vivid memories of what it had been like to have her eager and pliant in his arms.

Then he felt her fingertips on his face and he came back to awareness with a jolt, every sense working and sharp. He focused on Destiny's face, wind-whipped and glowing, her eyes half-frightened yet filled with longing. She reached up to him, and he lowered his mouth.

He wasn't looking for the hot passion of their youth, or even hoping to tap that longing he saw in her eyes. She didn't want to acknowledge it yet, and it surprised him that he understood that. He wanted simply to communicate that he cared, that he had finally reached a point in his development where what she wanted was more important to him than what he wanted. He wanted her to know that she would always be safe in his arms.

And Destiny felt that security. It had been years since any man had held her, and five long years since she had lain in this man's arms. She felt strangely virginal, skittish and nervous, filled with longing but afraid.

Yet Rafe's arms closed around her with such tenderness, his mouth claimed hers with such sweetness that she went limp against him with a little sigh.

Rafe's lips were cool and mobile, wandering the planes of her face, the hollow at her ear, and hesitating at her throat with studious attention. She took that time to run her lips along the hairline at his temple and to trace his muscular neck with kisses. Then he steadied her face in his hands and lowered his lips to hers once more, the kiss deep and long, filled with reassurance and affection and promise.

They pulled apart, looking at each other in surprise. Her arms still looped around his neck, Destiny asked in a husky voice, "How long have you been that sweet?"

He laughed softly, his hands loosely at her waist. "How long have you been that amenable?"

Destiny studied his face, seeing the mature man he had become overlaying the young man to whom she'd been married. This particular posture, with her arms around him, seemed so familiar yet very different. He had always been the one in control when they made love, but she knew now that this embrace could go either way and the choice was hers to make. She could simply reach up again for his lips and let the passion stirring within both of them lead them where it would, or she could retreat for now and he would not complain.

Her eyes went to his mouth, her own lips parting as she considered throwing caution to the wind and following her inclination to let his kisses take her. Yet this newfound link with him was so precious, she wanted nothing to threaten it. And their passion had always been so all-consuming.

She heaved a little sigh and dropped her hands to his shoulders, looking warily into his eyes, her decision made.

Taking her wrists in his hands, he pulled them from him, kissing the palm of one hand and then the other. Then he tucked her right arm in his and walked on. "So what's on your agenda tomorrow?" he asked.

She drew a deep breath of the purifying air, wrapping both arms around his in a warm gesture of affection. Knowing that he understood her feelings made her almost giddy. That was indeed a new luxury in their relationship.

"I've been thinking about my designs," she said, kicking at a rock that lay in her path. "I might even be ready to try a few rough sketches."

He looked down at her with sincere interest. "Tell me about it."

The breeze strengthened to a wind, and she tucked her shoulder behind his. "Remember how I always used to wear your clothes?"

He nodded. She had always worn his pajama tops to bed, his white shirts and sweat bottoms to work in, his bandanas in her hair. After she left him, the spicy-rose smell of her on one of his shirts had almost driven him over the edge. "I remember."

"Well, I loved them because they were really comfortable. The concept isn't fully developed yet, but I'd like to go for a look that's dressier than sweats but comfortable. Masculine styling but in soft fabrics."

He gave her a curious look. "You mean by letting you wear my things I've contributed to a fashion innovation?"

"Something like that."

He put his arm around her shoulders to lend support as they reached a hilly section of the lane. Unconsciously, going on with her explanation, she put her arm around his waist, grabbing a fistful of his jacket.

"The square lines of men's clothing give a woman comfortable moving room. You can swing your arms, lengthen your stride, bend, turn, reach without fear of splitting a seam or providing a peep show."

He slanted her a wicked grin. "Now let's not take all the fun out of girl watching."

She landed a light punch in his ribs. "Please pay attention. Try to visualize what I'm talking about. However comfortable a woman would like to be, she still wants to be attractive to the male. Would that look appeal to you?"

He thought about that. "There is something very vulnerable and delicate about a woman in a man's shirt," he said finally.

Destiny looked up at the sky, her hair whipping back in a gust of wind. "But today's woman is very conscious of her capability, her durability. Would she want a look that makes her appear...vulnerable?"

"Why not? Vulnerable doesn't mean weak, it means human. And there's nothing more appealing to a man than a woman who isn't perfect."

"Really?" They reached the top of the hill and she stopped to look at him skeptically, her green eyes reflecting the shadowy sky. "You don't want goddesses, or earth mothers, or geniuses?"

Rafe shrugged, an easy smile on his lips as he looked down at her, the wind puffing out the back of his jacket. "I don't. I just want a buddy who'll move from day to day with me, understanding my struggles and wanting to help me—letting me help her."

Something cautioned Destiny against bringing up their relationship at this point, but she ignored it. She wanted to relate what he had just said to their struggles of five years ago.

"When we were married," she said, the wind stealing her words so that he had to lean down to hear, "you wouldn't let me help you."

He straightened and studied her wind-whipped cheeks. "You offered financial help, and I didn't want that. I wanted to know that you cared about me, about us. It seemed like you were always working and taking every opportunity to do the jobs that took you away from home."

That was true. She had thought about those final months of their marriage quite a lot in the past five years, and she'd finally come to terms with her share of the blame. Instead of reacting to what she thought of as his macho tyranny by standing her ground and insisting on her rights, she had simply been flagrantly defiant. She had deliberately taken on projects that took her out of town because she knew Rafe hated it and missed Cara. She'd been getting back at him in a way that was childish, seeking to hurt him for not understanding her rather than trying to explain to him what she wanted and needed.

"I was so young," she said as he took her hand, and they started slowly down the way they had come. "I guess I expected you to read my mind. I was hurt that you didn't instinctively understand me, so I just did everything I knew you'd hate just to get back at you."

"And that gave me more excuse to yell at you because

I needed some contact with you and holding you was out of the question.''

Out of all those grim memories she found a giggle. "I was a little prickly. Remember the argument in the tenement hallway...?'' The giggle turned to laughter and she went on, fighting for breath, "When I hit you ...with Mrs. Laferrier's laundry!'' It had been a pillowcase full of Mr. Laferrier's jeans left in the hallway to be picked up by the local laundry service. It had packed quite a wallop.

Rafe, too, laughed. "And I landed in the Hennesseys' living room. I remember.'' He had reeled backward, off balance at the very moment that their neighbor across the hall, Pat Hennessey, had opened his door and bent down to pick up his evening paper. Destiny would never forget the view through the open door and the look on Maureen Hennessey's face as Rafe somersaulted into her.

Rafe fixed Destiny with a threatening glance. "I'm still planning my revenge for that one. Do you think we'd be any different now?''

"As a couple, you mean? I don't know. We've still got a lot of the same old problems. I still want to work, and you probably still want a pink and lacy little thing who'll bring your slippers and—''

He stopped her in the middle of the lane. It was darkening now as night fell, and the tall trees bordering the walk cast shadows that crowded out most of the remaining light. The wind was fragrant and strong and stung her cheeks as he framed her face in his hands.

"What if that isn't what I want anymore?'' he whispered.

Her heart was thumping out of control, and her swallow was audible. A wild, reckless response was on the tip of her tongue, but she forced herself to reply cautiously. "I'm not sure. I don't think I know what I want in a man.''

Her eyes stung, and she wasn't sure if it was from the wind in her eyes or if tears threatened because everything in life was so fragile and so complicated. Something inside her still yearned, burned for this man, but the mature woman she had become wanted to protect herself from another mistake.

He smiled and anchored her swirling hair with a gentle hand. "You're still very important to me."

She was able to nod in agreement. "And you to me."

He nodded to himself as though in satisfaction, then pulled her into his shoulder and started back toward home. "That's not a bad basis for a relationship."

"What kind of a relationship?" she asked warily.

"Don't complicate things by getting technical," he cautioned on a laugh. "I don't know what kind. I just think that we should have one and build it on whatever's handy. We care for each other. That's enough to start with, don't you think?"

That sounded dangerous and basically unsound. But she liked it. "Sure," she said, feeling bold and daring. At least it gave each of them some latitude. Or so she thought.

Chapter Six

For the next week clouds hung low over Digby Head. The breeze was cool, the rain intermittent. But Destiny was at work in her new office and was unaware of the outdoor gloom.

Cara and Jenny religiously devoted an hour every morning and every afternoon to learning their lines, then spent the rest of the day with board games or television and often went to Jenny's house to play with the baby. Cara's only concern seemed to be a fear that her unpredictable awkwardness would cause her to fall on stage during the play or knock something over, or that she would forget to tuck her tummy in.

Destiny became increasingly aware of subtle changes in herself. She felt good. It had been ages since she had sat up in bed in the morning, taken a deep breath and smiled over the prospect of breakfast and a new day. There was color in her cheeks and a new zest in her spirit that made her eyes sparkle.

While working on her first sketches for Havilland House, Destiny felt a stirring of excitement. She wanted very much to make this career change, and with every stroke of her pen the confidence to give it her best began to develop. She could do this.

It was several days before Destiny produced a sketch she was pleased with, and then she studied it for a long time, wanting to see the lines and folds of the completed garment to be sure the concept was correct.

With a thought on how she could see immediate results on her design, she went in search of Rafe. She found him in the garage sanding a large piece of composition board. He was kneeling on it on the concrete floor, his back muscles rippling under his white T-shirt while he worked.

"What are you doing?" she asked.

He looked at her over his shoulder and smiled. "Jeff informs me that your daughter also volunteered us for set design."

Destiny raised an eyebrow. "My daughter?"

"Yes. Today she's your daughter. Something I can do for you?" He sat back on his heels and looked up at her, his dark hair attractively mussed, his brawny body completely distracting.

"I was wondering if I could borrow one of your shirts and your pajama top," she asked casually.

He looked surprised for a moment, then apparently unable to make sense of the request, replied uncertainly, "There'll be a shirt in the closet in the room you're in and a pajama top in the middle drawer. Do I want to know what you're doing with them?"

"I'm going to try them on. Thanks."

"Hey, wait a minute!" he called as she started away. "Do I get to see you in them?"

"If you like," she replied, "but you might be disappointed. They're going to be worn over my sweatpants."

Obviously trying to visualize that picture in his mind's eye and failing, he grimaced at her. "Are you sure peepshow clothes wouldn't be a better idea?"

She laughed. "Trust me," she said, and ran back to the house

The strange combination wasn't quite the right look, of course, but actually seeing it, being able to study her reflection in the long mirror on his closet door, gave Destiny ideas for fabric and alterations in the pajama top's, or jacket's, construction.

Doing a turn in front of the mirror, Destiny tossed the tails of the top back and pulled up the collar of the white shirt.

As she unknotted a scarf from around her neck and tied it in her hair, she noticed Rafe standing in the doorway, looking skeptical. She gestured him toward her as she studied the touch of the scarf.

"Try to imagine these things in my size but with a big look."

He considered her request, then shook his head as he wandered around her. "I'm sorry, sweetheart. It'll never replace the bikini as male bait."

She turned to him in exasperation. "Rafe, try to be helpful. It isn't male bait we're after. It's something a woman can be comfortable in while maintaining a certain style and still present an attitude that will appeal to a man. Now..." With her fingertips to his shoulder she urged him back against the wall and went to the opposite side of the room. "Try to be objective. Just pretend we're strangers walking along the same street. Try to analyze whether or not the look appeals to you. Walk toward me," she directed as she started toward him, arms swinging as she pretended she was looking in shop windows, turning her head from side to side.

He played the role perfectly, his eyes running the length of her in a very close imitation of a man meeting an attractive woman on the street. When he went past her without a word, Destiny thought ruefully that he disapproved—until he caught the back of her shirt in a large fist and spun her around.

"Pardon me, miss," he said, "but there's something I've got to say to you."

Unable to withhold the smile, Destiny thought resignedly, *here it comes—the put-down of my design.*

But the only thing put down was her body on the bed.

His lips came down on hers, and she found herself lying across the bedspread. He lifted his head to look down at her, and for a moment she was still, designs and career changes forgotten. The length of his body pressed her deep into the mattress's softness; and the memories that had been at the root of her fantasies all those years came to her in brilliant detail. Every sense clamored to be recognized, and she felt her lips part in anticipation as the darkness of his hair and eyes swooped down on her again.

Nine years ago Rafe's gentleness when making love to Destiny had generated a warmth for him inside her, which all the arguments and the divorce that followed had never damaged. He had been experienced and older than she, a man who sought the thrills of a duel against nature in the North Atlantic. But when his hands reached out for her they were always tender, always mindful of her slenderness and her innocence.

There was that kindness about him now as he kissed her, his large hand wound in her hair, pulling the scarf from it. His lips were cool and dry, his tongue a darting, teasing tickle inside her mouth. His free hand covered a breast, shaping it to the form of his fingers, and for a moment she stiffened at his exquisite touch, even through the cotton of his shirt.

This was her night fantasy come to life, and she rose to his touch, arching her back to move against his chest, against the long, strong legs tangled with hers.

He took instant advantage of her compliance, an arm slipping under her to clasp her to him as he rolled onto his back. The hand tangled in her hair held, and she wound her arms around his neck to lessen the distance between them. The coarse hair under her fingers, the muscular cords in his neck, the width of his shoulders, which gave her slender fingers such a long way to travel, suddenly conspired to ignite the passion she'd fought so hard to hold in check the past few days. Her fingers nested in his hair as he dipped his head to nibble at the tempting swell of breast in the vee of her shirt.

At her little gasp of pleasure he followed the line of her throat with his lips, ending at her ear, following the intricate invitation with the tip of his tongue.

Destiny descended on his lips challenging his teasing tongue with her own invasion of his mouth. She nipped at his jaw, nibbled his ear and traced a torturously slow path inside the collar of his shirt. Reality was beginning to slip away when she felt him cup her head with his hand. He rolled their bodies until she was on her back and he beside her, drawing a long breath.

He studied the flush across her cheekbones that brought out her freckles and the splay of golden hair on the bedspread. His dark eyes, passion banked in them, ran the graceful arch of her neck as she gasped for breath, her head thrown back. He watched the rapid rise and fall of her breasts.

"You are still," he said with quiet reverence, "every bit as delicious as my sweetest memory of you."

Destiny sat up, trying to steady the spinning world. Her heartbeat was suffocatingly strong and rapid. She looked at Rafe with an unsteady smile. "You could safely say my body hasn't forgotten you, either."

There was a moment's heavy silence. "And your heart?" he asked.

"My heart's not to be trusted at the moment." She uttered a little laugh and fanned her flushed face with her hands. "It's out of control and not to be held responsible for its judgments."

Rafe sat up to put a hand over her heartbeat. It slammed against his palm, and he smiled into Destiny's eyes. "It wants more," he said.

"I know." She whispered agreement but firmly removed his hand. "But it can't have it. My head has to think."

He looked at her closely, trying to gauge, she was sure, whether or not the idea of more appealed to her despite her protest. She closed her eyes, not wanting to admit anything, but not before she saw his smile. He gave her one eye-opening, punctuating kiss, then got to his feet, pulling her with him.

Her head spun from being pulled up so swiftly, and he stopped a moment to steady her.

"The only thing I don't like…" he said, his eyes running over the slightly bizarre outfit, "I mean, it is attractive, somehow, but a man likes to see a little…delineation in a woman's clothes."

Destiny nodded. "That's the beauty of the right fabric. It'll cling to a thigh, mold a breast…"

He covered her mouth with his hand. "Stop or we won't make dinner." Then, with a smile, he turned her toward the hallway and gave her a gentle shove.

THEIR AFTER-DINNER WALK was a quiet excursion, Cara joining them this time, content to keep pace with their un-hurried steps. After the episode on the bed Destiny felt introspective, a thousand warnings clamoring to be heeded in her mind. But her sexual self had come back to life this afternoon, and she had the most unsettling feeling that all the warnings were futile.

She felt Rafe's energy in the large hand that held hers and an indefinable tension that was different from anything that had ever passed between them. Their first lovemaking all those years ago had been relaxed, easy—a happy end to the long wedding ceremony and the noisy reception. They had come together without the nervousness or re-straint that often characterized a first time.

Now she was nervous. Though there had been no sug-gestion that they make love, the inevitability of it passed between them like an electrical charge. She could no more have denied it than she could have flown. She made every effort to appear relaxed but she read in Rafe's casual pe-rusal of the dark clouds overhead that he wasn't fooled.

The air was heavy, the clouds hanging as though they

bore a great, dark weight. The tall trees were still, the air warmer than Destiny had observed since she'd arrived.

"That storm's going to hit us tonight," Rafe predicted. Then he looked down at Destiny, but she studiously avoided his glance. She didn't want to see what she knew would be in the dark depths of his eyes. Despite the building roar in the core of her being, she wasn't ready. Her defenses were down, and she seemed unable to draw them up again.

"More rain?" Cara grumbled. "The Morrisons were going to go on a picnic tomorrow, and I'm invited."

"Could be fine by tomorrow," Rafe assured her. "Once this storm finally does its thing, it should be sunny and warm."

"Will it thunder?" the child asked.

"Yes, I think so."

Cara looked dubiously at the sky. "I don't like that."

Rafe smiled gently down at her and smoothed a disheveled ponytail. "You get that from your mother. She doesn't like it, either."

Cara looked up at Rafe with a half smile.

"I know. When it thunders at home we get up and tell each other cheerful stories."

Rafe grinned at Destiny. "It's allowed to thunder in Beverly Hills?"

"A limited number of times," she replied, "as long as the storm is of short duration."

Rafe looked up at the sky again. "I don't think this storm will fit those requirements. Let's go. We'd better get back before we get caught in the rain."

The storm began in earnest shortly after midnight. Destiny lay alone in her bed, recalling with a wince the way she had avoided Rafe all evening and finally run off to bed at nine o'clock with the feeble pretense of a headache. Rafe had smiled at her knowingly for her carefully acted casualness and most appropriate excuse. Embarrassed, Destiny had turned away quickly, collided humiliatingly with the door, then left the room.

Thunder crashed a short distance away. She tossed the blankets aside and shrugged into her robe, crossing to the window to look out at the silvery sheet of rain. Thunder crashed again, rattling the window; then a twisted fork of lightning flashed and thunder exploded directly overhead. Destiny backed away from the window then turned and collided with a thick, naked shoulder. Rafe's hand covered her little scream of alarm. She sank against him in relief, her arms gratefully circling his broad middle as the thunder threatened to break her eardrums.

"Lord!" she complained. "Give me Beverly Hills thunder any day."

He laughed softly. "Come on. I'll fix you a *linguica* sandwich and pour you a glass of wine."

"That sounds wonderful," she said gratefully, shrinking against him as the incessant noise began again. "I'd better check on Cara."

Rafe flipped on the hall light at the same moment that Cara's bedroom door burst open. The child raced out into the hallway, ponytails askew, wide, myopic eyes frightened. Seeing her parents, she stopped in her tracks, looking very relieved. "Are we gonna tell stories?" she asked.

"We're going to raid the refrigerator," Rafe corrected. "Get your robe and slippers."

Cara ran into her room, then into the hall once more, glasses, robe and one cat-faced slipper on, the other defying her hopping efforts to don it. Finally, wearing both slippers, she followed as Rafe led the way to the kitchen.

While Destiny and Cara sat together at the table, Rafe made sandwiches and poured the wine and a glass of milk. He indicated the only sandwich cut across instead of diagonally as he put the plate on the table. "Peanut butter and jelly for you, Cara." He winked at Destiny. "She doesn't appear to have inherited your passion for *linguica*."

"It's a little spicy." Destiny selected a triangle from the

plate with obvious anticipation. "I'm sure when her palate grows up she'll change her mind."

Thunder crashed again, still loud but no longer directly over their heads.

"I wonder how Frances is sleeping through this?" Destiny thought aloud.

"She snores louder than the thunder," Cara replied, then collapsed in giggles when Rafe and Destiny looked at each other, trying to decide whether or not to laugh.

"I hope she didn't hear that," Rafe said, "or you'll be eating only green vegetables for the next week."

Cara rolled her eyes eloquently. "You have to come with us to rehearsal tomorrow," she informed her mother while munching on her sandwich. "So Mrs. Barnes can talk to you about the costumes."

"Cara, I wish you'd tell me these things," Destiny said with mild impatience. "I hope I have a little time to get them done. And Mr. Morrison had to tell us that you volunteered us for set design—you seem to have forgotten to mention that. You and I are on vacation, but your father does have other things to do."

"He's on vacation, too."

"And maybe he wanted to relax."

Cara looked at her father as though she hadn't considered that possibility. "Are you mad, Daddy?"

"No," he said immediately, "but it would have been nice if you'd remembered to tell me. It'll take some time to put together. And..." he reminded a little judiciously, "I still have to learn my lines."

Apparently confident he could do both, Cara turned to Destiny, her sandwich finished, the last swallow of milk going down as though she were competing in a contest. "Dad has to have a costume, too. A period one just like the rest of us. He's supposed to be a gentleman of the time."

"A gentleman?" Destiny gave Rafe an assessing glance, then said, as though she doubted she could pull it off, "A

good costume can lend authenticity to an otherwise doubtful role."

Cara frowned. "What does that mean?"

"It means," Rafe replied threateningly, "that your
mother is flirting with trouble."

"I don't get it."

"Your mother will."

The rumble of thunder seemed suddenly quieter. Destiny
hoped it meant the storm was finally moving away. Rain
continued to fall, but the drumming was less hectic, its
rhythm almost soothing.

Cara gave a huge yawn and her eyelids drooped. "I'm
sleepy. You guys better not stay up too late," she advised,
her tone grave and adult. "With all the costumes and the
set and stuff you need your sleep. Good night, Mom." Cara
hugged Destiny, then Rafe and disappeared, her footsteps
sounding on the stairs.

Rafe and Destiny finished their sandwiches to the comfortable accompaniment of the rain, then his eyes met hers
across the table. "Feel better?" he asked.

About to express relief over the quieting of the storm,
Destiny was startled out of her chair an instant later when
a brilliant flash of lightning destroyed her hope that it had
abated. She put her hands over her ears as thunder crashed
directly overhead, its powerful voice seeming to roll on and
on despite her attempts to shut it out. The lights went out,
plunging the cozy kitchen into menacing darkness.

"Rafe!" she screamed, her heart rising in her throat.

"Here, Des." His warm, strong arms closed around her.
Through the light fabric of her robe, his hands pulled her
close and stroked gently up and down her back. "It's all
right," he said, laughing softly. "It happens all the time.
We may as well go up to bed; it'll be a couple of hours
before power is restored."

"No!" she protested, horrified at the thought of being
left alone in the dark while thunder beat her nerves to
shreds. She snuggled into his naked chest, asking hopefully,

"Can't we stay down here? Don't you have candles or something? We could play cards or Scrabble..."

Rafe's voice was quiet and filled with gentle amusement. "There's an oil lamp in the bedroom you're using."

"There is?" She looked up at him in the darkness, seeing nothing but the brightness of his eyes. She had noticed the beautiful hand-painted globe on the lamp beside her bed but she had thought it merely decorative. She still hung back, certain she didn't want to be alone, even with a light.

"It's only noise, you know." Rafe's voice was conversational as he anchored her to his side with an arm around her shoulders. He started to walk toward the living room and the stairs. "If you're going to be afraid of something, it should be the lightning."

As he spoke lightning flashed brilliantly, as though on cue, flickering before it faded, announcing its noisy companion. Destiny wrapped both arms around Rafe and held him while thunder slammed against her eardrums and left her paralyzed with fear.

"*Cara linda*, it's all right," he assured her.

"It isn't all right," she denied vehemently, tearfully. "It's too damned loud!"

With sudden resolve Rafe lifted her in his arms. She settled against him like a kitten, her nose burrowed in his throat, her arms so tight around his neck that he smiled, considering Destiny a more serious threat to his health at the moment than the storm.

"You need a diversion," he suggested, walking carefully up the stairs. "And not cards or Scrabble."

Thunder crashed again, and she held on tighter. "What could possibly distract us from all..."

And then she understood what he meant. She lifted her head from his shoulder abruptly, shifting her weight. Rafe stopped, planting his feet firmly.

"No sudden movements, my love," he warned. "We're on the stairs."

Silently she settled back against him.

"I don't want to," she said softly, her voice small and unconvincing against the warm plane of his shoulder.

They had reached Cara's open door, and Rafe paused to peer inside. The sound of the child's soft snore filtered out of the darkness. A funny thump issued from the foot of Cara's bed, followed by a questioning whine.

Rafe laughed softly. "Good boy, Joe. Stay. I think he wants to convince us that he's protecting Cara, but frankly, I think it's the other way around."

Destiny couldn't quite focus her attention on what Rafe was saying, concentrating instead on the suggestion he had just made.

He walked into her bedroom, placed her carefully among the now-cool sheets and blankets, then fumbled in the bedside table drawer. A scratching sound produced a small flame. Rafe pulled the fat globe off the lamp, put the match to the broad wick, and a soft light bloomed in their corner of the room.

Rafe sat on the edge of the bed studying Destiny, who was cross-legged and clutching a pillow, her eyes jewel-bright and filled with a fear unrelated to the storm.

"Why not?" he asked, as though the conversation had never been interrupted. His eyes were deep and warm and so brimming with the knowledge of her innermost secrets that she had to look away.

"Well, we're no longer married, for one thing," she pointed out judiciously. She chanced a look at him and found an irritating smile on his lips.

"Yes," he agreed. "The court granted us a divorce, but the tie was never broken between us, Des, and you know it."

A clap of thunder reverberated through the house like some divine punctuation to his statement. A primitive sense of self-preservation made her inch backward, away from him.

He shook his head at her, his eyes amused. "And distance doesn't diminish what we have. Haven't you learned that?''

She couldn't breathe, and yet her heart was pounding so fast. Everything he said was true. After all the years and an entire continent between them, she wanted him every bit as much as she had when they were married—more, perhaps, because everything seemed more real to her now, as though when they were married they'd only been playing at having a relationship, like actors with a script.

Her hands yearned to touch him; her body longed to be touched. But was it safe? Of course it wasn't. Surrender to Rafe in any form was a risk. It was frightening to be able to admit to herself that she was willing to take it.

Rafe's dark eyes, lazy with passion, roved her rumpled hair, then her anxious features.

"Afraid of me suddenly?" he asked with a puzzled frown.

She shook her head in a frantic little gesture and pushed away to sit with her back turned to him.

"Not afraid," she denied, her voice husky. "Just confused."

"About what?"

"Oh, Rafe." She turned to look at him, excitement and anguish a curious combination in her wide green eyes. "I want you, and I won't be coy about that. But is this wise? Can we just…just jump into bed as though all the problems that drove us apart no longer exist?"

Rafe came to stand over her, looking down into her face. Then he knelt in front of her, his curly hair in rakish disarray, his dark eyes bright with understanding.

"Have you forgotten so much?" he asked gently, cupping her face with his hands and lifting it until she was forced to look into his eyes. "We've never jumped into bed." He combed the tumbled hair out of her face with a tender caress. "We always approached it easily, one well-orchestrated step at a time." For a long moment he studied her eyes; then, smiling at something he saw there, he held her face and kissed it. It was a gesture meant to comfort, but to Destiny, who had dreamed this very scene a hundred times in the past five years, it was fuel to the flame.

"I could fall in love with you again so easily," she admitted in a hoarse whisper, while she tried to hold him away with fingers that bit into his tough forearms. "You may be sure you've learned something in five years, but...I'm not sure I have."

"We haven't failed, Destiny," he said, moving to sit beside her. "We just haven't succeeded yet. Love still lives between us like something unresolved, and I'm not letting it get away. I'm going to love you—" he drew her back with him to the mattress, pulling at the buttons on the yoke of her nightgown "—and love you..." He slipped a hand under her to work the gown clear of her hips. "And love you..." It sailed over her head to the chair. "Until all you can do in self-defense is love me back." Rafe and Destiny were atop the silky bedspread, her satiny flesh against his brawny muscle.

He touched the peak of her breast with the warm palm of his hand, stroking it, circling it with an index finger, putting his lips to it, then the gentle tips of his teeth until Destiny thought she would go mad with pleasure. She wanted to feel his body under her fingers, to trail them down his hard chest to his waist, but a bud of fear held her back and she clenched her hands.

Rafe took one of the small fists at his chest, gently forced it open, then kissed the palm. Mooring her against him with an arm around her shoulders, he held her still while his other hand teased the backs of her knees, stroked her thighs and her taut bottom, then gently invaded where she hadn't been touched in years.

She gasped, her stomach muscles constricting in reaction. She dropped her head against his shoulder with a sighing breath, her body still, afraid to shatter the delicious sensation.

She ran her small hand along the hard steel of his shoulders, across the ripply hardness of his torso to his tapering waist. Then she stroked lower, into the taut, pelted plane of his stomach and felt his body react to her touch.

Pushing her gently onto her back, Rafe hovered over her for an instant—then he was inside her. Destiny cried out, the sound half pain, half delight as his hands behind her knees pulled her up, fitting her to him. Then he freed her legs and lay atop her, cradling her in his arms to begin the tantalizing, maddening undulation that she remembered in explicit detail, though she'd known it only in her fantasies for the last five years.

The wave approached slowly, just a ripple of feeling at first, a teasing promise dancing just out of reach. Then it came on with the force of the driven tide and she was helpless before it, a victim of its delicious, tormenting pleasure. For minutes the storm raged around her, Rafe as much a victim of its power as she. They writhed together, her little cries forced into the hollow of his shoulder.

Then it was over and she felt as though they lay wrapped in a bolt of Thai silk. It was moments before Destiny realized that Rafe was leaning over her, his eyes catching the lamp light as they explored her face, his hair a damp, curly frame for his grave expression.

"You haven't had anyone since me," he said, his voice breathless as though the suspicion astounded him.

She shook her head, brushing the hair out of her face with the back of her hand. Rafe stilled the movement, taking the task over himself with infinite tenderness. "Why?" he whispered.

Destiny looked back at him silently, still surprised as she had been all those years ago by the wild feelings they could stir in each other, by the fact that the tough, demanding skipper could be such a caring lover.

"I never wanted anyone but you," she admitted, reaching a caressing hand up to his face.

His eyes almost melted as he turned his lips into her palm. Rolling onto his back, he pulled her on top of him, grinning at her. "You're going to be sorry you said that," he warned, his hands stroking the length of her back and hips, stirring feelings that made her body tauten, awaiting the return of pleasure.

"Oh, I don't think so," she whispered, moving against him in invitation.

He crushed her to him and buried his lips in her hair. She could feel the restraint in his powerful hands. "God, Des," he said softly, his voice ragged. "Do you know how many times memories of a night like this have haunted me? How many fantasies I've had that we'd share it all again?"

"I know." She kissed his shoulder and felt his whole body stir under her. "I've lived on fantasies and memories, too. But this is real, isn't it?"

"It's real," he confirmed. Then he rolled her onto her back to provide proof.

THE WEEK THAT FOLLOWED was a procession of sunny days, each more golden than the one before, and each moment of every day as precious to Destiny as any of the considerable fruits of her success. She spent every morning at work on her sketches. In the afternoons she and Rafe picnicked with Cara and Jenny and Frances; they went to town, to the movies; they took long walks.

Destiny was now often looking forward to meals and was able to add foods to her diet she wouldn't have been able to look at a month ago without being ill.

"Must have been Portuguese food deficiency," she told Rafe one morning at the breakfast table after she had finished an egg, a slice of toast and a small piece of sausage.

He laughed and pushed away from the table. "Funny you should mention that. A package arrived this morning—special delivery."

Destiny frowned. "And?"

"And," Rafe supplied, crossing the kitchen to reach to the top of the refrigerator for a large white box, "it's addressed to you, and it's from my mother."

Destiny looked puzzled. "What could it be?"

He slit the box open for her with his pocketknife. "Open it. If it's edible, you have to share."

Destiny parted the flaps of the box and found a small, cream-colored envelope on top of an aluminum foil-wrapped package. She read aloud from the note. "'Hi, Destiny. Rafe says you've been missing some of our Portuguese favorites, and I remember how much you loved these. The grandchildren are visiting so I'm not sure I got everything in the right proportions. But Toby tried one and said it was okay. Hope you like them. Love, Josephina.'"

Destiny looked up from the note and smiled impishly at Rafe. "It doesn't say a word about sharing."

"But I'm bigger," Rafe reminded, peering into the box as she pulled aside the foil. "I can take the box away from you."

"Malassadas!" Destiny exclaimed. A dozen fat, sugary doughnuts were arranged in two neat rows, and a whiff of the sweet dough made Destiny's mouth water.

"Oh, Rafe," she cajoled. "Would you make more tea?"

"Do I get one?"

She wrapped her arms possessively around the large box. "No. They're mine. Your mother said so. She didn't say anything about sharing."

Cara walked into the kitchen with Jenny and sniffed the air, closing in on Destiny's box like a hunting animal on the scent of its prey.

"Grandma's *Malassadas*!" Cara clapped her hands in delight and reached into the box for one, stopping belatedly to fix a wheedling smile on her mother. "Can I?"

Destiny sighed defeatedly. "Why not."

As the girls poured milk, Rafe turned the burner on under the kettle and leaned against the counter with a grin. "Cheer up. If you ate them all yourself, you'd get fat."

"You're the one who's been forcing food down my throat for the past week and a half!" she accused over her shoulder as she took a plate from the cupboard. "Now that

I've gained a few pounds, I suppose you'll want me to eat only salads and green things cooked in a wok!''

Just as Destiny concluded her exclamation, Joe raced into the kitchen through the door the girls had left open. With a deep-throated "Woof!" he leaped at Destiny. She overbalanced, making an awkward attempt to save the plate. Rafe's grab for her arm was too late to save her from sprawling gracelessly on the floor as the plate crashed and broke.

Rafe knelt beside her as Joe ran to her side, dropping his leash on her chest with an anticipatory whine.

Destiny stared at the ceiling and asked with forebearance, "What did I do that time?" She held up an empty hand. "See? No keys."

After a serious bout with laughter, Rafe replied unsteadily, "You said w-o-k. Unfortunately, Joe can't spell. It sounded like w-a-l-k to him."

Destiny groaned, then glared at the girls as they giggled helplessly.

Rafe put two strong hands under her arms and lifted her to her feet, dusting off her jeans as she tried to fix the dog with a threatening stare and failed. Instead she turned the look on Rafe who was battling with another round of laughter.

At her expression, he sobered immediately. "Are you okay?" he asked in a strained voice.

Watching his valiant attempt to be solicitous, Destiny was finally overcome with giggles herself and they fell against each other convulsed. Only Joe, sitting patiently beside his leash, found nothing amusing in being kept waiting.

Chapter Seven

Alice Barnes was a small, energetic woman with mousy brown hair, nondescript features and a voice that belonged on the Shakespearean stage. She rounded her vowels, enunciated her consonants and rolled her *r*'s in a way that gave her stature and turned her gray corduroy pants and white sweater into an Elizabethan gown.

"Carrra," she told Rafe and Destiny with an elaborate gesture of her hand toward the child under discussion, at play with Jenny on the high school steps, "has prrromise as an actress. I'd like to talk to you about it privately some time."

Destiny glanced at Rafe in surprise, not knowing what to say. Then the girls joined them, giggling, and Mrs. Barnes began an explanation of the play, efficiently producing a sketch of the costumes.

"This is basically what we need. Of course, I wouldn't presume to tell you what to do. Cara boasts that you're a very professional seamstress. But we would like the costumes to be as authentic as possible."

With a completely straight face, Destiny nodded. "I understand."

"As you see, we have a cast of nine. Mr. Forrester, his wife and their two daughters. Then there's the ship's captain, three members of the crew, and you, Mr. Janeiro—the narrator. We'd like you costumed as a well-to-do gentleman of the period."

Remembering Destiny's gibe concerning his role as a gentleman, he gave her a dark glance. Mrs. Barnes looked down at the sketches before handing them to her costumer.

The director sighed. "I'm a stickler for doing things properly. I teach drama at the high school, and I try to impress on my students that we should strive for excellence, even if we are at the back of beyond and can't hope for an audience of more than one hundred." She smiled and patted Destiny's hand. "Still, you are just a volunteer and I can't push you around as I do my students. Just do what you can, Mrs. Janeiro. I do appreciate your volunteering to help. The two spinster sisters who usually costume the plays during the school year are spending the summer with friends in Virginia. I was beginning to panic until your daughter told me that you sew." Mrs. Barnes removed her glasses and studied Destiny with narrowed eyes. "I understand from Cara that you've just recently moved here to Digby Head. But you do look familiar. Is there a reason I should think so?"

Destiny returned a look of wide-eyed innocence. "None whatsoever. Thank you for preparing the sketches. I'll try to have a sample of Cara and Jenny's costumes for you by rehearsal next week. If you could have names and telephone numbers of the cast for me so that I can contact them for fittings, I'd appreciate it."

Surprised by that display of efficiency, the director nodded absently. "Of course. Thank you, Mrs. Janeiro. And you, Mr. Janeiro." Alice Barnes called herself back to the matter at hand. "The narrator is a very important role. You cut just the dashing figure we need to stride across the stage and keep the audience well informed. See you next week, same time. And thank you again. Oh, and Mr. Janeiro?"

Rafe turned in the act of shepherding Destiny and the girls toward the car. "Yes?"

"You're in charge of sets, aren't you?"

"Yes."

"Would it be too much to ask you to add a square rigged ship to the dock set for the last act? Our play is about the ship, after all."

Destiny hid a grin as Rafe took a hard swallow.

"I'll give it my best, Mrs. Barnes," he said.

"Thank you!" she said with such resonance that Destiny half-expected to hear *Twelfth Night*'s "I can no answer make but thanks, and thanks, and ever thanks."

Once the door closed behind her, and Rafe slid into the driver's seat, the laughter Destiny had been holding back burst forth.

Stabbing the key into the ignition, Rafe turned in his seat to face her before starting the motor. Cara and Jenny leaned over the back of the front seat, interested.

"What's so funny?" Rafe asked, barely holding back laughter himself.

Unable to contain herself, Destiny giggled uproariously, pointing at him. "You have to make four sets and… *and*…stride across the stage…and—" she had to swallow and draw breath "—and make a ship!" The words out, she sank against the seat and laughed harder.

"Laugh it up, Sweetheart," Rafe said dryly. "You have to make the sails."

Destiny sobered instantly. "Oh."

Then it was Rafe's turn to laugh as he pulled out of the high school parking lot. Cara turned to Jenny with a frown. "Do your mom and dad ever act like that?"

Jenny nodded instantly. "All the time. Grown-ups are weird."

BY MIDSUMMER two of the sets were completed and the third sketched out in charcoal on a primed piece of composition board. Mrs. Barnes had approved Jenny and Cara's costumes and had applauded Destiny's skill and attention to detail. Then she had studied the younger woman once more as Destiny led the girls to the car.

Frances was canning and pickling as though there were no tomorrow, or, rather, many famine-filled tomorrows. Cara and Jenny paid dutiful attention to their lines, Cara practicing her stage walk while balancing a book on her head.

"What's she doing?" Rafe whispered as he and Destiny passed Cara's room and found her walking while trying not to lose a copy of *Anne of Avonlea* that was perched on her uneven ponytails.

"You know how she is about being awkward..." Destiny began to explain.

Rafe frowned down at her. "I've never understood that. She's so beautiful, and so charming, with a great sense of humor and..." He stopped enumerating his daughter's virtues when he noticed Destiny's teasing smile. He winced. "That smacked a little of fatherly pride, didn't it?"

Destiny laughed. "Just a little. Anyway, learning to walk with good posture will make her feel better about herself. Come on. If she catches us watching, she'll be embarrassed."

Destiny pulled Rafe away to the dinner table, a twinge of uneasiness beginning to grow inside her. While she respected the love Rafe and Cara had for each other, she had to fight a growing jealousy over their closeness. Though it should have pleased her that they cared for each other, the uniqueness of their situation made approval hard for her. Was it because Cara seemed to understand her father and be able to earn his love with such ease when she, Destiny, found it difficult to commit to him? Or was it the subtle suggestion that he'd taken advantage of her weakness to be near his daughter for the entire summer, rather than the brief six weeks usually allowed him?

Feeling guilty for allowing the thoughts to form, Destiny pushed them from her mind.

One hot afternoon in July Rafe had gone to town for a part for the lawn mower. Destiny had taken a break from the costumes for the play, a project she had well in hand, to work on her sketches for Havilland House. Her ideas did not seem to want to translate themselves to paper, and she felt hot and mildly headachy.

In her room next to Destiny's, Cara, left behind today when the Morrisons went to visit an ailing grandmother, was studying her lines. She had been restless all morning, feeling lost without Jenny's companionship. The same lines repeated over and over with very professional but distracting change of tone and accent were thinning Destiny's patience and disturbing her efforts to concentrate on her designs.

Destiny pushed her sketches aside and went to Cara's room. As she stepped across the threshhold she was struck in the side by an outflung arm. Cara, unaware of her mother's presence, had gestured vigorously, prepared to deliver her dramatic lines in the second act. The gray bear sat on her bed, a rapt audience.

"Ooops!" Cara giggled. "Sorry, Mom."

After a moment to regain her breath, Destiny suggested diplomatically, "Darling, could you work on your lines downstairs? I know they're important to you, but I'm having trouble concentrating on my sketches."

Cara drew a long breath, looking completely deflated. "Frances chased me up here from downstairs."

"I'm sorry." Smiling, Destiny unfastened a ponytail located over Cara's ear and moved it higher, putting it in balance with its evenly placed twin. "It's a beautiful day. There must be a quiet spot somewhere outdoors where you can work."

Cara fixed Destiny with a pained look. "The acoustics are terrible outdoors!"

Destiny bit her lip desperately as her daughter relented. A delicate cough disguised the laughter.

"All right. I'll go. But don't forget to call me for dinner. We're having spaghetti."

"Promise."

Scooping up her copy of the play, Cara headed downstairs.

Destiny was working on a rear-view sketch of a loosely belted dress several hours later when a series of excited barks heralded Rafe's and Joe's return. Looking out of the window she saw Joe leap across the back lawn after his master. Then there were squeaky, athletic-shoe footsteps in the rear of the house and a door slammed in the kitchen. A tiny flame leapt in Destiny's breast. Rafe was home.

It took very little lately to ignite that flame, she thought while she heard the sound of his footsteps as he walked up the stairs. The sound of his voice, a hand on her arm as he moved past her in the corridor, a warm look across the dinner table were enough to bring a flush to her cheeks and to quicken her pulse.

Her reaction to Rafe was alarming, even more volatile than it had been all those years ago. Maturity seemed to have intensified her need for him rather than diminished it.

She slept the night through every time he made love to her and he teased that it was a delicious cure for her insomnia.

"Gotten to my costume yet?"

At the sound of his voice, Destiny turned in her chair, steadying herself for the onslaught on her senses.

In jeans and a plain white T-shirt, he wandered into her office and perched on the edge of her desk, facing her. He picked up the sketch from the desktop.

Destiny's heart hammered at the nearness of the well-muscled thigh on the edge of the desk and the large hand that held her sketch, the hand whose fingertips could caress her body until the universe exploded around her. His handsome face bent over the design, Rafe finally looked up at her with an affectionate grin. Every nerve ending in her body reacted.

"I don't think this dress is me," he said.

"You're right." She snatched the sketch from him and

put it in the folder with the others. "We have to hide your knobby knees."

He hiked up his pant leg and studied his foot and what he could see of his leg covered by an athletic sock. "Knobby? I thought I was superbly muscular."

She patted his knee consolingly and stood. "Most of you is Rafe, but your legs are funny."

Feigning hurt feelings, he yanked her toward him. "I wouldn't say that to you."

She smiled complacently. "That's because I have great legs."

He fastened his arms around her waist to pull her closer and swatted her bottom. "You're damned right, so you can afford some compassion for legs that have steadied me on a broiling sea."

She fell ready victim to the laughter in his eyes and leaned down to plant a light kiss on his lips. "I'll make you some high boots. The audience need never know. Come on. The spaghetti smells wonderful."

He yanked her back again as she tried to pull away. His eyes were inky and warm. "Don't change the subject."

She fought to maintain a casual attitude. "Subject? How long can you talk about boots?"

"Not boots," he corrected. "Love."

"We weren't talking about love."

"I'd like to." With a hand between her shoulder blades he pulled her closer still and planted a kiss in the hollow of her throat. "I love you, Des. I don't know if I'll ever be able to let you go again."

With kisses and nibbles he traced the cord of her neck to her earlobe. Fighting for composure, drowning in his languorous eyes, Destiny pushed halfheartedly at his shoulders.

"You said we didn't have to feel pressured," she reminded softly.

"We don't," he assured her, moving to take her lips in

a lengthy, breath-stealing kiss. Then he raised his head and smiled at her. "But we can feel loved."

Swallowing and breathing deeply, she suddenly realized she was sitting on his knee. She put on a judicious face. "What you're feeling, Rafe Janeiro, is lust."

He nodded agreeably. "Yes, I am. But I am also feeling love. I thought about you all the way to town, while I was there and all the way back. And it's different than it was the first time. It isn't a light bouncing all around me, blinding me, disorienting me. It's a beacon—" he indicated his heart with a jabbing thumb, his eyes suddenly serious "—here. And one day, Destiny Janeiro, it's going to lead you home."

"Dinner, you two!" Frances's voice filtered up the stairs. "There'll be plenty of time for that later."

Destiny had to share a laugh with Rafe. Yes. There would be.

"You'd better tell Cara," Rafe said, standing and planting Destiny firmly before letting her go. "I'll get cleaned up."

"Didn't you see her outside when you came in?" Destiny asked.

"No. I just presumed she was in here with you."

Frowning, Destiny went to knock on Cara's door, then opened it. The room was silent, empty of Cara's presence, the gray bear awaiting her return.

"Maybe the Morrisons are back," she thought aloud.

Rafe shook his head. "Their car wasn't there when I came home."

She looked up at him, a flicker of alarm showing in her eyes. He took her arm and led her toward the stairs.

"I'm sure Frances knows where she is," he said reassuringly.

Frances did not. "She left with a handful of cookies in the middle of the afternoon and was going out to the porch to work on her lines." She frowned in concern. "You've checked everywhere upstairs?"

Rafe went up while Destiny ran out to the front lawn. The front door was hardly ever used, and most of their family living was done in the back of the house. But she was running out of options. A deep green lawn sloped down to a plateau and a drop of ten feet or so to the ocean. It was bright and blue this evening, reflecting a cloudless sky. It rippled brightly in the quickening evening breeze.

Destiny's heart began to throb slow, hurtful beats that made her breath catch as she walked toward the brink of the cliff. Could Cara have come out this way, looking for the quiet place to study? Could she have sat on the edge of the bank, perhaps to dangle her legs comfortably and…

"Don't even think it," Rafe ordered firmly as he joined her. "She knows she's not to play in the front. Maybe she went for a walk. We'll trace the way we go every night, and Frances will stay home in case she phones or comes home."

"Where could she have gone that she'd phone?" Destiny demanded, her voice beginning to sound panicky.

"I don't know," was Rafe's calm reply as he pulled her toward the house. "Maybe she went walking and got farther than she expected. Mackey's Store is about two miles down the road."

"But she was looking forward to having spaghetti."

Rafe didn't answer that, simply put an arm around her shoulders and led her through the house to confer with Frances. Once out the back door he whistled up Joe who was dozing by the garage. Eager to join their expedition, the dog ran out ahead, turning back every few yards to be sure his master followed.

Ugly possibilities pelted Destiny's brain as she and Rafe walked up the long winding driveway that led to the lane. Every crime perpetrated against children came to mind, and she shuddered as she realized the loneliness of living this far from town.

Feeling Destiny tremble, Rafe pulled her closer to his

side. "Now don't let your imagination run away with you," he cautioned.

"I can't help it." She clung to him gratefully. "She wouldn't stay away willingly; I know she wouldn't. So she's either lost or hurt or—"

"Stop it! That's not going to help. Joe!" Rafe shouted at the dog as he cut across the lawn suddenly to stop several hundred feet away at the foot of an ancient sugar maple.

"Joe!" Rafe called again, and when he was still ignored by the usually obedient Lab, he stopped to watch the dog.

Joe barked up at the tree, then jumped at the trunk and barked again, his tail wagging. Then they heard the faint cry. "Mom! Daaady!"

Rafe took off at a run for the tree, with Destiny in hot pursuit. He was under the umbrella of overhanging branches and parting the sprays of leaves to look upward when Destiny reached him. She immediately noticed Cara's script for the play in the grass at the foot of the tree.

"Cara!" Rafe called.

A tearful voice replied weakly, "Hi, Daddy."

Rafe swallowed, pushing at the branches. "Are you okay?"

"Yeah. But I'm stuck!" And she began to cry, a reaction so unlike Cara that Destiny's fear deepened.

"Rafe, she must be twenty-five feet up!"

"The branches are closely spaced," he said, rubbing his hands on his jeans. "She's just too scared to manage. You be ready to take her from me."

"Rafe, be careful!" Destiny cried as he leaped for a clump of branches farther up to boost himself so he could plant his feet on the lower limbs as a base from which to begin the climb.

"I'm too scared to move, Daddy!" Cara cried as Rafe worked his way carefully up the jagged, gnarled trunk.

"That's fine," he called back. "Right now I don't want you to move."

Destiny, both hands at her mouth, watched Rafe's body

grow smaller as he climbed higher. She strained to see Cara, but a small glimpse of blue denim and a tennis shoe were all she could spot through the branches and foliage.

Then Rafe stopped and steadied himself before reaching his left arm out to the side.

Destiny couldn't hear the quiet words exchanged between father and daughter, and her nerves were screaming for some sound, some sign of movement from the leafy aerie. Then she watched, her heart in her throat, as Cara caught Rafe's shirt in one hand and climbed onto his back with the guidance of his free arm. Destiny could hear the child's soft sobs as Rafe began his careful descent. Cara's face was hidden against the back of his shirt, her legs wrapped around his waist as she held tightly to his neck.

It seemed to take forever for them to make any downward progress. It was longer still before they were close enough for Destiny to see them clearly. She half-expected to see a branch break any moment or Rafe lose his hold. But he continued slowly, cautiously from branch to branch until Destiny, on tiptoe, could reach Cara's legs.

"I've got her!" Destiny cried, and tried to pull Cara to safety. But the child wouldn't release her hold on Rafe. "Cara, you can let go. I've got you."

"No," she said, her eyes tightly shut.

"Cara," Rafe said gently, "you have to let go. I'll have to jump down, and I can't do that with you on my back. We'll both get hurt."

"No."

"Honey, you're safe now. Mom's got you."

Destiny pulled and Cara fell into her arms, slipping all the way to her feet. With a well-aimed leap, Rafe landed beside them. For a moment the three simply stared at each other, sharing amazement that the episode had ended safely.

Then as Destiny drew a breath of relief and moved to comfort her daughter, Cara turned, her face crumpling, into her father's arms. Destiny tried not to be hurt as jealousy tainted her relief at Cara's safety. The child didn't need the softness of her mother's arms at the moment, she tried to reason, but the strength of her father's.

"I don't know how I got up there!" Cara sobbed. "It was so big and green and quiet. I...I tried one step and...and then another." Cara pulled away to look up into Rafe's face, her amber eyes spilling tears. "I guess I...I forgot how c-clumsy I am. I didn't know I had gotten so high. Then I couldn't come down."

Rafe pulled her back against him and bent over her, shushing her, rocking her gently.

"Well, you're down now and you're safe so don't think about it anymore."

"But I almost fell!" Cara pulled away again and pushed the heels of both hands across her eyes. She looked at Rafe seriously, her face puffy and tearstained. "If you and Mom hadn't come..." Her voice cracked as she said, "I know I'd have fallen."

Rafe smiled down at Cara, bracing his hands on his knees and looking into her eyes. "That's what parents are for: to get you out of tight spots."

Cara frowned and shook her head. "Mom couldn't have done it."

"I guess..." Rafe glanced over Cara's head at Destiny, the emotion in his eyes at war with the quiet calm in his voice. "That's why it's good to have a dad as well as a mom."

Cara gave that suggestion a hearty nod. "Yeah! For the tough stuff."

Rafe straightened and gave one of Cara's ponytails a tug. "Are you hungry?"

"Starved!"

"Then let's go." He offered his hand to Cara, and they started toward the house. Destiny hung back, not certain there was a place for her in this moment. But Rafe and Cara turned toward her simultaneously, and the child extended her hand. "Come on, Mom!" Cara said impatiently. "We're starved!"

Cara ate heartily, and Destiny watched her surreptitiously as she sprinkled Parmesan cheese on her spaghetti. She was chattering to her father about the play, and Destiny fought an overwhelming feeling of alienation. It was childish and unworthy, she readily admitted, but she couldn't help it.

Rafe glanced up at her, catching the broodingly warlike look in her eyes and arched a questioning eyebrow. Destiny looked down at her plate and speared a meatball with a vicious stab of her fork.

Cara fell asleep that evening while watching television, her head leaning against Rafe's shoulder. Destiny, too, felt exhausted, the strain of that potentially dangerous episode taking its toll on her.

"Looks like I'd better get you both to bed," Rafe said, noting Destiny's weary yawn. "Want to help me with Cara?"

Destiny supported Cara's head so Rafe could slip out from under her and lift the child into his arms. He looked down at the angelic face at his shoulder for a moment and swallowed hard. When he turned to Destiny, there was pain in his eyes.

"I can't get over," he said heavily, "how much she's grown, or the thought of how much of her life I miss out on."

Destiny swallowed a painful lump in her throat, moved by his vulnerability and the real sadness she saw in his face. But the next moment, as he held the child against him and started up the stairs, she felt suspicion nibble at her consciousness again. He loved Cara so much. Had he invited her, Destiny, for the summer simply to have his daughter for a longer period of time?

Without turning the light on, Rafe deposited Cara on the bed and paused in the shadows to look down on her. If things didn't work out between Destiny and him, how was he ever going to be able to let them go? Sending Cara back to her mother after her time with him was always hard, had become more difficult every year. But this year the three of them had been together, and he wasn't sure he'd ever be able to live with less again. Pain moved inside him, real and alive.

Cara stirred and reached a hand out, groping on the sheet beside her. She raised one heavy eyelid.

"Hi, Daddy," she murmured sleepily. "Where's bear?"

"We forgot him on the sofa." He stroked her flushed cheek and then stood. "I'll get him," he told Destiny, and hurried out of the room before emotion overtook him.

He didn't like Destiny's expression. She said nothing, but she was feeling pressured; he felt it. He'd been beginning to think all the old threats of the past were gone, but he felt this one like a tangible presence even if he didn't understand it. For some reason, his rescue of their daughter had pushed him back a step in his relationship with Destiny.

When Rafe returned with the bear, Destiny had helped Cara into her pajamas and was pulling a thin sheet over her. The sleepy child put her arms up for the bear and laid it beside her, burrowing her nose in it. In a moment she was asleep.

Rafe looked at Destiny across the bed and knew that a chasm had opened between them.

"I've got work to do," he said quietly, moving toward the door. "I'll sleep in my office so I don't disturb you when I come to bed. Good night." Without giving her a chance to comment, he was gone.

Standing alone over Cara's bed, Destiny felt strangled by emotion and guilt. She sank quietly onto the edge of the bed, trying to find comfort in her role as mother. But that was the problem: she wasn't as necessary to Cara as she used to be. This afternoon, when she was frightened, Cara had run into her father's arms.

To compound her problems, Destiny knew Cara had completely lost the concept of a visit and was thinking of the three of them as a family again. But how could she, Destiny, commit to a man who, in all probability, was working toward a reconciliation more to have his daughter back than his wife?

Depressed and confused, Destiny tucked the covers around Cara and went to bed.

The following morning Destiny awoke to gales of laughter coming from downstairs. She took little time getting dressed, suspecting from their hysterical giggles that Cara and Jenny were into something potentially dangerous. But halfway down the stairs in hastily donned white pants and a brightly striped shirt, she caught a deeper masculine note in the laughter and Frances's high cackle.

Destiny followed the sounds to the kitchen and walked in to find Cara and Jenny leaning against each other, giggling helplessly. Frances was sitting at the table with a cup of coffee, her hand covering her eyes as she laughed. Rafe, with his back to everyone, was flipping pancakes on a griddle.

"What's happening?" Destiny asked, looking from one face to the other.

"Oh, Mom!" Cara straightened away from her friend and strained to catch her breath. "Have you seen Dad's fish imitation?"

Destiny cocked an ear toward her daughter, afraid she had misunderstood. "What?"

"Dad's fish imitation," Cara repeated on the brink of laughter again. "Do it for Mom, Daddy!"

"Oh, Cara…" he resisted.

"Please!" The girls shouted simultaneously, joined by Frances. Surrendering to pressure, Rafe put down the spatula and turned toward Destiny. Before her eyes his beguilingly handsome face became a caricature of a fish, eyes bulging and crossed, mouth somehow elongated and perpendicular, pursing and then opening like that of some eccentric form of sea life.

The girls and Frances collapsed into laughter again. Their camaraderie irritated Destiny, and she glared at Rafe, who was himself once again. "Obviously a deranged fish," was her pronouncement as she took a place at the table.

Noting the quarrelsome quality in her voice, Rafe picked up his spatula and studied her with controlled impatience. "How many pancakes?" he finally asked.

"None," she replied, looking away from him. "Just tea."

"No reversion to bad habits," Rafe countered. "How about just one pancake?"

"Is there any point in refusing?" she asked, her irritation deepening.

His gaze was level. "None."

"Then I'll have one pancake."

"We're going to Jenny's," Cara announced, crossing the room to hug Destiny. Then she went to Rafe and reached her arms up to him. He put the spatula down again and leaned down to give her a noisy hug.

"I love you, Daddy," she said. "Even when you're a fish."

"And I love you," he responded, "even when you're up a tree."

She grimaced at him. "That's funny today, but it wasn't yesterday."

He laughed and hugged Cara again, then turned her toward the door. "Have fun."

Breakfast was quiet, the strain between Destiny and Rafe increasing as she toyed with her small meal, and he made short work of a score of pancakes.

Destiny finally pushed her plate away and looked at Rafe with grim reluctance. "I have to get your measurements for your costume sometime today."

He laughed mirthlessly over the dread in her tone. "And I'd love to be alone with you, too." He stacked their plates and took them to the counter, turning to the table to challenge her. "I'm free. How about now?"

The last thing she wanted at the moment was the intimacy required in taking his measurements, but the fact that he knew she was reluctant made her look at him with exaggerated bravado. "Why not?"

Rafe wandered around Destiny's workroom picking items up and putting them down while she rummaged for her tape measure.

"A cheese grater?" he asked, holding up the item obviously commandeered from Frances's kitchen.

"For breaking down the fabric I used for the girls' skirts. The weave was too fine."

He walked across the room to where several finished garments hung and held aloft a pair of embroidered linen hosiery. He wiggled his eyebrows wickedly. "Wow!" he said. "Look at these."

Destiny looked up at him quellingly. "They're yours."

He put them down as though they had suddenly become toxic. "They are?"

"Every gentleman of the period wore them."

"Well, I guess for the sake of authenticity…" His voice trailed away as he moved to an area of the wall covered in corkboard. Her sketches were pinned there, and he studied the one of himself. "Doesn't look like much of the stockings show between the boots and the bottom of the cape."

"We have to bear in mind your knobby knees, remember. Are you ready?"

They had teased about Rafe's knees repeatedly during the last several weeks, but this time the remark carried a trace of vitriol.

He turned to face her as she placed a sheet of paper and a pen on her worktable and beckoned him toward her, shaking out the measuring tape.

"Do you want to tell me what's on your mind?" he asked, walking over to her to stand in an aggressive attitude, arms folded. He looked impatient with the morning's bantering and close to anger.

"Lean toward me please, so I can measure your head. The only thing on my mind is your costume." Destiny snapped the tape around his head, read it carefully and made a note on her sheet of paper. Then she measured over his head from ear to ear and recorded her findings.

"That's a crock, sweetie," he said.

She was measuring his neck and then measured a second time to be sure she was correct. She glanced up into his bright, dark eyes, then down at her sheet of paper.

"Are you claiming the ability to read my mind?" she asked coolly, placing the tape at his neck, measuring to his shoulder.

"I'm good at reading the weather," he paraphrased, his arm moving obediently as she bent it to place his hand at his waist so that she could measure his outer arm. "There's a storm blowing, Des."

She did not reply, but instead reached around him to measure his chest and then his waist. The action put her in contact with his brawny torso. Her annoyance grew as she felt her pulse react to his nearness. She drew a shaky breath and jotted the measurements down.

"It started whipping up last night, didn't it?" he asked. "I could feel it when we put Cara to bed."

Without answering Destiny measured his hips, keeping a clinical attitude and a steady heartbeat with Herculean effort. She measured the inches from his waist to the floor, then the circumference of his calf.

"I don't know what you're talking about." She managed to make her voice sound preoccupied as she walked around him and took back measurements.

Suddenly Rafe spun around and grabbed her by her forearms, ignoring her little scream of surprise and the startled expression in her eyes.

"Look, Destiny, I think I've got your measure," he said angrily, snatching the tape measure from her and flinging it onto the floor. "And I didn't need a tape to do it. You don't like it that Cara and I get along so well, do you? I saw your face this morning in the kitchen." He frowned down at her as though unable to believe what he saw in her eyes. "I can't believe that you're jealous because Cara loves me."

"That isn't true!" Destiny yanked away from him, marching across the room toward her sewing machine.

Rafe followed her. "Yes, it is true!"

She turned on him impatiently, her cheeks pink, her eyes snapping anger. "I know she loves you. What isn't true is that it's jealousy making me afraid of your relationship."

Rafe folded his arms, his manner doubtful. "Then what is?"

"What do you care?" she screamed at him, tears forming, burning behind her eyes. She wasn't sure she could explain coherently how she felt; she didn't entirely understand her feelings herself. She just knew that their increasing closeness made her feel threatened, pushed, guilty. "Cara thinks we're a family again." Her tone accused him of being responsible for that fact. "She'll never be able to get along without you now. Isn't that why you came for me in the first place? To get Cara on a more permanent basis?"

His arms unfolded slowly and he blinked, a look of complete surprise on his face. Then he put his hands in his pockets and shifted his weight to his right foot.

"You have a poor memory," he said quietly. "I wanted you ten years ago, before there ever was a Cara."

"Yes," she agreed tearfully, bitterly. "So much that when I left you never tried to make me come back."

He shook his head in exasperation. "Destiny, I say what I feel and I do what I feel I should do. I can't be held responsible for the fact that you don't operate that way. I thought you left because you wanted to go, not because you wanted me to make you come back. That doesn't even make sense!"

"Well, nothing makes sense now, either," she sobbed, falling into the chair at her sewing machine. Even loneliness had been better than this muddle in her mind. "Why didn't you just leave me alone?"

Rafe crossed to the window seat, moving aside the pillows she had made with scraps from the costumes, and sat down, leaning his elbows on his knees. "Because I needed you. Because you needed me, Des. You need me now. That's what you really don't like about all this. Not that Cara loves me, but that you do. You never knew that feeling five years ago."

She gave him an indignant look as tears slid past her jawline. "That isn't true."

"I think it is," he insisted. "I was committed to keeping a pretty doll by my side, one who would give me pleasure and buoy my sometimes flimsy sense of self with her adoration—and you were committed to hurting your mother for all her husbands and your uncertain childhood by marrying a lowly fisherman and living the romantic role of rich girl giving up everything for her love. When reality set in, we couldn't take it—either of us."

Destiny swiped at the tears on her face and stood frowning at him. "I loved you!"

He nodded. "I know. And I loved you, but we loved each other for what each could get from the other rather than what we could give." He caught her hand as she paced by him and pulled her beside him on the window seat. "It's the real thing this time, Des."

She looked up into his dark eyes and seeing sincerity there was able to admit candidly, "Rafe, I don't know what's happening. Part of me would like us to be a family again." She wove her fingers in her lap and stared at them. "But I...I just can't go back to that until we know for sure we can make it work. I've learned too much about life and about myself. I've been very independent. I can't give that up."

"Is the freedom really worth the loneliness?" he asked.

She gave a mirthless laugh. "Do you know how little freedom there is in raising a child and being under contract to a studio?"

"I know you don't want to be free of responsibilities,"

he replied. "You want to be heart-free. I suppose that's the most appealing and most lethal freedom of all. It gives you everything you think you want, then the solitude slowly kills you."

Had a record been kept, heartbeat by heartbeat, of the past five years of her life, it could not have read more accurately. But her every argument would be lost if he knew that.

Destiny stood up and walked away from him, not turning until she'd reached the middle of the room. "It isn't fair to Cara to let her think everything's going to work out and that we'll all live happily ever after."

"Do we have to say anything until we're sure it won't work?"

"Every day we spend here," she said coolly, conscious of needing moving room in this debate, "pushes me, forces me into what you want and what Cara wants. I feel trapped!" Her voice had risen in frustration and she drew a deep breath, making a conscious effort to be calm. "I feel trapped."

It was a simple statement, swiftly spoken, an honest expression of her feelings at the moment. But she heard the selfishness in it even as she spoke; she felt the change in the room's atmosphere instantly.

Anger emanated from Rafe as he straightened and got slowly to his feet.

"The only thing trapping you," he said heavily, "is your own inability to trust yourself." He stabbed a hand into the pocket of his jeans, then took her hand and slapped a silver key ring into her palm. "Here are the keys to my car. Go. You've got color in your cheeks, and you've put on a few pounds. Your sketches look great. I've done what I set out to do." He looked hurt and moody and thoroughly fed up. "You're a whole woman again, but inside you're still the classic brat who lived with me on Belleville Avenue. Anything that requires you to trust someone is a trap!"

The blood draining from her face at his unexpected re-action, Destiny tried to treat his statement as a bluff.

"And what about Cara?" she asked with a tremor in her voice as he crossed to the door.

"Had she been here alone it'd be time for her to go back anyway," he replied, his hand on the knob. "Just explain to her that you feel trapped," he added on a note of sar-casm. "I'm sure she'll understand." Rafe yanked the door open.

"Wait!" Destiny shouted.

He stopped, the action suspended as his shoulders rose and fell. He drew a deep breath then turned to face her, his brow unfurrowed but the eyes under it so dark and angry that Destiny found it required all her courage to walk to-ward him.

"Don't walk away from me," she said forcefully, stop-ping two steps from him. "I was trying to tell you how I feel."

"Yeah, well if you're going to tell me that you're think-ing of this place as some sort of cage..."

She folded her arms and looked up at him intrepidly. "You didn't let me finish the thought."

It would be so satisfying to take that spun-gold hair in one hand and shake her, Rafe thought. That made him the chauvinist she always accused him of being, he supposed, but she was going to drive him to drink—or worse. He hadn't felt turned inside out like this since...since the last time he had fought with her, five years ago, just before she left him. With a few well-chosen words she could make everything inside him hurt and fill him with a fear so pow-erful he'd never seen its like—even in forty-foot swells when the boat heeled so far over he was sure they were going to capsize.

Trapped! How could the fire and the tenderness he felt for her ever be considered a trap? As he forced himself to hold his temper, to try to be calm, he wondered if it was his fault. Was he unable to communicate the feeling to her with the same purity with which he felt it?

Rafe jammed his hands in his pockets, walked to the worktable and sat on the edge of it. He tried to look receptive to whatever she wanted to tell him, but he could feel the stiffness in his face, in his thoughts. *So, Janeiro,* he told himself with a bleak flash of humor, *you haven't come as far as you thought you had.*

"All right," he said, the stiffness in his voice, as well. "Finish the thought. I apologize."

Destiny hiked herself up next to him on the table. She could feel the rock hardness in him, in the bicep brushing hers. She could feel the control she knew he was exerting over himself. She gave him a weak smile, appreciating how difficult it was to listen when one really wanted to rage.

"I apologize also for a poor choice of words," she said in a low voice.

He turned to her, his eyes, his mood softening.

"What I was trying to explain," she went on, making every effort to speak calmly and clearly, "is that I could love you again so easily. I've told you that. I think a part of me always has. The problem is that the part of me that grew without you while we were apart has learned to trust in me because I accomplished a million things, big and little, that I didn't know I had in me—from replacing a washer on a dripping faucet to earning the respect of the movie industry. Rafe…I know I can depend on me."

God. How many hits did he have to take? But he made himself ask, "And you're not sure you can depend on me, is that it?"

"No!" she said so vehemently that he looked at her in complete confusion. "I mean that…this per- son—" she spread a hand against her breastbone and looked at him earnestly "—has become very strong. I don't know if I could fit her into a permanent relationship."

He turned slightly and put a hand to her back. "Des, what's the point of being strong, if there's nothing or no one to be strong for, or with—" he smiled dryly "—or even against, for that matter?"

"I don't know." She patted the knee beside hers in a way that was totally fraternal. "I just feel like an important part of me has developed, and I don't want to lose it. And you're so strong—" she smiled again, disarming him completely "—I don't know if I could stand up against you, and I'm afraid to take the chance."

"Could you stand up beside me instead of against me?" he suggested.

She looked doubtful. "Look at us. How long did it take for this argument to work itself around so that we could listen to each other?"

"But it did. Isn't that the important point?"

She considered that a moment and finally nodded. "I guess so. We could have never done this five years ago."

"True."

"You know what I think?"

The hand at her back rubbed indulgently, the look in his eyes a distinctly masculine one from the old days. "I wouldn't dare hazard a guess."

She ignored his teasing and told him seriously, "I think our sleeping together is getting in the way of our thinking together." She had been as eager as he to take up their physical relationship and she hastened to explain, not wanting him to think that she was denying responsibility for it. "It's too easy for us because we're so good together. But if we want to see if we can live together again...we have to let getting along instead of getting in bed pull us together." She swallowed, hating the very thought herself, sure he would protest. If he offered a good argument on why they should continue in the same bed, and she knew there were many, she wasn't sure she could hold out against him. But that was the entire issue, wasn't it?

She looked at him levelly. "Agreed?"

Rafe's eyes ran over her face, full of protest, irritation and a very basic lust. Then they settled on her eyes, and she watched their expression change reluctantly to one of patience.

"Hell, no," he said. "But I'll do it." Then he gave her a grim smile and offered her his extended arm. "Any other vein you want me to open for you?"

She took his fist, examining the knotty blue vein in the vulnerable underside of the forearm he offered her, filled with his life's blood.

"Open your hand," she said ambiguously.

His fingers opened like some large, rough flower. She leaped off the table and slapped the car keys he had given her into his palm. "I'll leave when I'm damned good and ready," she said, and closing his fingers over the keys, she kissed them and left the room.

Chapter Eight

By the end of July Destiny had the sails finished for the ship to be used in the Digby Day set, and all of the costumes ready for the production, except Rafe's. Fitting and measuring created an intimate atmosphere between actor and costumer, and Destiny wasn't anxious to confuse the friendly relationship they were trying so hard to build by draping his naked torso with the slit-sleeved shirt she was making, by testing and tucking and making the judgments only fingertips in touch with the body could do accurately.

Rafe was complying dutifully with her request of that afternoon in her office. Though they were together every afternoon, sometimes with Cara and sometimes alone, he was studiously careful not to hold her or touch her or even catch her hand. They laughed together, discussed their daughter, the play, his family, whatever subject arose—careful to let each other speak, to disagree without being disagreeable, and found to their mutual surprise that there were many subjects on which they could agree.

But what Destiny had so hoped to achieve had built-in snares. They were learning so much about each other through the simple act of listening that their respect for each other was growing. As warmth developed between them—something that was completely different from the fire that had always been there—she felt an increasing desire to put her hand to his face or his shoulder, to take his arm, to put her arms around him and to feel his lips at her throat. The physical side of their relationship that she was trying so hard to separate from the personal side, was growing, as well. She had the distinct feeling that it was about to elbow her constraints aside and assume control. Afraid of herself, she fought desperately against it. She worked longer in the office; she began to break their regular routine of walks after dinner, of afternoon trips to town, of sitting on the porch steps in the darkness and listening to the crickets.

Cara became confused. A knock on Destiny's office door was followed by a blur of cotton plaid and blue jeans that landed in her lap. More ebullient than usual, Cara put both arms around her mother's neck and hugged.

"I think I finally know all my lines!" Cara announced with contagious delight. "Daddy says I sound just like Karen Crane."

"Well!" Destiny widened her eyes dramatically. "She collected her second Oscar in a row this year."

"Someday I'm going to do that," Cara confided. "Do you think somebody built like me and clumsy could ever be an actress?"

"I dressed Karen for both roles and I always had to compensate for a thick waist. And you're not clumsy."

"A thick waist? Really?" Cara looked incredulous.

Destiny nodded. "Really. If you demand me to dress you in your contracts, I'll hide every figure flaw you might have. Though by the time you're old enough to do a film, your body will be mature and you may not have figure flaws."

With crossed eyes and distorted lips, Cara looked comically doubtful. "I'll probably grow up just like I am now—fat up and down."

"I hate to keep repeating myself, but you're not fat and you're not clumsy. You just have to wait for your coordination to catch up with your growth."

Cara kissed Destiny's cheek and bounced to her feet.

"Oh, well. Daddy says if I don't want to worry about being glamorous all the time, character actresses get good roles and make a lot of money."

"And he's right," Destiny confirmed. A part of her felt hurt that she hadn't been the first to share Cara's thoughts on her future. But another part of her was pleased, realizing that for the first time in a year Cara seemed less plagued by how she looked than how she felt. Cara was happy.

"I thought so. Well, bye, Mom." Cara started for the door, then turned to study her mother thoughtfully. "Mom?" she asked with a frown, her voice softening from her earlier excitement. "Do you think we'll...you know...stay?"

Destiny's heartbeat accelerated, but she replied steadily, "We agreed just to come for a vacation, Cara. You know that."

Cara took several steps toward her mother. "I think Daddy would like us to stay," she said. Then she added uncertainly, almost as though afraid it would be considered betrayal, "I'd like to stay."

Destiny closed the gap between them and put her arms around Cara, holding her close. "I know, darling. But we'll have to wait and see, all right?"

Cara looked doubtful about that. "But we're going backward, aren't we? About being a family, I mean."

Destiny frowned at her, uncertain what she meant. "I don't understand, Cara."

"You know," she began to explain, her eyes downcast, her manner mildly embarrassed. "Daddy doesn't sleep in your room anymore. When he did sleep there, I thought for sure everything was gonna be all right." The extent of her concern was apparent in her wide amber eyes. "I thought you liked being here. I thought you liked Daddy."

Destiny put an arm around her daughter and held her close, remembering how difficult it had been to make another adult understand how she felt. What chance did she stand with a prejudiced child? "I like being here, and I like your dad," she said, "but...a marriage needs stronger stuff than liking."

Cara nodded. "I know. Loving. But loving is only liking real hard, isn't it? Can't you just like him harder?"

If there was a good, logical reply to that, Destiny couldn't think of it. She simply hugged her philosopher again and smiled.

"We're doing our best to learn to be friends again. Can you settle for that for now? Just concentrate on the play. Maybe everything else will take care of itself."

Cara looked dissatisfied, but let the matter drop. "Did you know that Daddy talked to Grandma and Grandpa Janeiro this morning?"

"No, I didn't."

"They're going to come and see the play." Cara's face brightened at the prospect. "And Uncle Manny and Aunt Michelle and Uncle Mike and Aunt Augusta and all the kids are coming, too."

Destiny swallowed the groan that rose to her lips and forced a smile for her excited daughter. "That's wonderful," she made herself say.

"I'm invited to Jenny's for dinner and to spend the night. Is that okay?"

"Sure."

Cara nearly strangled Destiny with a hug and skipped away, adding over her shoulder, "Oh, Daddy says the boat's almost ready. He wants you to come to the garage with the sails and see if everything fits okay. Bye."

Destiny was terrified at the thought of seeing Rafe's family again. And coming face-to-face with his father would give her nightmares, she was sure. How could he make these plans without even telling her?

Destiny fumed, snatching the heavy sails from the corner of her worktable and stalking down the stairs and out the back door to the garage. Her angry stride was halted by the sight of the ship. The complete forward half of a seventeenth-century merchantman dominated the space usually occupied by the Mercedes and the old truck.

Rafe rose above the gunwales of the ship, sandpaper wrapped around a block of wood in his hand, perspiration gleaming on his face and naked chest in the dim light of the garage. He leaped gracefully to the concrete floor to stand back and survey his handiwork. Destiny shifted the heavy sails in her arms, and he looked up, a ready smile on his lips until he read her expression. Then he frowned.

"What's the matter?"

She walked up to the boat, snapped "Nothing!" and draped the sails over the rails, rubbing her arm against the scratchy weight of the canvas. There was no mast that she could see. She turned to him, hands on her hips. "Do I hang the sails on thin air?"

He advanced slowly toward her and she felt a sudden, instant sense of déjà vu. The angry tension between them reminded her of every argument they'd ever had in their five years together.

He stopped in front of her, wiping his hands on a rag. He tossed the rag inside the boat. "No," he said evenly after a moment. "You hang it on the mast, which we can't raise until I push the boat out into the driveway."

The ship stood on a platform, resting on a trailer for ease of transfer.

"Then what are we waiting for?" she demanded.

He moved to the front of the trailer, ready to push. "For you to get out of the way." His reply was mild but pointed as he indicated her presence in the path of the ship. She stepped aside, giving him a poisonous look, and watched while he put his shoulder to the trailer and pushed the boat from the garage into the bright sunlight. He went back into the garage and emerged with two long poles, one slightly shorter than the other, that served as mast and yardarm. The larger one fit neatly into a hole he had drilled in the bottom of the ship.

"You didn't tell me your family was coming." Her tone

was accusatory though quiet. He looked down at her from inside the ship, his appearance disturbingly appealing, like that of some pirate peering from the rigging under a Jolly Roger.

"I didn't know until two hours ago," he said equably. "You know how they are about Cara. She invited them, and they jumped at the chance to get together. Hand me the large sail, please."

She passed the heavy bulk of sailcloth up to him. "You could have told me," she insisted petulantly.

"You were working in your office, remember?"

"Have you forgotten where it is?"

They looked at each other across the space separating them, his glance impatient, hers angry.

"I thought you were hiding there as usual," he finally replied. He went to the garage for an aluminum ladder and set it up inside the prow of the boat. With the sail in hand he climbed it. "I didn't think you'd want to be disturbed."

"I wasn't hiding."

"There's some rope lying on my workbench," he said, ignoring her denial as he temporarily laid the sail across the horizontal spar to take the weight off his arms. "Would you get it for me, please?"

She did as he asked and handed him the loosely coiled cord.

"You're going to have to come up here and help me," Rafe directed. "Put your foot here on the trailer wheel and give me your hand."

Then she was in the boat beside him, holding the sail out while he climbed the ladder and eased the cord through the grommets along the top of the sail.

"I wasn't hiding," she said again as though their conversation hadn't been interrupted.

"I heard you." He moved several steps down the ladder. "I just didn't believe you. Take up the slack."

She didn't press that because she wasn't sure she told the truth anyway. "I won't know what to say to your father,'' she blurted defensively, moving aside as he got off the ladder to move around the sail and judge the authenticity of its appearance.

"Don't worry about it," he said absently. "He probably won't know what to say to you."

"I'm sure he'll think of something mean to say immediately."

Rafe put the yardarm in place. "That's because he doesn't know what else to say." At her look of confusion he added, moving, then climbing the ladder, "It took me a while to figure that out. The way he treats me doesn't mean that he hates me; it means that he doesn't know what to make of me. I'm not just like him and therefore, confuse him." He looked down at her from the top of the ladder. "Sail."

She handed the second piece of canvas up to him. "He just doesn't like me."

"No, he doesn't understand you." He fastened the sail in place. "Portuguese women, though they're full of fire and spirit, are supposed to do what their man tells them. At least that was the way it had always worked before. The twentieth century finally caught up with him when you joined the family. But he's mellowed a little. I wouldn't worry about it."

"Easy for you to say," she grumbled.

"No, it's not!" he shouted, his temper finally breaking through his attempts to smother it. "I'd like it better if I got along with him—I'd like it better if you got along with him. Hell, I'd die of gratitude if anybody got along with anybody! Knife!"

She handed it up instantly, half-expecting it to turn into a cutlass in his hand.

"You're shouting," she pointed out.

"I know!" he shouted again, yanking the line taut. Was the tension getting to him, too, she wondered. He climbed down several steps, fed the line through the last grommet and tied it off. "I just don't see what the big deal is," he said moodily. "Why is it so hard for people to just let other people be who they are and love them anyway?"

Holding the sail steady, Destiny shrugged. "I suppose because we're imperfect."

The sails set, he leaned against the ladder to frown down at her. "Then why do we expect other people to meet our needs perfectly?"

As far as Destiny could tell, that question ranked close behind Cara's analysis of loving being just like liking only harder. She could think of no plausible reply.

"Don't ask me," she replied, a small flare of humor softening her distress. "I have trouble enough with the simple stuff. When are they coming?"

"A few days before the play. They'll stay about a week, make a real family thing out of it." He glanced at her dryly as he folded the ladder, then he leaped out of the boat. "I hope it isn't too miserable for you."

She studied his back as he walked around the boat, checking details, and tried to judge whether or not that had been a snide remark. Unsure, she decided not to comment.

He came to join her as she admired their craftsmanship. "So what do you think?" he asked. "Should we go into the boat business?"

She tilted her head to the side, considering. "Well, aesthetically, we've got it all over ChrisCraft."

"Our styling is classic," he contributed.

"But we'd have to learn to make the back part, too, don't you think?" She gestured to where the large model disappeared into nothingness beyond the audience's view.

Rafe turned to her, hands on his hips. "Five years married to a fisherman, and you still call it the back of the boat?" He sounded horrified. "It's the stern, Des."

She rapped a fist on her chest. "Forgive me. The stern."

"To make up for that gaffe, you have to help me take it down."

Rafe and Destiny climbed into the boat to reverse the rigging process they had just completed.

"Want to go out to dinner?" Rafe folded a sail and handed it down to her. "Cara's gone to Jenny's, and Frances would probably appreciate an evening off. Besides..." He looked down into her suspicious expression. "You look like you could use a change of scene."

Rafe handed her the second sail, folded the ladder, leaped off the boat, then hefted the ladder on his shoulder and carried it to the garage. He returned to remove the poles that served as mast and yardarm and carried them also to the garage.

Trailing in his wake, Destiny asked sulkily, "Am I looking matronly again?"

He looked at her over a naked, muscular shoulder. His eyes were dark and analytical. "No. But you do look stressed."

That was putting it mildly, she thought. She felt a sudden need to scream and throw things. How could he be so calm and controlled? Didn't he miss her in bed as much as she missed him? Didn't he ache and burn and want her back in his arms? He didn't look stressed. In the face of his containment, she felt vulnerable and very, very annoyed.

"Look, if you don't want to go..." he began.

"I'll go, I'll go!" Destiny accepted the invitation with ill grace and stormed off to take a shower. Damn. If he could take it, so could she.

LIKE EVERYTHING ELSE in town, the Digby Head Hotel was decorated in a nautical theme, but with a certain authenticity that made it particularly charming. The dining room was small, and the dance area a mere patch near the raised dais where the band performed.

Rafe looked across the table at her, only his eyes visible above the tall menu. "You want cod, right?"

She hated cod and he knew it. He'd been teasing her mercilessly since they'd left the house, almost as though he were deliberately trying to ease this afternoon's tension. She'd always been susceptible to Rafe's charm, and now when it looked as though sitting across a table from him was all the intimacy she could hope for for a while, she felt herself relax, determined to enjoy it.

Giving Rafe a warning arch of her eyebrow, she stopped the maître d' as he passed their table with an ice-filled bucket containing a bottle of champagne.

"Sir, this man is bothering me," she complained, indicating Rafe, who had suddenly turned urbanely innocent.

The tall, slender man slipped his glasses down his nose and frowned at Rafe. "You again," he said with severity. "What did I tell you the last time we asked you to leave?"

Rafe thought hard. "Never to come back?"

The man nodded judiciously, and Rafe hung his head. "And here you are again, harassing lovely innocent women. For shame." With a commiserating look at Destiny, the man began to walk away, then turned to Rafe. "Incidentally, Claude says we need thirty pounds of scallops for a banquet next week. I was supposed to call you."

"You got 'em," Rafe assured him.

As Destiny watched the maître d' walk away with a salute for Rafe, she turned to her companion with a grimace. "You certainly got off easy. Friend of yours?"

He was studying his menu again. "We've been supplying their seafood for three years. He wasn't fooled by your accusation for a moment. He knows what a fine and noble paragon I am."

Destiny put her menu down, feigning illness. "I don't think I could eat anything after that."

He leaned across the table toward her. "Behave yourself or I'll take you home."

"Oh," she murmured consideringly. Wondering if she could tease a reaction out of him, she leaned toward him with a suggestive smile. "To do what?"

For a moment he looked darkly dangerous, as though he would take advantage of her overt suggestion and carry her off to the car. Her heart picked up an erratic beat. Then he looked down at his menu and asked conversationally, "I don't know. What do people who are learning to get along rather than get in bed do at night?''

So. He was determined to hold firm against her. She was tempted to run the toe of her shoe along his sock and into his pant leg and offer a few suggestions. But noting his apparent unconcern as he closed his menu and looked at her as though she were just another scallop, she sighed wearily and shook out her linen napkin. ''They go to town and have dinner.''

Rafe tasted nothing of his Shrimp Kiev. His mind was totally occupied with keeping his senses under control. He didn't know how much more of this he could take.

Destiny was goading him; he recognized that expression from the old days. She was probably wondering if she had pushed him to the limit yet, if she could prod him past the strict rein he'd kept on himself for the past two weeks. She was testing his fortitude, and it had to match or surpass hers if they were ever to be husband and wife again. And he knew with certainty that he wanted that for their future.

He pushed his half-empty plate away and looked up to find Destiny watching him with such longing that his resolve wavered dangerously. She indicated the small dance floor, where couples moved in tight patterns to avoid colliding with other couples. It was the kind of situation they used to love when they were first married. It was a good excuse to lean against each other, barely moving, bodies close and preparing for the inevitable end to a romantic evening.

He didn't have to pretend the look of regret though he was sure it didn't convey a fraction of what he felt. ''Sorry. I pulled a tendon or something when I hauled the boat out today.''

Destiny fell back against her chair with a pout. And the spurned expression went a long way toward stiffening his resolve. Concealing a smile with a sip of wine, he determined that she would weaken before he did.

After they left the restaurant Rafe also refused a moonlight walk along the waterfront, pleading the soreness of his pulled tendon. Destiny subsided in the passenger seat without a word until he pulled into the driveway of his home. She peered through the windshield at the low-slung, obviously powerful and expensive car in the path of their headlights.

"One of your brothers?" Destiny asked.

Rafe made a sound of appreciation for the fine machine before turning off his lights. "No. Manny's got a van and Mike's got a wagon. Nobody's got a Lamborghini."

Destiny frowned at Rafe as he held her door open, a disturbing sense of foreboding settling over her.

"Maybe Frances has a wealthy boyfriend," Rafe suggested, taking a last look at the car in the light from the porch before following Destiny up the few steps.

The front door swung open abruptly, and they stood looking at a beautiful blond woman, framed in the doorway by the soft light from the living room.

Destiny froze on the top step as her instinct of foreboding materialized. The unsatisfactory evening fell into total ruin. "Mother," she said faintly.

Chapter Nine

Destiny allowed herself to be wrapped in an embrace of St. Laurent chic and Valentino perfume. She felt silky hair against her cheek, and her mother's still coltish slimness under her hands.

Serena Fleming held her daughter at arm's length and smiled. "It is good to see you, darling."

Rafe was looking at her over Serena's shoulder and she read the message in his eyes very clearly. Good manners, please, Des. She's a guest in my house.

"You look wonderful, Mother," Destiny replied. That was something she could say honestly. At fifty-plus, the ingenue who had taken Hollywood by storm was still visible in her, even if her makeup was a little more carefully applied and small lines now radiated from her eyes. Her well cared for skin was pink and creamy and still flawless. Her body, in a casual yellow jacket and matching pants, was three inches taller than Destiny's and had always made her green with envy.

"What brings you here of all places?"

Serena looked surprised by the question, but only for a moment. "You, of course, Destiny. I wanted you to meet Brandon." She reached behind her for the hand of a man only slightly taller than she with fair features and a male-model smile. He looked like Robert Redford with curly hair. She judged his age at somewhere around her own. He was young enough to be Serena's son. "Des, this is my fiancé, Brandon Gates."

It wasn't until Rafe reached around her to shake the man's hand that Destiny realized she was staring. "Have you eaten?" Rafe asked his guests.

"We had dinner on our way up," Brandon said. He had a deep, clear voice and a relaxed manner that annoyed Destiny. How dare he be twenty years younger than her mother and not feel uncomfortable about meeting her family. "Frances made us very comfortable. We don't want to put you to any trouble."

"No trouble," Rafe insisted, guiding them back toward the sofa and chairs. "Sit down and I'll see if I can find some champagne."

"Oh, Rafe, don't fuss…" Serena began.

He took the hands the older woman held out to him in protest and squeezed them. Destiny looked on in disgust. She had always hated the fact that they liked each other.

"Sit down, Serena. It's too late for you to be on the road; you'll have to stay the night. So let's have champagne while we get acquainted with Brandon."

"Thank you," Brandon said graciously, pulling Serena out of Rafe's path to the kitchen. "We'll enjoy that very much. Sit down, love."

"I can handle it." Rafe gave Destiny a knowing smile as she tried to follow him into the kitchen. "Keep your mom entertained."

Destiny perched uncomfortably on the edge of the love seat facing the sofa where her mother and Brandon sat together. She hated this game she played with her mother. Serena always acted thrilled to see her, and Destiny always behaved as though she, too, was pleased. She was sure Serena wished as much as she did that she were somewhere—anywhere else. And now she was faced with Brandon Gates, as well.

I've got him pegged, Destiny thought as she studied his open, friendly expression. An actor. With those good looks and that voice, he had to be. She was sure his relationship with her mother was the classic story. Serena's connections would serve him well on the way to the top.

"So, what do you do, Mr. Gates?" Destiny asked politely.

"I'm in retail," he replied—a little too quickly, she thought. He probably clerked in a men's store between acting jobs. He looked at Serena, and they exchanged a small smile. Then he looked back at Destiny. "Call me Bran. Please."

"How did you meet my mother?"

"At a party." He reached a blunt, square hand out to pat Serena's knee. They exchanged another smiling look. "We were both bored and wandered out onto the lanai. A real cliché, I suppose, but it's the best thing that ever happened to either of us."

Sure. Destiny looked at her mother, watching for some sign that she was aware of being duped, but there was none. She looked disgustingly happy. It amazed Destiny that after three husbands, she still hadn't developed a sense of self-preservation.

Anxious to interrupt another of their loving looks, Destiny asked, "Where are the dogs, Mother?" Serena seldom went anywhere without her three poodles.

"Home with Celestine. Brandon said I'd be too busy fussing over him to pay attention to them."

Destiny looked at Brandon with fresh interest. Someone who could part her mother from those dogs had to be someone to be reckoned with.

"Frances told us that Cara is staying the night with a neighbor," Serena said. "I'm so anxious to see her."

"She's just down the road. She'll be home for breakfast." The question, "When are you leaving?" was on the tip of Destiny's tongue, but when Rafe came into the room with a tray bearing a bottle of champagne and glasses she quickly rephrased it to, "How long can you stay?"

"We've got to be on our way tomorrow," Brandon replied. "We're going to New Brunswick."

"Brandon's sister had a baby," Serena explained. "She and her husband have a small farm there."

"Babies are something this family understands," Rafe said, efficiently popping the champagne cork. "My brothers are trying to outpace each other. So far the count's four to three."

To Destiny's astonishment her ex-husband and her mother's fiancé continued to talk babies while Rafe poured champagne and passed glasses. Then Rafe raised his glass in a toast.

"To Serena and Brandon."

As Destiny lifted her glass she wondered if crossing one's fingers during a toast negated it, as the same action negated a lie.

Rafe took a seat beside Destiny, having shed his jacket and put Brandon's away. "Are you involved in Gates Business Systems?" he inquired of their guest.

Brandon nodded, obviously surprised. "I am."

"I thought I recognized you from a photo in *Forbes* magazine." Now her mother's fiancé looked a little embarrassed. "I was interested because we just put in your interbranch coordinating system." He lifted his glass again. "My compliments. The communication system works beautifully."

"I'm glad to hear that. We…"

Destiny lost the thred of their conversation as it went on at length about Rafe's particular system and a new project Brandon was working on. Calmly sipping champagne with his hand on her mother's knee, Brandon Gates decimated Destiny's theory about him and left her in a state of perplexity.

As she tried to focus her attention on him she learned that he was born into a wealthy family in Rhode Island, struck out on his own in computers and at thirty was a member of the Millionaire Club. That piece of information came from Serena as she watched Destiny, apparently waiting for comment. All she could think of was an inane, "How nice."

"You're probably exhausted," Rafe said finally when glasses were empty and the clock read 2:00 a.m. "The sofa bed in my office is very comfortable. Des, why don't you take your mother upstairs, and I'll help Bran with their bags."

While the men were occupied Destiny put fresh linens on the sofa bed, noting with relief that Frances must have taken the ones Rafe was using when she did the laundry today. She wasn't sure why it would have upset her to have her mother know she and Rafe weren't sleeping together. They'd been divorced for five years, after all.

"You don't look at all ill," Serena observed, helping Destiny adjust the fitted corners. "Your decision to come here must have been a wise one." Then she added with a tone of approval, "The years seem to have made Rafe even better looking than he was before."

"Yes," Destiny admitted.

"And you've never stopped loving him. Can you admit that now?" Serena plumped a pillow and tossed it down.

Destiny looked up at her to meet an observant gaze. From her mother that surprised her. "I'm trying hard to be sure I don't make another mistake." The reply was politely spoken, yet the implication that Serena, with her many failed marriages and her young boyfriend, wouldn't understand about that, was very clear.

Serena's brow puckered in pain, and she turned away to pull the blankets up. "That's very wise, of course," she said quietly. Destiny felt guilty instantly and hated both herself and her mother for it.

Rafe and Brandon arrived with the bags, still talking business.

"If I oversleep, please call me when Cara comes home," Serena asked as Rafe and Destiny said good-night.

"I will," Destiny promised; then she turned away from

her mother and the fit young man standing beside her. "Well..." she said to Rafe, horrified to feel color creeping into her cheeks. "We'd better get to bed."

Totally ashamed of herself, yet unable to behave differently, Destiny was sending him a silent message, asking him to pretend that they were going to bed together. She saw awareness of her ploy flicker in his eyes, followed by amusement, then finally, after what seemed an eternity, his consent.

"Right. I'm beat." With a "see you at breakfast," he put a proprietary hand at Destiny's neck and closed the door on their guests.

Her blush deepening, Destiny felt Rafe follow close behind her to the bedroom. She went inside and he stopped in the doorway, leaning against the molding with dark, taunting eyes.

"You should look embarrassed," he said very softly as she finally turned, pink-faced, to look at him. "What are we proving?"

Grabbing his arm, Destiny yanked him inside and closed the door. "I don't know!" she whispered harshly, leaning against the door as though a tiger waited on the other side of it. "I just...I just had to let her think—" She broke off in self-disgust and glared at him as she walked to the window. "I don't know why it was important, but it was."

"I know why you did it," he said, watching her from the middle of the room.

She spun around. "Why?" she challenged.

"Because at fifty, your mother's got an obviously adoring lover who's twenty years younger. While you, in your prime, don't even have your husband in your bed."

To her complete surprise, Destiny heard herself admit in a weak voice, "That's true." She folded her arms and turned away from Rafe, leaning against the window frame and staring out at the darkness. "What's the matter with me?"

"It's been a long day," Rafe replied gently, coming up behind her. "You've been working hard and you're tired."

She shook her head. "No, I mean what's the matter with me that…that I can't love her."

His hands fell softly on her shoulders. "You do love her. But you don't seem to like the fact that you do."

Destiny turned to look up at him, her eyes brimming. "Rafe, he's probably only thirty!"

His grip on her shoulders tightened, and he gave her a small shake. "Did it look to you like that bothered either one of them?"

"He's got to be using her!"

"For what? He's got more money than I have. And if all he wanted was a body, with his looks and money he could get some nubile seventeen-year-old."

She pulled away from him and paced the room. "Well, it'll never last."

"You don't know that."

She stopped, and her expression became judicious. "She blew it three other times and those husbands weren't half her age."

"Don't be judgmental," he advised, the quality of his voice changing from gentle to stern. "We blew it pretty well once, too, and she's not throwing it in our faces."

Destiny folded her arms. "I don't like him."

"You made that painfully apparent." He went to the head of the bed to toss the covers back. "Try to do better in front of Cara, will you?"

Rafe walked to the door and began to open it.

"Where are you going?" she demanded in a whisper.

He closed his eyes, obviously summoning patience. "To check on doc. I'll be back. I won't humiliate you by sleeping on the living room sofa, so just relax. We'll do our best to give every appearance of intimacy."

As the door closed behind him, Destiny changed into pajamas and got into bed, turning her face into the pillow. When Rafe returned she listened to his quiet movements as he prepared for bed, feeling guilty about her playacting fiasco. He flipped a switch, and the room was bathed in darkness.

When she felt him climb into bed and curl onto his side, facing the door, she called his name. "Rafe?"

There was a moment's silence. "Yeah?"

"I'm sorry," she said.

"Forget it. Go to sleep."

"Rafe?"

The silence was a little longer this time, his reply a little more tense. "Yeah?"

"How come you've always liked my mother?"

Rafe sighed wearily and rolled onto his back, turning his head to look at her. His dark eyes caught the moonlight from the window behind Destiny.

"I guess because I could identify with her," he said quietly. "She could never quite be what you wanted of her, either."

"She's had three husbands, Rafe." Destiny's voice was urgent though she fought to keep it down. "And several affairs. That's hard for me to admire."

"Can't you just admire and respect the part of her that loves you and Cara," he asked, "and try to understand the lonely woman looking for love? Forgive her for not being the perfect mother you wanted and just let her be who she is—the mother who loves you. All any of us can do is the best we can."

Destiny stared at the ceiling and relaxed into her pillow, letting her tired body sink into the old bed. For the first time that she could remember, she forgot the frustration she had felt at adjusting to a new stepfather, a new neighborhood, a new school, and tried to think what it had been like for her mother. She had always seemed so happy in her new relationships, radiantly beautiful, and then the little arguments had begun, the silences, and finally the move back to the house in Beverly Hills. Destiny had grown to resent her mother for what she thought of as her weakness.

Even as Destiny grew up enough to understand such things, she had always thought of Serena's many marriages and relationships as a search for sex and excitement—never as a search for love. Certainly love was worthy of a more noble effort than a brief commitment that ended in anger or in silence?

"Some people—" she sighed thoughtfully "—make it seem so easy. Like your mother. She married your father at seventeen, and at fifty-eight she still loves him."

He moved down farther in the bed, raising his head a little, then settling it back down in his pillow. "Maybe because she was lucky enough to give her love to the right man. For all the qualities you dislike about my father, he loves my mother with every old-world, chauvinistic, hard-nosed bone in his body."

"I wonder why some people pick the right partners and some people don't. And sometimes," she persisted, "it seems like even when the right people get together—it still doesn't work."

"That's because it's hard for any of us to be more dedicated to the unit than we are to ourselves as individuals. It's hard to give up or to compromise the things that are important to us in the interest of keeping the marriage together. Like my temper and your independence."

They lay staring at the ceiling for a long time, a foot of cool sheet separating them. Then Destiny reached out to Rafe, tugging at the arm that lay across his waist until she found his hand. She laced her fingers in it and with an uneven sigh leaned her forehead against his upper arm.

"Good night, Rafe," she said.

He rested his cheek against the crown of her hair. "Good night, Des."

CARA WAS DELIGHTED to see her Grandmother Fleming. Across the breakfast table she carried on in great detail about the play in which the entire family had become involved. Then she asked unexpectedly, "The play's in two weeks, Grandma. Will you be coming back from your trip by then?''

Destiny's eyes widened, knowing what was coming next. She looked at Rafe for help but he was feeding a begging Joe his last piece of *linguica*.

Serena looked at Brandon. He nodded. "We certainly can be.''

Cara looked delighted. "Then you could both come, too. Everybody's going to be here. Grandma and Grandpa Janeiro and…'' She went on to list every aunt and uncle and cousin.

"The kids will all be camping out in sleeping bags on the living room floor,'' Rafe said. "So we can promise you a bed to sleep in, but whether or not you'll ever get a turn in the bathroom is another story.''

Brandon laughed and put a gentle hand to the nape of Serena's neck. She leaned into it like a satisfied cat. "We'll take our chances. Sounds like fun. What do you think, love?''

Serena turned to Destiny, who forced herself to smile. Destiny knew her mother read the negative in her eyes despite her attempt to look hospitable. She couldn't remember Serena ever being able to read her mind before, and it made her uncomfortable.

Serena turned to Rafe. "We'd love to come, if you're sure we won't be in the way.''

"Of course not,'' Rafe assured her quickly. "Cara would love to have you and so would we.'' He smiled at Destiny, the gesture a curious combination of encouragement and threat. "Right?''

She didn't hesitate to reply, knowing there would be little point.

"Right.''

"Fine.'' Serena stood, planting a kiss on the top of Brandon's curly head. "Excuse me, darling. I'll go get our things together. We'd better be off before lunch. Want to come with me, sweetie?'' Serena asked of Cara. "We've brought something for you."

As the two walked off hand in hand, Rafe wandered away with Joe and Destiny excused herself from the table on the pretext of preparing a thermos of coffee for the trip to New Brunswick.

Frances was doing laundry and Destiny puttered around the corner of the kitchen nervously. She didn't like the way Brandon was watching her. It was as though he saw past all her efforts at civility to her discomfort around her mother and her distrust of him. Her suspicions were confirmed a moment later when he brought a stack of dishes to the counter and leaned against it, several feet from where she fitted the stopper on the thermos.

"What is it that you don't like about me?'' he asked without preamble.

She looked up at him, her surprise, if not her innocent expression, genuine. "I don't even know you."

He nodded. "And you don't particularly care to."

"Really…'' She began to phrase another denial but he interrupted her.

"Please. Your mother's the actress, not you." He studied her profile as she put the cup top in place. "Your mother loves me,'' he added quietly.

"I know,'' she said, her tone casual. "My mother has a great capacity for loving." It was a criticism and not a compliment, and Brandon's blue eyes darkened with instant anger as he recognized that fact.

"You apparently have no idea how true that is,'' he said. "How sad that you've inherited her beauty and none of her heart."

Destiny looked up at him, all attempt at civility stripped away by his candid observation. "And what are you hoping to inherit?''

His anger deepened at her implication and flashed hot and explosive in his eyes. But as he opened his mouth to reply Cara burst into the room, breathless.

"Gr…ah…Bran…ah…Mr. Gates."

Cara stood in the middle of the kitchen in obvious confusion. He turned to her, his expression softening.

"Grandma says she needs you," she reported. Then giggling over her stammering efforts with his name, she admitted with childlike honesty. "You're too young for me to call you Grandpa."

He took her face in his hands and kissed the irregular part in her hair. "Mr. Gates is pretty awful. How about Bran?"

"Okay."

With a playful tug on her ponytail, he disappeared into the living room.

As Rafe came through the open back door, Cara raced past him with a "Hi, Daddy! Goin' to Jenny's, Mom!"

Destiny turned to the thermos, fussing with the lid. It was apparent from her glimpse of Rafe's judicious expression that he had overheard at least some of her conversation with Brandon.

"That was cool, Des," he said, pouring himself a cup of coffee. "You managed to insult the woman he loves and accuse him of being out for her money in the space of thirty seconds."

She turned away from him and wandered to the kitchen door. "What about what he said to me?"

"About you having no heart? There are times when I'd call that an astute observation."

Destiny spun around to confront Rafe. A waft of delicious deep summer breeze floated around her, strangely at odds with the resentment boiling inside her. Rafe put his cup down on the counter with a bang and regarded her from several feet away, his hands loosely on his hips.

"That was a cruel thing to say about your mother and a thoughtless accusation to toss at him. You have been cold and flinging innuendos since they arrived. Were I Brandon, you'd now be wearing the contents of that thermos."

"Yes, well, we all know what a gentleman you are."

She spoke sarcastically, turning away from him with a haughty toss of her head. She uttered a little shriek of surprise as he took hold of her upper arm and pushed her firmly onto the porch. He closed the door behind them and forced her into a corner, imprisoning her there with one hand on the side of the house and the other on the railing.

"I have tried, Des," he said. Keeping his voice down was an obvious effort but his eyes were shouting adequately. "But the more I try to be understanding and to pull back and let you find your way, the more I wonder if it's worth it. You make all these demands on people—your mother isn't right, her fiancé isn't right, I'm not right. Yet you are free to turn a cold shoulder on your mother, accuse her fiancé of being a philanderer and stomp around in my life as though the only thing we all have to work toward is what you want. Well, there are things we need from you!" He stabbed her shoulder with an angry index finger. She felt as though it went through to her back. "I'd soft-pedal your self-righteous attitude until you've fulfilled some of your obligations."

Cornered, wounded by his verbal attack, she glared at him with brimming eyes. "What about the stability I never got from her or the freedom to grow I never got from you?"

"We both stand guilty," he admitted without pause, "but what about what you did get? I know your childhood wasn't a picnic, but she kept you with her, unlike many of your friends who spent their lives in boarding schools. Your life was disrupted, but her love was constant." His voice softened and he added, his eyes filled with anguish, "As was mine, even if I didn't know how to give it. But now that I think I do, you still keep slapping it aside. All summer we've been working according to your rules for establishing the kind of relationship you think we should have, setting standards and limits as you see fit—unless it suits your purpose to change the rules, like our little game of pretense last night."

With a sigh Rafe straightened away from her, jamming

his hands in his pockets. "Well, I'm not playing anymore, Destiny. I care about what you and I had, and I accept much of the blame that our marriage didn't make it. But there's a limit to what I'll put up with to make it work again." He sighed once more, his expression grim as his dark eyes went over her pink and tearstained face. "That isn't really what you want anyway, is it? You just agreed to come here to put me through my paces. Well, it worked. My life was hell without you, but if it's not going to be better with you, what's the point?"

Suddenly laughter and the bump of suitcases hitting the floor came from the kitchen, and Rafe reached into his pocket to pull out a handkerchief. He handed it to Destiny. "Mop up," he instructed brusquely. "I'll stall them for a few minutes."

Destiny managed to wave the travelers off with a smile, returning Brandon's polite thanks for their hospitality with a just-as-polite denial that it had been any trouble. His expression was wry as he gave her stiff body a brief hug for her mother's benefit, then turned to shake Rafe's hand.

When their car disappeared in a cloud of dust, Destiny hurried inside to her workroom and closed out the world while she put the finishing touches on her designs. She had yet to complete Rafe's costume but couldn't face the prospect of being confined with him for that purpose.

The first day of her incarceration, she worked and cried. The second day, she worked and fumed. By the third day she was able to recall their conversation without bursting into tears or throwing her drafting pen across the room. By the fourth day she could analyze what they had said to each other. And by the fifth day she could grant Rafe a few concessions.

Over the weekend Rafe and Cara were in town from morning until night for rehearsal, and Destiny ventured into the kitchen in search of food. Frances took the opportunity to stuff her with chicken and vegetables and challenged her to a game of Scrabble.

After half an hour of the game and the same amount of time spent with Destiny staring into space, Frances's gaze narrowed on the board. She leaned closer to look at the word formed by the collection of letters Destiny had put together.

"Yxwadu?" Frances asked, leaning back in her chair, her all-seeing blue eyes rolling heavenward in exasperation. "That'll make you a lot of points but it doesn't spell anything."

Destiny refocused her eyes on the board. "Are you sure?"

"I could consult a Swahili dictionary to be certain."

Destiny pushed away from the table with a defeated sigh. "I'm going back to work."

"How long are you going to hide up there?" Frances asked.

"I'm not hiding, I'm working," Destiny corrected, pushing her chair in, "and it's none of your business anyway."

"My caring doesn't stop at seeing that your house is clean and your stomachs full."

"It should." Destiny turned away to the door. "That's all I pay you for."

Destiny was ready to push through into the living room before she actually heard what she had said, registered the cold selfishness of her remark in her brain. She went back to the table and sat down, covering Frances's hands on the table with her own. "I'm sorry," she said, pulling her hands back to cover her face. "This summer has turned me into a monster."

Frances dismissed her apology. "It's all right. You've always been a monster. You're just lucky that some of us love you anyway. So what's happened between you two?"

"Nothing new. Another quarrel."

"You seemed to be doing pretty well until your mother's visit."

Destiny rested her forehead on her hand and closed her eyes. "She just reminded me how fragile marriage is, at the same time that Rafe realized what a poor bet I'd be a second time.''

"You are a little hard on your mother."

"She made life pretty hard on me."

"And you're determined to make her pay?" Frances made a scolding sound with her tongue. "I thought that kind of attitude went out with the advance of Christianity. No wonder Rafe gave up on you. I don't imagine any man would want to trust his love to a vindictive woman.''

"I'm not vindictive!" Destiny said loudly, dropping her hand. "I don't like her; she doesn't like me. We're uncomfortable together. Why pretend?''

"If she's uncomfortable around you, it's because you make her that way. She loves you."

"And I love her. I just don't like her!''

A sudden flash of Cara's wisdom came to Destiny's mind. 'Loving is liking, only harder.' According to that philosophy, if she loved her mother, there had to be something about her she liked.

"I like her." Frances squared her ample shoulders. "So she is a little nuts about her dogs, and she enjoys having the best of everything. She's always smiling and always kind and I'm sure, though she may have hurt you at times, she never meant to. And she loves that Mr. Gates. He's nobody's dummy, you know. I'd trust his judgment.''

Destiny leaned across the table toward her housekeeper. "He'd be her fourth husband, Frances."

"At least," the housekeeper said meaningfully, getting to her feet, "she isn't afraid to try again."

Watching Frances march away in a huff Destiny wondered why it was so difficult for her to assess and solve her problems, when solutions seemed so simple for everyone else in her life, including her housekeeper.

Chapter Ten

Destiny awakened Monday morning to the roar of the lawn mower. She glanced out her window as she passed on her way to the shower and saw Cara skip up to her father, reach her arms up for a hug, then scamper off toward Jenny's house. As Rafe moved on in an ever-diminishing square, Joe danced along beside him, barking, reacting ecstatically to an occasional pat on the head.

Under a hot shower Destiny forced herself to remember in detail their argument on the back porch the day her mother and Brandon left. Had she really been unfair to her mother all these years?

Turning her face into the hot spray, Destiny tried to remember a conversation she'd had with her mother during the summer between Destiny's junior and senior years in high school. Serena was planning to marry Roland and seemed to feel the need to explain to her daughter why her marriages hadn't worked.

"I was on the stage at three years old," Serena had said, sitting at the foot of Destiny's bed. "My mother emphasized my looks so much, and all she talked about was the money I made. I grew up judging myself strictly by those standards, and when men admired me for those qualities, I was ripe for the trap." Destiny remembered the heavy sigh that followed as Serena explained her first disillusionment. "Your father made such promises, but all he really wanted was a few nights with me and an introduction to my director."

Her memories sharp and vivid, Destiny recalled how disgusted she had felt at that revelation, wondering what would become of her mother when she was no longer glamorous enough to make money. With typical, youthful self-involvement she had felt no pity and no compassion, only superiority. And all she'd felt for her father was relief that she hadn't known him.

Destiny turned the shower off and stood quietly in the stall, listening to the distant hum of the mower. Now her mother was over fifty, still beautiful, with a young man anxious to marry her for whatever reason and a career that was still going strong.

And here she, Destiny, was—not yet thirty—feeling stalled between careers, with the only man who had ever loved her giving up on her.

Wrapping herself in a towel, Destiny went back to the bedroom, stopping to watch out the window as Rafe pushed the lawn mower into the garage. Her foreshortened view of him made him look all shoulders. Literally and figuratively, he had shoulders a woman could lean on. She had to smile as he disappeared into the garage. He had tried hard to break free of the macho traditions of his upbringing to understand her and be sensitive to her needs. He was ambushed occasionally by a still-volatile temper and a perfectly understandable successful man's tendency to think himself right in every confrontation—but he was never defeated by it. How many times over the summer had she seen him swallow his temper in the interest of reaching a compromise with her? How many times had he simply given in to whatever she wanted—and nobly, without the martyred air she often attached to her concessions.

As she pulled on a pair of khaki shorts and a pink sweater she tried to total up a list of things she had done to salvage their relationship. She sat down defeatedly on the foot of the bed when she realized the total sum of her efforts seemed to be that she had them sleeping in separate rooms.

The ring of the telephone jarred her out of her thoughts. She heard Frances answer it, then call, "For you, Destiny!" from the bottom of the stairs.

She picked up the receiver, her voice grim.

"Mrs. Janeiro?"

It was the play's director, Mrs. Barnes. Destiny tried to sound bright and in control. "Yes. How are you?"

"Frantic!" came the honest reply. "I would just feel a little more at ease if you could reassure me that you have the costumes under control and that they'll be ready for dress rehearsal Thursday evening."

"Everything's ready," Destiny fibbed. "And everyone's fitted."

"Ah!" Mrs. Barnes breathed a sigh of relief. "And the sets?"

"Finished."

"The ship?"

"It's beautiful."

"Bless you and your husband. You're bringing everything by Wednesday night?"

"Right."

"Bless you again. See you then."

That was it. She could stall no longer. Destiny went to her workroom and shuffled through her notes for Rafe's costume. The silk shirt and velvet jacket were nearly finished, waiting only for their final fitting, but the fabric for the pants remained on the table, as yet uncut. The argument they had when she had taken his measurements had left one vital statistic of his body unmeasured. She had procrastinated as long as possible in rectifying the problem. But if everything was to be finished and fitted in the next two days, she had to work on the pants now.

She approached Rafe with the news when he came in from mowing the lawn and was pushing his way into the bathroom to shower.

"Rafe?" She stood in the doorway to her office, trying to appear businesslike. But she was full of longing and mysterious regrets.

He turned to look at her, his disheveled hair and sculpted face, shiny with perspiration, making mincemeat of her efforts. His eyes were quiet, waiting. "Yes?"

"When you're finished in the shower, I'd like to try the shirt and jacket on you and get...another measurement."

He frowned. "You've run that damn tape from my head to my ankles," he said with sudden ill humor.

She sighed. "I missed something."

"What?"

She forced herself to look him in the eye. "The inseam."

He studied her a long moment, his eyes darkening. "You're kidding."

She studied him, too. "I wish I were. I forgot to take the measurement—we began to argue, remember? I've got to have it. We can't have the host striding the stage in ill-fitting pants."

He shook his head. "God forbid. I'll be out in about fifteen minutes."

Every inch of her body trembled as she yanked the tape measure out of her basket, brushed imaginary lint off the jacket and then paced the room to the accompaniment of the drumming shower.

Why was she so nervous? Where was the businesslike attitude she was so proud of? Her staff at the studio often laughed at the detachment with which she could take the most intimate measurements of a man.

She knew why her fingers were trembling, but it was difficult to admit it to herself. For all her noble words about their learning to get along before getting in bed, she wanted to be there with Rafe now, this moment, in that familiar indentation in his parents' old bed. She had longed for him for weeks.

Destiny was staring out her window at the neatly trimmed lawn when her office door closed behind her.

She turned to find Rafe standing just inside the room in white cotton Jockey shorts, his clothes slung over his right arm. He pitched them at the room's only chair and approached her with obvious reluctance.

As he moved toward her Destiny couldn't help her head-to-toe perusal of his beautifully proportioned, virile body. He was all carved angles and rippling muscle under brandy-colored skin. Curly dark hair covered his forearms and the long-muscled calves of his legs, triangled his chest and disappeared into the waistband of his shorts.

Her eyes ran up his body to his face and clashed in meaningful silence with his dark ones. She wasn't sure for a moment what she saw there; anger flashed, then confusion and uncertainty. Those emotions were so alien to the man she knew that she too felt confused, uncertain. To cover herself she became brisk.

She crossed the room to whisk the shirt off the hanger and hand it to him. As he pulled it on and shrugged it into place, she turned away to the jacket, her breathing shallow, hardly there at all.

"Well?" he asked. She had to turn around to inspect the fit.

She walked around him, trying to compose herself, checking the shoulders, pulling his arms forward to check the reach in the sleeve. It was perfect. He was perfect. Without the jacket he was a pirate in the silky white billowing sleeves. With his hot black eyes and shiny, dark hair, curly and wet from the shower, he looked every inch the brigand.

"That's good," she said, moving behind him. "Now the jacket."

He slipped it on, and she smoothed it across his shoulders, pleased to see that the puffy-sleeves fit beautifully. She came around him to pull the front together and judged it perfect. In the jacket, Rafe went from pirate to gentleman, his strong, swarthy face made more dramatic by the lace collar at his throat.

There was nothing left to do but take his inseam measurement. Destiny glanced up into Rafe's eyes to gauge his mood and then she saw it—fear. At this moment, under these conditions, Rafe was afraid of her. But why, she wondered, pulling at the tape around her neck. What did he have to fear from her? Unless he hadn't grown as casual about their relationship as she believed. Unless he really cared very much.

She turned away, taking the jacket from him and hanging it up so that he couldn't see the plot forming in her eyes. Hadn't five hard years on her own taught her that lack of success was not necessarily defeat—that you hadn't lost unless you hadn't the spirit to try again? How painfully simple, she realized with a sudden rush of adrenaline.

She took the shirt Rafe handed her and hung it up as well, carefully adjusting it on the hanger as though her life depended on it. She finally turned to him and knelt before him, suddenly able to assume the businesslike manner she had been afraid she'd lost. But her heart was pounding.

With an audible sigh Rafe planted his feet apart and folded his arms across his chest, prepared to endure Destiny and her tape measure.

Carefully she placed the tape at the juncture of his thigh and groin and held it taut to his ankle.

"Please don't squirm," she said coolly. "It's a critical measurement."

"Would you hurry, please?" he asked with much self-control.

"I'm trying," she said, dropping the measure and taking hold of his thigh to move him into a firmer position. "Now, be still. Please." She positioned the tape again, less careful where she placed her fingers.

"Destiny…" he said, his voice a groan.

"Yes?"

He did not reply, and she moved to the other leg.

"They're the same, Des," he said, his voice now strangled. "I've walked on these legs for years. They're the same."

"I can't guess, Rafe," she insisted, placing the tape again. "A hundred people will see you. There could be a fractional diff—"

Biting hands lifted her to her feet, then shook her. "Destiny, what are you...?"

And then he stopped, his angry eyes ensnared by something he saw in hers. Destiny had seen that particular scene of fury arrested by sudden passion filmed dozens of times while working for Olympus Films. She had always thought it phony until now.

She knew what Rafe saw in her eyes the moment he touched her. Desire rose in her and billowed, like smoke in a closed place. Her lips parted with the force of it, and her eyes grew dark with longing. She breathed his name, and her hands went up instinctively but hesitantly to his shoulders.

He pulled her to him, covered her lips with his hot, thirsting mouth and she caught fire. The kiss drew every spark of feeling from deep inside her, and for a moment combustion was out of control as his hands embossed her body with the texture of his own. Then he pulled back and studied her face for any sign of refusal. When he saw none he lifted her in his arms. She looped her arms around his neck and planted kisses in the warm hollow as he carried her to her bedroom.

She was divested of shorts, sweater and undies with his fascinating efficiency, and his shorts joined the pile as they settled into the indentation several generations of loving bodies had made in their old bed.

She felt like a different person suddenly, still composed of the same qualities that made her Destiny Black, but she felt like Destiny Janeiro at that moment—something she had never really felt even in the early years of their marriage.

And that understanding of herself made her bold. As

Rafe leaned over her on an elbow, she pushed gently on his shoulders, forcing him onto his back. She pulled herself astride his waist, reacting with a small convulsion of passion as his hands closed on her bare midriff. She half-expected him to protest her assumption of power, but he seemed ready to enjoy the advantages her position afforded him as his hands moved to mold her breasts. His eyes were smoky with desire, his hair a crisp black ruffle on the white pillow. His smile was languorous and wicked.

"Des," he whispered, bringing her face down until their lips touched. He covered her eyes, her nose, the line of her cheekbone and her jaw with kisses.

Destiny dotted his chin and throat with kisses, planting them along his shoulders, across his chest, teasing his nipples with them and the jut of his ribs.

Her hands swept over him, working magic, feeling his flesh come alive. The soft sounds of his pleasure spurred her on. She left kisses along his long muscular legs and started working up his body, stopping short of her objective when he sat up suddenly and brought her down on top of him.

He stroked the backs of her legs, her bottom, and moved his hands between their bodies to enclose her breasts. Then he crushed her to him until they were truly one flesh, stroking over her hip to part her gently and tease the warm, moist heart of her to life.

One hand held her fast against him and the other transported her to heaven and beyond. She lay against him in perfect stillness, poised on the maddening crest of ecstasy.

His sudden movement to tip her onto her back surprised her back to awareness and she resisted, pushing against him. After a moment's hesitation he lay back, and she put his hands one atop the other at his waist.

"My present to you," she said, leaning down to kiss him gently.

Then she worked her hands down his chest, over his hipbones, and this time, would not be stopped. His groan of pleasure fired her own, and she caressed him with her hands and her lips until he pleaded hoarsely, "Destiny! God..."

She led him gently into her, and for a moment the sensation of being filled with him was paralyzing. Then she moved slowly, carefully, a dancing rose on a stem, the breeze from the open window wrapping her in fragrance.

Pleasure teased her for only a moment before crashing in on her in a breath-stealing, overpowering undulation of feeling. She rode with it, Rafe drawn with her. It was excruciating and gentling at the same moment and she felt laughter and tears on her lips as they crested together, hands laced between them on the final wave of a shuddering climax.

When they lay quietly facing the sunny window, Destiny shaped into the spoonlike curl of Rafe's body, he kissed her shoulder and enveloped her in his arms.

Destiny leaned against him, absorbing his warmth and his love with a sense of wonder. She felt unalterably linked with him now—not merely because of the act of making love but because, between them, lovemaking was a communication beyond the physical. Wrapped in each other's arms, each seemed to become the essence of what they really were at heart—he, gentle and protective, she, generous and warm.

Why had she never understood that before? She'd been so full of anger and frustration when they were married, and he'd been trying so hard to prove himself that somehow the communication was lost. And earlier in the summer the renewal of their physical relationship had been such a heady experience there'd been little opportunity to analyze.

She turned in Rafe's arms to face him, her head lying on the pillow beside his, her hand reaching tenderly for his face. She traced his bottom lip with the pad of her thumb, then put her lips to his mouth in a gesture of affection. His dark, lazy eyes watched her, filled with satiated passion and touching tenderness.

"I love you," she whispered.

"I love you, too, *cara linda*," he whispered back. "See? This getting-along business isn't so tough after all."

Destiny laughed softly and settled into his shoulder as he shifted onto his back. "Maybe we're just slow learners."

Suddenly there was a sound like a herd of buffalo on the stairs, followed by a loud knock on the bedroom door.

Rafe looked at Destiny questioningly.

"Cara and Jenny," she said softly, then shouted at the door, "Yes?"

The door burst open and Joe was on the bed in a second, lying along Rafe's body and kissing both him and Destiny as though they'd been separated for weeks.

"Joe, get down!" Rafe shouted, while Destiny, laughing, protested.

"Oh, Rafe, he was just…" And then she noticed Cara, Jenny and two other little girls she'd never seen before standing in the doorway, staring.

"Cara!" Destiny gasped in reprimand, instinctively pulling the sheet up.

Cara looked instantly contrite. "Oh. Sorry. Mom, this is Candy, and this is Malinda. They're Jenny's cousins. They're visiting for a few weeks, and Mrs. Morrison was gonna take us all to the pool. Can I go?" Then turning to her father, she said in a pleased tone, "Hi, Daddy!"

Destiny considered explaining that it wasn't the lack of any introduction she was protesting, but rather the sudden audience disrupting an intimate moment. The four little girls looked so wide-eyed and interested that she gave it up. She smiled at her daughter's obvious delight at finding her father in her mother's bed.

"That's fine. Just make sure you obey all the rules and stay with the group."

"Okay." The foursome started to turn away when Cara turned back to add, "Oh. Grandma Janeiro called while you guys were in the workroom."

"Why didn't you come and get us, baby?" Rafe asked.

"I was going to," she said, shrugging, "but I saw you carrying Mom into the bedroom and closing the door, so I figured I'd better not."

Rafe closed his eyes, while Destiny bit back a peal of laughter. "I see. Thank you. What did Grandma say?"

"She said to tell you that the Janeiros are on the move. They'll be here tomorrow night."

It was Destiny's turn to close her eyes.

"Okay. Thanks, Cara. Remember what Mom said about the pool."

"Right, Daddy. Bye." With a quick kiss for each of them, Cara was gone, the foursome with Joe trooping down the stairs with the same deafening clamor with which they had come up.

Rafe settled back against the pillow, and Destiny cuddled into place against him. He was laughing over the intrusion of Cara and her friends while Destiny was frowning at the prospect of seeing all her in-laws again.

At best their sheer number and the level of their Latin enthusiasm and volatility was terrifying. Now she'd be faced with a sister-in-law she'd never seen before. Five of the seven nieces and nephews were strangers to her; and her father-in-law had never liked her and had never been shy to apprise her of her faults. Her mother-in-law was wonderful, but Destiny was plagued by guilt that she'd not kept in better touch with her, though she'd been careful to see that Cara did.

She came out of her thoughts as she became aware of Rafe gently tugging on her hair.

"Are you listening to me?" he asked.

She looked up at him and smiled, forcing down her fears, trying to hold on to her new victories. "Sorry. What?"

"I asked if you wanted to go to town this afternoon, since Cara's occupied and the horde will be descending on us tomorrow."

She kissed the hair-covered plane beneath his pectoral muscles. "Sure. Sounds great."

He made a small sound of pleasure, reacting to the touch of her lips. "Or we could stay right here."

"Let's go to town. And we'd better get groceries on the way back." Destiny got to her knees, ready to get out of bed, but Rafe caught her and pulled her back to him, her small breasts pressed against his muscle-plated chest. He noted her bright smile and his eyes rose past it to study the clouds in her green eyes.

"Everything will be fine," he said, surprising her with his perception. "No one in the family bears grudges, and I've always made it clear that I was equally to blame for our divorce. I'll try to keep my father out of your way."

Her concerns swamped by his kindness, Destiny kissed his throat and then his lips, and smiled again, sincerely this time. "I want you to enjoy this visit. I'll be fine, I promise." Then she frowned, remembering his costume. "But I'll have to seclude myself for a day to finish your costume."

"I'll personally stand guard at your door." He rose, pulling her to her feet. As she landed beside him on the soft carpeting he waggled wicked eyebrows. "In case you need a last minute measurement or something."

"How thoughtful. And you and Cara have dress rehearsal tomorrow night, don't forget."

"I'm starting to get nervous about this," Rafe admitted and, taking Destiny in his arms for one last hug before turning to the wardrobe closet, added feelingly, "this is going to be one hell of a week."

Chapter Eleven

Added to all the wonderful discoveries Destiny was making about Rafe was that he did indeed possess the gift of prophecy: the days that followed did compose one hell of a week.

Often during the next few days Destiny fought to find a private corner where she could revel in the memory of the idyllic afternoon she spent with Rafe in Digby Head. They had eaten a late lunch on the waterfront, at the end of a pier that stabbed out into the never-ending blue ocean. They fed a flock of hungry, fearlessly friendly sea gulls, then walked through the sunbaked streets of town hand in hand, sometimes talking, sometimes quiet. They went from one end of Digby Head to the other, then paced the same distance along the beach. Destiny had never felt so...so united with Rafe, and yet so free. It was as though whatever made them a unit, gave her some awesome power within herself as an individual. She tried to analyze that paradox and failed.

They came home with the trunk and the back seat of the car full of groceries and spent an hour helping Frances put them all away. Afterward they sat on the porch with Cara, Destiny leaning against Rafe, the child sitting on his other side, her arm in his.

"This is nice," Cara said softly as the sky went from cobalt to midnight blue and bright stars appeared. The breeze smelled of roses and salt, and the tang of fall.

"Yes, it is," Rafe agreed, hugging her closer. There was a pregnant silence, then Cara prodded warily, "So are we gonna stay together?"

When there was no reply for a moment, she added in a businesslike manner, "I'm only asking 'cause pretty soon it's gonna be time to unroll me for school."

"Enroll you," Rafe corrected with a laugh. "Although you do get pretty wound up. Unrolling you might work, too."

"You know what I mean," the child scolded.

Rafe's tone grew serious. "Yes, I do. Would you like to live here?"

"Not without Mom," Cara said, reaching out to cover Destiny's hand resting on Rafe's knee. "But I don't want to live in Beverly Hills without you anymore, Daddy." Large tears pooled in Cara's eyes in the moonlight as she looked at her parents. "What'll we do?"

The answer to that question as yet hadn't been formally discussed by Rafe and Destiny. Destiny felt a subtle tension in him as he waited for her reply. She didn't know if their relationship had developed to a point where they could safely remarry, but she knew beyond doubt that her world would come to an end without him. And the thought of separating father and daughter again after watching them together was too painful to contemplate.

Destiny turned her hand to hold her daughter's. "We're going to stay together," she said, leaning into Rafe's shoulder as he pulled them both closer. "Right after the play we'll enroll you in school and hope that we get good news on my sketches."

As though aware of her parents' inner struggles, Cara appeared relieved but not elated. There were variables, she knew, in an adult's world, and though neither parent had ever broken a promise to her, an occasional one had been altered to adjust to the unforeseen. Though she hadn't like it, she had understood it.

"All we can do," she said philosophically, quoting

something she'd heard both parents say when she was concerned about a particular challenge, "is the best we can. Right?"

Destiny's throat was too tight to answer, and she heard the emotion in Rafe's voice as he concurred. "Right. I love you, Cara."

"I love you, too, Daddy." Her declaration was followed by a mighty yawn.

"Sleepy, baby?"

"No," Cara replied, no longer philosopher, but again a typical child.

Rafe chuckled as she moved to settle herself in his lap and went promptly to sleep.

"How did you and I," he asked Destiny in quiet wonder, "with all our individual quirks, ever make this brilliant, beautiful child?"

Destiny sighed, pulling her cardigan sweater off and draping it over her daughter. "A miracle of some kind," she suggested. Then she tilted her head back, reaching her mouth up for his kiss. He gave it gently. "Or a love sprung from us as pure and generous as we intended it to be when we fell in love."

"We have to talk about getting married," Rafe said, startling her out of the comfortable neutrality she had been prepared to continue for a while.

She looked up at him in the dark and saw the light from the kitchen window gilding his strong profile. "Do we know that we're ready?" she asked softly.

For an instant he didn't move, then he looked down at her in grim surprise. "You just told Cara you were staying."

"Yes." Her agreement was instant, urgent. "Neither of us could live without you."

He studied her closely, as though trying to make sense of her reply. "Then doesn't that mean we're ready?"

"I guess it should." She looked away from him and out

to the darkness closing in around the porch. "But I'm afraid to promise you before God that I will be a perfect wife."

"The ceremony says nothing about 'perfect.'"

"No, but it has a lot of requirements I found hard—even impossible—to fulfill last time."

"Des!" Cara stirred at Rafe's raised voice. He shushed her, and when she relaxed against him he began again in a whisper, "Des, you keep confusing the last time with this time! Can't you see the difference?"

"Yes. I can. But I want to be sure."

Sure, Rafe thought, bracing his back against the pillar and shifting Cara in his arms. *Who the hell was ever sure about anything? With experienced savvy and sophisticated calculations you could plot the spot to drop the cage in the water and for reasons the most experienced skipper couldn't explain, the scallops weren't there. You could deal honestly, trade fairly, and every once in a while lose a customer to another company whose price was higher than yours. You could love a woman till you ached with it and have her turn to you with eyes that ripped your heart open, and tell you that she wasn't ready to promise you forever.*

You had to love the whole damn thing—the fish, the business, the woman—to have the heart to stay with it. The fact that he did was all that gave him courage.

He turned to Destiny and found her watching him, her eyes big and scared like a cornered cat's. He put his hand out to her, and she took it firmly.

"So, we'll talk about it again after the family leaves, okay?"

She looked grateful and relieved. "Okay."

Patience, he told himself with conviction. Patience.

His mother had left an appropriate message, Rafe thought, as he watched the three cars that comprised the family caravan pull into his driveway. "The Janeiros are on the move," she had said. They were like an army, and one half-expected to see the scenery change, trees felled and large craters made in the earth as they passed. There was Manny's van, Mike's station wagon and his father's ten-year-old Cadillac. Children peered out at them from every window.

Rafe tightened his grip on Destiny's shoulder and pulled her with him down the steps and across the lawn. He felt her momentary resistance, and then she moved with him in just the way he had begun to think of her, like the right half of his body. Car doors opened and children poured out, running toward them.

"Brace yourself," Rafe warned in an undertone. "Mikie thinks he's a soccer ball...oof!" A boy of about three, as round as he was tall, came running at Rafe, screaming, and launched himself as high as he was able, which was about the level of Rafe's thigh. The man reached down to scoop him up, bearhugging him as he giggled delightedly. Then Rafe was overwhelmed by the onslaught of the rest of the children while Destiny, stepping back to let them all close, felt left out and forgotten in a moment of lonely panic. Then a dark-eyed girl about Cara's age but of slighter frame came toward Destiny with a warm smile.

"Hi, Aunt Des," she said.

"Josie?" Destiny asked, cradling the upturned face in her hands. "Is that you?" Manny and Michelle's oldest child had been born just six months after Cara, and Destiny and her sister-in-law had swapped baby-sitting duties on a regular basis. Nervousness fell away as warm memories took hold.

Then Destiny's sisters-in-law descended on her with a horde of children, and she was occupied with trying to catalog them in her mind. Their peas-in-a-pod beauty and the black eyes, which seemed to be a part of each one's inheritance, would make it difficult to remember who belonged to whom.

Rafe's brothers were upon her, with bone-crushing hugs, behaving in the same affectionately abusive manner she'd been treated to the first time she was invited to the Janeiros for dinner all those years ago. A lump of nostalgia rose in her throat and threatened her composure.

"You leave her alone!" An imperious voice spoke at the same moment that a pudgy hand wielding a paper fan smacked Mike's arm. As he backed away from Destiny, protesting dramatically, Josephina Janeiro, half a head shorter than Destiny, came forward to put her arms around her.

"*Querida*," she said, her voice filling with emotion. "I'm so glad you're here." Josephina pulled Destiny away, gave her a long, tearful glance, then hugged her again. "So glad."

Over Josephina's shoulder Destiny saw her father-in-law approach and braced herself, clinging a moment longer to Josephina, loath to separate herself from the warm embrace.

Toby was shorter than all of his sons, but it was apparent that their good looks came from him. Though well over sixty, he was still handsome, with a thick shock of gray hair, a strong nose and eyes that saw and passed judgment on everything.

"So, Pop, how's it going?" Rafe appeared beside Destiny and advanced to embrace his father.

Toby gave Rafe what Destiny presumed was an affectionate slap on the back as he hugged him. It looked to Destiny as though that gesture, delivered with the same vigor in the right spot, could be fatal.

"So, genius," Toby said as he and his son pulled apart, "You made us all a bundle this year."

Sweet, Destiny thought. You probably haven't seen your son since Christmas, and the first thing you can think to talk about is money.

As though he read her mind, Toby Janeiro's alert dark eyes swung to Destiny, their expression not condemning but not entirely welcoming, either. Then Toby glanced up at his son, reading a subtle threat in Rafe's carefully calm expression.

"Good to see you," Toby said, taking Destiny's shoulders and giving her a token embrace. Then he added deliberately, "After so long. You're looking well."

"I am well, thank you," Destiny replied serenely. Around them, children and adults were shouting and laughing and carrying suitcases inside. Joe was barking as he and Mikie raced around the house. Destiny blotted the whole scene from her consciousness to devote every ounce of her attention to maintaining control.

"But I thought you were supposed to be ill?" Toby insisted, obviously implying that she looked fine to him.

"Rafe did bring me here because I was ill," Destiny agreed evenly. "But I'm better now. Will you excuse me? I should see that everyone gets settled in the right places."

As Destiny walked to the house, catching Mikie as he flung himself at her declaring a terrible thirst, she congratulated herself on keeping cool despite Toby's innuendos. Though she wasn't sure how far Toby intended to go with the taunts about her illness, she was sure he could unnerve her with them. She resolved to stay out of his way as much as possible.

AT DINNER the children sat at card tables in the kitchen with Frances supervising, and the adults were served in the house's elegant dining room. It was the first time it had been used since Destiny had arrived. The loud, teasing banter that had always been part of this volatile Latin family ran rampant. Dark eyes sparkled with laughter, curly dark heads bobbed and wove as they met in conversation, then leaned across the table to join another discussion.

Destiny was absorbed in the family's high spirits as though she hadn't been absent for five years. Mike and Manny teased her about her rise to prominence as a costumer and wanted to know just how naked the male stars were when she dressed them.

Everyone around the table fell silent, waiting for her to answer. Toby looked particularly interested.

"It depends on the particular actor's feelings about modesty," she replied with a quick glance at Rafe, who was also watchful. "If they're modest, there are dressing rooms in my studio. If they're not—I'm totally unaffected by a naked male. Sort of like a doctor." She shrugged her unconcern and found herself facing her indignant father-in-law.

"You work with naked men?" he demanded, his swarthy face darkening.

Destiny struggled to maintain her composure and save the evening's festive mood.

"They're usually wearing shorts," she said, surprised at finding herself on the brink of laughter.

"Doesn't that put you in a dangerous position?" he insisted.

"Not at all," she replied, the laughter bubbling up. "I'm the one holding the pin cushion. One wrong move and he'd be dressed to play a porcupine."

Everyone else's laughter joined hers, except Toby's. He looked at Rafe with the mild condescension that seemed to mark all his dealings with him.

"You allow that?" Toby asked.

"It wasn't my position to 'allow,'" Rafe replied quietly, stressing his father's choice of words. "We weren't married at the time. Anyway, it's a requirement of her job. If there ever was a problem," he said, a grin flying across the table at Destiny to remind her of the episode in their tenement hallway, "she's stronger than she looks."

Toby's reply was a snicker. It clearly said that Rafe had never had his wife in hand. Destiny took exception to Toby's attitude, but for Rafe rather than herself. She picked up the empty roll basket and got up from the table. "My attitude toward the man I'm dressing is always professional," she said, moving toward the head of the table where Rafe sat. "Besides..." She leaned over Rafe's back to nip at his earlobe in bold familiarity. "I've had Rafe's body. How could any man hope to compete?"

As hoots and cheers rose from Manny and Mike, and

finally from Toby, Destiny went to the kitchen for more rolls.

WITH RAFE AND CARA gone to dress rehearsal that evening, Destiny was forced to cope with Rafe's family by herself. Used to the large family get-togethers, Josephina and Augie had organized the older children to help clear the table and clean the kitchen, while Michelle started baths for the little ones in preparation for winding down what must have been a long day. The men wandered to the living room with glasses and a bottle of Madeira, and Destiny smiled to herself at how little some things had changed.

Destiny was running to the laundry room for more towels when the doorbell pealed. She smiled at the three men seated in the living room and walked past them to answer. Standing on the porch were her mother and Brandon.

For a moment Destiny just looked at them in surprise. She had almost forgotten in the hubbub of the Janeiros's arrival that Cara had invited her Grandmother Fleming to see the play.

"Hi!" Destiny finally said brightly, pulling them inside. She was surprised to feel like a beleaguered fort commandant whose reinforcements had arrived. "Come in, Mom. Brandon. How was New Brunswick?"

"Beautiful," Serena replied, caught off guard by Destiny's effusive welcome. "We took lots of pictures." Then she noticed the three men who had gotten to their feet and went toward them with the wonderful stage presence that had made her such a star. "How nice to see you all!" she exclaimed. "It's been so long."

WHEN RAFE AND CARA arrived home at eleven o'clock, the din from the living room was deafening. Cara ran off to find Josie, and Rafe smiled at the sound of laughter and excited voices. Destiny filled another plate with cookies and Frances's nut bread.

"Sounds like you've got everything under control," he noted.

She smiled at him over her shoulder. "Actually, you may attribute the success of the evening to my family. Mother is listening to your father's and your brother's stories with complete attention, and Brandon has hopelessly disarmed your sisters-in-law and your mother."

"What did my father say about Brandon?" Rafe asked warily?

"Nothing. I could tell he was thinking unkind things but he's been very polite."

Rafe looked heavenward. "Thank you, Lord," he said emphatically. Then he looked into Destiny's eyes with an expression that was not at all prayerful. "Are you ready for a romantic night in the garage?"

She asked with a grimace, "The garage?"

"There's not an unoccupied room left in this house. And I cleaned it up before I started building the boat. There's an old wreck of a sofa bed in there but it'll do." He leaned down to plant a small but fervent kiss on her lips. "And we can have some privacy."

Even when the decision was finally made to retire sometime after midnight, it was another half hour before everyone was settled and Rafe and Destiny were able to wander off to the garage. Rafe had already opened the sofa and placed a double sleeping bag on it.

"How come a single man owns a double sleeping bag?" Destiny asked him as he turned out the overhead fluorescent light. "Or is that a silly question?"

"I own it," he replied, climbing in beside her in the deliciously comfortable cocoon, "because I bought it in town this week expressly for tonight."

"You're so organized. No wonder you're so successful." She snuggled into his shoulder and let the warm contentment envelope her. Then a thought that had nagged her all evening came to mind and had to be expressed. "Rafe, why does your father treat you with such...I don't know...is it resentment?''

"Oh..." He considered the question a moment in the silent darkness. "I guess because I took over for him before he was ready to relinquish the helm of the business."

"It wasn't your fault that he broke his hip."

"I know." She could hear a small smile in his voice. "But it was my fault that I didn't fail."

She made a small gasp of confusion. "But why isn't he proud of that?"

"Some basic insecurity in himself, I guess. Through no fault of his or mine, I grew up to be very different from him, and we became almost like male animals in the wild, fighting each other for supremacy. When I got old enough to understand, at least somewhat, I stopped fighting him, but the time was right for new methods and a new approach and he resented the fact that I understood them. I guess I threatened his position and continue to do so."

"But he's retired. Can't he just be pleased that you've made the business such a success—that you still care so much about your family?"

"A man like my father never really gives up power. He's on the board, and he still fights me every step of the way. But the fight helps him forget the constant pain in his hip. It gives him a reason to get up every morning and have coffee with his cronies to discuss the wimpy, computerized younger generation. We all need a reason to keep going."

Destiny contemplated the complexity of Rafe's relationship with his father and the simplicity of his continued love and devotion.

"But doesn't it bother you that he treats you that way? He snickered at you at the dinner table!"

Rafe laughed and held her closer. "That was a very flattering remark you made in my defense. Thank you. Sure, it bothers me. But I'm tough and he's old, and I know he loves me—he just can't tell me. And I hate to ruin our get-togethers for everyone else by taking a stand. This has gone on for a long time, Des. We all just ignore it.''

She cuddled close, placing her arm around his waist as though to ward off the hurt she knew his father's attitude caused him. Rafe changed the subject with a chuckle. ''I think our play is going to be a hit. Your daughter, Sara Heartburn, is frighteningly good. I wouldn't be surprised if she's doing Shakespeare before she's twelve!''

Destiny laughed, looking up at him in the dark. ''She's that great, huh?''

''I don't pretend to know anything about theater, but she seems absolutely comfortable on stage, completely without fear. I was terrified, but she seemed quite at ease.''

''She probably gets it from her grandmother.''

Rafe held Destiny a little closer. ''Isn't it time you straightened things out with your mother?''

''Why?'' she resisted. ''She'll marry Brandon, then get divorced, and she probably won't visit me again until Cara gets married.''

''She doesn't visit you because you don't make her feel very welcome.''

Destiny thought about that and admitted to herself that it was true. Everytime they saw each other after a long separation, she expected her mother to be different. She expected to see regret in her eyes for all she had put her daughter through with her many marriages. Yet every time Destiny opened the door to Serena there was that same, hesitant hope in her eyes, that same wistful look that said maybe this time her daughter would understand her and be kind. It never failed to annoy Destiny that Serena thought the problem was her daughter's and not her own.

She tried to explain that ambiguous thought to Rafe.

''Yeah, I think I understand it.'' He wrapped both arms around her and kissed her forehead. ''It's a lot like my problem with my father. The trouble is, when you continue to try to make the other guy understand how you feel when he can't see it, it continues to keep you apart. All you remember is being hurt and scared, and all she remembers is that she loves you. Just put all that away and try to find someplace to start over. She's finally got a man who loves her for what she is rather than who she is. That can make everything in her life clearer. Give her a chance, Des.''

Wrapped in the warmth of Rafe's embrace, Destiny thought starting over with her mother didn't seem like an impossible task. Agreeing to remarry him seemed very logical. But she knew both decisions would change her life in the light of day. Standing on her own two feet, they would take on far more intimidating proportions. Yet she knew she had to do something about both, and soon. But for now the haven of Rafe's body made her push all difficult decisions aside and concentrate on being warmed and made to feel secure.

Chapter Twelve

In the front row of the Digby Head High School auditorium, nervously seated between Frances and Betsy Morrison, Destiny tried to clear her mind of problems with her mother and Rafe's father so that she could relax and enjoy the performance. But she found herself wringing her hands. No movie or stage presentation she had ever worked on had ever left her in such a state of panicky anticipation. She knew how hard Rafe, Cara and Jenny had prepared for this, and she knew she would die a little if one of them was embarrassed.

The theater lights went down, and the high school band struck up a sea shanty. Destiny turned her attention forward to see Rafe swagger across the stage. She settled down in fascination as he took a spot center stage and turned to the audience, arms akimbo, to begin the play.

There was a round of applause and shouts of laughter from his family and friends as he was recognized. He returned the greetings with a smile, never losing a word of the lines he delivered with all the authority Mrs. Barnes could have hoped for. Pacing back and forth, one hand loosely holding the hilt of a sword Destiny had designed and he had fashioned out of wood, Rafe played to a rapt audience.

His costume fit perfectly, Destiny noted with pride. Every muscle of his legs was perfectly outlined in the clinging pants; the square cut of the jacket gave him a larger-than-life look; the fussy lace trim made him even more formidable.

As he pointed to the parting curtains with a sweep of his hand and took a position stage right, the audience applauded.

Various characters made their entrances on stage—the shipbuilder, his wife, a seaman. Rafe reappeared to move the story along with an expository line or two, then Cara and Jenny ran onstage hand in hand.

Destiny braced herself and felt Betsy Morrison draw a shaky breath.

"The ship is ready, Father!" Cara cried, Destiny mentally repeating the lines she also knew by heart. "Mr. Longworth says you're to come to the dock immediately."

Destiny silently began Jenny's first line and realized in alarm that it was not being said aloud by Jenny. The child simply stood there, apparently the victim of a classic case of stage fright.

"Oh, no!" Destiny heard Betsy whisper to Jeff.

Jenny's line, "Oh, do hurry, Father," was finally spoken by Cara who darted to the man as Jenny was supposed to have done. She began tugging on his arm.

The man gently pushed the child away. "Go and tell Mr. Longworth that I'll be along," he said, speaking the line he was supposed to deliver to Jenny.

"Right away, Father. Come on, Charity!" Cara grabbed Jenny's hand and ran offstage with her.

As the curtains closed for preparation of the next scene, Destiny put a comforting arm around Betsy, who had both hands at her mouth. Did anything horrify a mother more, Destiny wondered, than the prospect of her child's embarrassment?

The house lights went down, and Destiny and the Morrisons braced themselves again. The next scene belonged to Cara and Jenny for a full two minutes. They were to stand on the dock, staring at Rafe's beautiful ship and discussing the romantic notion of running away to sea.

It was supposed to be an exchange of dialogue, Cara being the adventurous sister who found the thought exciting, and Jenny the cautious one, who offered arguments against it.

When Cara's first statement was met by silence from Jenny, she played the scene through, delivering both their lines as though she were arguing with herself. Yet she managed to involve Jenny and prevent her from looking like a paralyzed stage fixture. With an arm around Jenny's shoulders she walked her through their blocking, talking to her, finally asking her a question to which Jenny, with obvious effort, managed a simple nod. Everyone in the first two rows, Morrisons, Janeiros, and Serena and Brandon, heaved a simultaneous sigh of relief. Life was beginning to spark in Jenny.

By the middle of the second act Jenny was speaking her lines, if a little stiffly; Cara had become a favorite of the audience; and Rafe looked as though he had ridden the North Atlantic on a stage rather than a scalloper. By the last act the play had ignited. The cast, seemingly aware of the effort put forth by Cara on Jenny's behalf, and finally by Jenny herself in response, gave the final scenes their entire enthusiasm. Their performance ensnared the audience, and the curtains closed to absolute silence. Then Rafe walked onstage to deliver his final monologue, summarizing the importance of that event in Digby Head's history and describing what it had meant to the future of its residents. Then, hands joined behind his back, he went slowly offstage, softly humming along to the closing music.

The audience roared its approval, getting to its feet to demand the reappearance of the cast. There were calls for Mrs. Barnes who finally appeared after members of the cast literally dragged her onstage. She shocked Destiny by appearing thoroughly embarrassed. Then she went stage left, where Cara and Jenny hung back together and, taking each child by the hand, brought them forward. The applause was deafening, and Destiny sobbed helplessly. She had been so tense throughout most of the performance that she was just beginning to realize what her daughter had accomplished.

The next two hours were chaos as the audience congratulated the cast, then adjourned to the high school cafeteria for cake and coffee.

Mrs. Barnes cornered Destiny while the rest of the family was occupied. "Cara is something very unusual, Mrs. Janeiro." She gave Destiny a pained look and uttered a small, embarrassed laugh. "Or should I say, Miss Black?" She looked into Destiny's smile, then covered her own mouth with both hands in a gesture of horror. "To think that I was telling you that I wanted the costumes to be authentic! I am so sorry! I'm ashamed that I didn't recognize you instantly or that I didn't suspect anything when you brought the first costume for my approval."

Destiny laughed, liking this more human side of the formidable woman. "There's no reason you should have known. And I appreciated your demand for authenticity; it was your right."

"One of the other mothers recognized you. I felt a perfect fool. And to think that your mother is..." She waved a hand in the direction of the punch bowl where a crowd had gathered around Serena. "Well! It's no wonder Cara has such stage sense. We were all amazed by her very professional reaction to a situation that would have given most adults a few bad moments. Now, let me tell you what I have in mind..."

The family caravanned home, the Morrisons riding with Rafe and Destiny. Cara sat on her mother's lap to make room for Frances. Rafe drove while singing the sea shanty to which he had made his appearance on stage, Cara and Jenny singing heartily in accompaniment. Jenny was all smiles and giggles, forgetting that she had frozen on stage, remembering only that she had finally remembered her lines and been able to speak them. Jeff and Betsy Morrison each gave Cara a hug when Rafe pulled into their driveway.

Once in the house the family's congratulations were deafening, and Rafe and Destiny happily sat back while the child was fussed over by everyone.

Serena was beside herself with excitement. "She's got it, Destiny," she told her daughter, slipping down beside her on an upholstered bench. "She's a natural. And you know that isn't just grandmotherly pride talking. I know the business. I talked to that Mrs. Barnes, and she agreed with me. You are going to let her be part of Mrs. Barnes's theater group?"

"Yes, I think so. As long as it doesn't interfere with school and all the other things she wants to do."

Rafe leaped up to arbitrate a disagreement between two of Manny's boys, which threatened to get physical. Serena asked Destiny cautiously, "Are you staying with Rafe, then?"

"At least for now," Destiny hedged. "Cara loves it here."

"So do you, darling," Serena said earnestly. "Why is it so hard for you to admit? It would be clear to a blind man how much Rafe loves you. I've waited all these years to see that look in a man's eye."

Before Destiny could phrase a reply, Cara ran up to sit in her lap. She was flushed and sleepy, and Destiny felt the sudden warmth of this too fleeting moment in the parent-child relationship. Cara would be grown before either of them knew what had happened.

As a natural extension of that thought, she considered her relationship with her own mother and tried to imagine herself kept at the careful distance at which she held Serena. And she felt the brutal tearing of real pain. Destiny's eyes focused on her mother's, and she saw that pain reflected in her mother's face as Serena watched her daughter and her granddaughter embracing each other.

"Don't tell me you're finally worn out." Rafe walked up to them, distracting Destiny from her heavy thoughts.

Cara giggled from Destiny's shoulder. "I was going to the kitchen to get some milk but Mom's lap looked so comfortable."

"Well, come on. I'll help you the rest of the way." Rafe scooped Cara out of Destiny's arms and added, grinning down at his wife, "Will you come along? We need someone to pour the milk."

In the kitchen they found a calm Frances dealing with a mound of dishes and Mikie sitting on the counter beside her, chattering away.

"Mommy's looking for you," Destiny said, playfully poking his round tummy with her index finger. Mikie giggled infectiously, trying to push her hand away.

Frances very capably slung him onto her hip and started off in search of Augie. "Don't touch a thing!" she ordered over her shoulder as Destiny stared in dismay at the confusion in the sink. "I have a system. Just leave everything alone."

As the door swung closed behind her Destiny looked at Rafe. "We're going to have to give her a bonus for this week."

He sat Cara on the counter, letting her lean sleepily against him. "And probably a long vacation," he said, chuckling. Then he turned his attention to his daughter. "I've been wanting to talk to you all evening," he said, "but you were so popular I couldn't get near you."

Cara leaned away from him as Destiny offered her a juice glass of milk. "Thanks, Mom." She smiled impishly at her father, her eyelids drooping dangerously. "If you hurry you can do it now before I fall asleep."

"I want to tell you," he said gravely, "how proud I am of you."

"But you were really good, too, Daddy," Cara praised. "I think everybody was even better than they were at dress rehearsal."

He nodded. "Yes. But I'm not talking about your performance, although it was very good. I'm talking about something more important."

She looked sleepily puzzled. "What?"

Rafe smiled at his daughter, a mist of emotion in his eyes as they focused levelly on her. "You know how you're always worried about being clumsy?"

"Yeah."

"Cara, you have grace of spirit—something many adults never acquire. Physical grace will come as you grow up, but the grace you have inside is uniquely you and it's beautiful."

Still somewhat perplexed, though beaming under the praise, Cara said in a small voice, "Thank you, Daddy."

"Do you know what you did tonight?" he asked gently.

She thought a moment and shrugged. "I...kinda... covered for Jenny. 'Cause she was scared."

"You did better than that. You covered for Jenny, and you saved the show, but you didn't do it to make a heroine of yourself. You did it in a way that shielded Jenny long enough for her to find her feet."

Her eyes widened slightly. "Find her feet?"

Rafe smiled, translating. "Relax enough to remember her lines."

"Oh. Yeah. And she was really good once she got going." Cara handed Destiny her empty glass and slumped back against Rafe's shoulder, a rakish milk mustache on her upper lip. "The play was fun, but I'm glad it's over. Now we can do all the Digby Day's fun stuff. I hope they have candied apples at the fair tomorrow. Maybe you could win me a doll, Daddy."

Cara's voice was waning, and Rafe lifted her off the counter, holding her tightly against him while reaching his free arm for Destiny. "We're losing her fast. We'd better get her to bed."

Mike and Manny were helping the boys settle into their sleeping bags in the living room while Destiny ran to the laundry to check on a load of towels she had put in when they came home from the play. She discovered that keeping glasses clean and bath towels ready were two of the major hazards to being successfully hospitable to this large group.

She returned to the kitchen to find Rafe, her mother and Brandon sitting at the table, having a last round of coffee. The trio turned to look at her expectantly, as though she had been their topic of conversation in her absence.

"Want some tea?" Rafe asked. His eyes were steady and watchful. Destiny had a vague feeling he was in complicity with Serena and Brandon about something and felt herself stiffen. She prepared to reject whatever venture they had planned.

"No, thank you," she replied, continuing to the door with her burden. "I have to take these to the bathrooms, then I'm off to bed." She forced a smile in their general direction. "I'll say good-night."

"Des." Rafe's voice stopped her before she could open the door. "Brandon and your mother would like to talk to you." He took the towels from her and put them aside. "Come and sit for a few minutes."

Reluctantly Destiny sat at the table in a chair Rafe pulled out for her next to her mother.

"Don't look so frightened, darling," Serena said with forced lightness, her blue eyes registering the wary look in her daughter's face. "All we want to do is ask you to stand up for our wedding."

This was it, Destiny knew, her opportunity to push the past aside as Rafe had recommended and start over. But the fact that Serena had circumvented her to propose the idea to Rafe first only served to confirm how difficult communication was between them. Her mother was wearing that hopeful look, but Destiny could only stare back at her, lips parted to speak, unable to reply to the question.

As Destiny remained silent, Brandon's expression began to darken and her mother's eyes filled with pain. Serena finally looked down at her lap.

"Cara will be in school..." Destiny offered the first feeble excuse she could think of.

Serena raised her head, her eyes brimming and her mouth unsteady. "It's all right." She swallowed hard and held on to her composure. "I know how hard you've been working on your fashion sketches but..." She shrugged helplessly, and Brandon put an arm around her. "Well... Don't give it another thought. We'll...manage." She pushed away from the table and stood. "Well. Goodnight. We'll see you in the morning for the parade."

"I'll be right up," Brandon said, a threatening glance bouncing off Destiny before he smiled up at his fiancée.

"Darling..." Serena, having caught the look, put a restraining hand on his shoulder. "Please..."

He took her hand in his and kissed it. "Go on," he insisted gently. "I'll be right there."

The moment the door closed behind Serena, Brandon opened fire. "That is the last time I will let you hurt her." His voice was quiet but his fury was unmistakable. "We are leaving tomorrow and as far as I'm concerned, the next move in this relationship is up to you." He drew a deep breath as though anger was sapping his energy. "Your mother loves very generously, but from what I've heard of her past husbands and what I've seen of you, she gives it in all the wrong places and doesn't expect enough in return." Brandon swallowed with emotion, and Destiny kept her own indignant tears from falling with sheer force of will. "And still, she's willing to trust her love to me. I feel honored and humble. Trust is a quality of hers you could learn from. You seem abnormally stingy with it."

He stood, and though Destiny stared at the tabletop, she felt him look over her shoulder at Rafe, who stood somewhere behind her.

"Please don't feel we haven't enjoyed your hospitality, Rafe, and your family. Thank you for all you've done."

"It was my pleasure," Rafe replied.

Brandon disappeared into the living room, now dark beyond the kitchen door.

A deafening silence fell on the kitchen. Destiny felt choked by anger, by hurt and guilt, and by what she felt had been Rafe's silent betrayal. He had set her up for this encounter and been silent during Brandon's diatribe.

"Thank you for coming to my defense," she said with cold sarcasm. She continued to stare at the table as her eyes burned with unshed tears.

"Sorry," he returned heartlessly. "You had no defense."

Destiny sprang to her feet and ran for the door, but Rafe reached it first, holding it closed.

"Des, don't run away from this," he said firmly. "Stop and look at yourself. I know this cruel little witch isn't you!"

She turned to face him, tears finally spilling over. Trapped between his chest and the closed door behind her, she glared as though she had the strength to move him aside.

"Frances said I was a monster; your father thinks I'm a pervert; Brandon and my mother think I'm heartless; and to you I'm a witch. It seems to be unanimous!"

Rafe lowered his arm and rested his hands on his hips, his dark eyes unyielding. "Then maybe it's time you did something about it."

She glared at him, injured pride and a disorienting guilt making it impossible for her to think straight. She spun away from him and went to the lineup of hooks by the back door. She snatched her blue windbreaker and shrugged it on over the gray-and-white silk dress she had worn to the play. She went back to Rafe and held her hand out.

"Give me your keys, and I'll get out of all your lives. I'll come back for Cara when your family leaves."

Rafe studied her hand for a long moment. Finally he took it in his own large one and pulled her after him toward the

back door. "You're looking for an easy way out," he accused, "and I'm not going to let you have it."

She pulled against him, dragging her weight until he had
to stop on the porch. She noticed irrelevantly that the night
was velvety and fragrant.

"You mean you're going to revert to your Latin, chauvinist upbringing!" she shouted.

"You're damn right." He slung her over his shoulder
and marched across the pitch-dark yard with her into the
even blacker garage. He moved toward the middle of the
room, then leaned forward and loosened his grip on her.

She fell backward with a little scream, clutching for and
missing his shirt. In the darkness, the sensation was like
falling down a well. But she landed safely on the bouncy
sofa bed as the overhead light went on. The bright fluores-
cents outlined Rafe's workbench and tools, tires, a small
boat and a myriad of things stored in corners and hanging
from the rafters. It gave their sleeping quarters a bizarre
quality she hadn't noticed before. Everything looked
strangely alien as did the angry man standing over her.

"How dare you!" she huffed at him, slamming both fists
into the mattress.

"Five years ago when you left me," he reminded her,
sitting on the edge of the bed, "you were hurt because I
didn't try to stop you. Well, I'm trying to stop you now,
Des. Think about it. Is it easier to walk away from me and
all we can have together than to admit to yourself that
you're being a selfish shrew about your mother and to do
something about it?"

She found it hard to breathe. A curious softness was
trying to force its way through the anger and the guilt, and
she felt strangled by the struggle.

"I do love her," she heard herself say.

"Then she'd have to be a psychic to know it." His reply
was swift and condemning. He grabbed her wrist as she
tried to turn away from him. "Destiny, despite all your little
innuendos during their visit and all the times you've turned

away from her, she put her pride on the line and invited you into her life again. How could you have thrown it back at her like that?''

Destiny tried to think back to that moment, to explain the hesitation she had felt. Her wide, troubled eyes looked up at Rafe. ''She'll only get hurt again. She's the same person she was in all those other marriages. It's…it's just like us talking marriage. Have you and I really changed that much? In the crunch, I'm still bitchy and you'll still throw me over your shoulder to make me do what you want me to do.''

He frowned at her, trying to see through to her reasoning. ''Why are your mother's marriage and ours connected in your mind?''

''Because she's failed!'' Destiny cried, her throat clogged with tears. ''And I've failed! She's made a lot of mistakes and I'm…I'm a good designer, but I can't make a pattern for my life with you to save me! How do we dare try again?''

''Sweetheart.'' He took hold of her shoulders, leaning down to look at her when she tried to avert her eyes. ''Brandon said it. Trust. We trust each other to commit to our relationship and to back it up with every strength and resource we've got.''

''But how can we be sure…''

''Destiny!'' He put a hand on her arm as she turned away from him in frustration. Her rumpled hair shimmered in the bright light and parted at her neck as she lowered her head. His chest constricted at the grace of the delicate line that curved from the tip of her shoulder to the pale flesh at the back of her neck, bare except for a few golden strands. He knew her vulnerabilities as well as he knew his own—but he knew Destiny's strengths, too, and all the shining qualities with which she, herself, seemed so unfamiliar. They had come such a long way from Belleville Avenue. He had to make sure she knew that. ''Des—that's the flaw in your argument.'' She looked up at him, a small pleat between her brows. "You don't trust in things that are sure, you bet on them. And how many sure things are there? You trust in things that are full of warts but show potential." He caught her hands in his and squeezed them. "So you can be a shrew sometimes, and I'm a quick-tempered brute, and your mom's insecure, and my father takes out his misfortune on me. You don't have to be perfect to be lovable, you just have to be making an effort."

Destiny's eyes narrowed on him in concentration. He pressed his advantage. "I threw you over my shoulder because I needed another chance to talk to you, to try and make you see. We're not the dumb couple we were in New Bedford, but that doesn't mean we won't make other mistakes. I'd put up with you yelling at me any day if the trade-off to avoid dealing with that was losing you. And Brandon and your mom aren't going to give each other up because it'd be easier if they were the same age."

He studied her earnestly, trying to gauge whether or not she understood. She still looked so confused.

"I do want my mother to be happy," she whispered.

He framed her face in his hands and held on. "Then forgive her for having made mistakes. Forgive Brandon for being younger than she is and loving her anyway. Just trust them to love each other."

She shook her head doubtfully. "You make it sound so easy. And what about us?"

"It's simple. Forgive me for being less than the perfect man you want and try to balance my weaknesses with the depth of my love for you. Des, I think you followed your mother from husband to husband thinking that the next place would be perfect, that the next man would be perfect. Nothing is. *No*body ever is!" Rafe spoke the two syllables with emphasis. "Just trust yourself to love me, Destiny. Trust me to love you, and I swear to God on Cara's life that every time you turn to me I will be there."

Rafe saw Destiny absorbing all he said, striving to believe him, to trust him. He reached into the side pocket of his jeans, then put his trust in her on the line by taking the biggest chance of his life. He took her hand, opened the small, tense fist and put his car keys in it.

"Here, Destiny. This is how far I've come from Belleville Avenue. If you have the smallest doubt in me, or if total independence is really what you want, you're free to go." Then he hugged her to him. "But I want you to go knowing I love you. Good night, Des."

The keys were warm from Rafe's body, and Destiny clutched them to her chest as she fell sideways onto the pillow, watching him disappear into the black night. The keys represented everything she had once felt so important: personal independence, freedom from the harrowing business of fitting one's life into someone else's. Freedom from the responsibility of finding a way to love her mother.

She held the keys against her with both hands, feeling their teeth bite into her palm. They were precious not because they meant freedom, but because now that she held them, she knew she didn't need them. She was already free—free to love Rafe, free to forget the past and all its insignificant injuries, free to love her mother, free to be imperfect because Rafe loved her despite her imperfections—so much so that he would let her go if that was what she wanted. With access to freedom from all her problems in her hands, she finally realized that escape was the last thing she wanted.

Chapter Thirteen

Destiny smoothed the dress she had slept in and donned her windbreaker for the brief run to the house. It was only shortly after seven, but she could already hear high-pitched giggles and commotion across the yard. The children would be up and eager to attend the parade and all the other Digby Day's festivities. Frankly, she was eager, too. With a smile she gave the key ring a confident toss and dropped it in her pocket.

Orderly chaos greeted her in the kitchen. An unruffled Frances supervised a horde of shouting, laughing children eating cereal and fruit. Jenny and her cousins were also at the table, adding to the high-spirited confusion. The housekeeper gave Destiny a cross-eyed grimace and rattled an empty cereal box.

Observing that all the bowls had been filled, Destiny laughed. "We'll get more after the parade." With a hug for Cara and another for Mikie, and a kiss blown toward the other children, Destiny went through to the dining room in search of Rafe.

"Mrs. Barnes called this morning and asked him if he'd loan the square-rigger to the parade," Manny told her. "He took it right down. He says if he's not back, we should go to the parade without him and he'll catch up with us later. Want some breakfast?"

Destiny smiled, heading for the stairs. "Thanks, but I'll

see if I can get a turn in the shower.'' She raced upstairs, love and life and energy flowing through her like a heady blend of oxygen. She barely noticed the steps, felt the water of the shower in the miraculously empty bathroom nor heard her blow-drier as she fluffed her curly blond hair into order.

In jeans and wearing one of Rafe's long-sleeved white shirts over a red-and-white checked blouse, she went to the second-floor railing and leaned over, spotting Mike and Manny still sitting over coffee. "Is Rafe back yet?" she called.

"Not yet!" Mike shouted back.

She braced her hands on the railing and drew a deep breath. Well, that was just as well. There was something she had to do before she could dissolve blissfully in his arms anyway.

She smiled at Augie and Michelle as she passed them in the hallway, the pair giggling over Michelle's large straw hat. She proceeded to Rafe's office, the room Brandon and her mother shared, then pausing to summon courage, rapped firmly on the door.

It was opened immediately, and Brandon stood there in casual khakis, a camera and a roll of film in his hand. He looked surprised and then apologetic. "Destiny, I..." he began. But she cut him off politely.

"Excuse me, Brandon. May I come in?"

"Of course." Brandon held the door ajar, and Destiny passed through as Serena turned away from the mirror. She wore a khaki slacks outfit that matched Brandon's, and Destiny found herself smiling at the unutterable sweetness of love—shared by anyone at any time.

"Good morning, darling." Serena, too, looked surprised and just a little tense. "Are we holding everyone up?" She glanced at her watch. "Is it time to leave for the parade?"

"No, there's plenty of time." Destiny's voice faltered, and she seemed suddenly to have lost access to every word in her vocabulary. Out of the corner of her eye she saw Brandon move toward the door.

"Excuse me, ladies. I'll just..."

"No." Destiny turned to stop him with an uncertain smile. "You needn't leave. In fact, this concerns you, too."

Brandon put the camera on the bed and came back to Serena's side, putting a protective arm around her. She seemed all eyes and pallor. Her hair was caught at the nape of her neck with a white ribbon, Destiny noted. With her perfect skin Serena looked youthful and astonishingly innocent. Destiny finally understood that her mother had never meant to hurt anyone. She was simply on a quest, just like she, herself, was, like everyone was. But she hadn't been lucky enough until now to find the right man to trust with her love.

"I love you." Destiny heard the words before she knew she had spoken them and marveled at how simple they had been to say—how free she felt now that they were said. "I love you, Mom. I wanted to be sure you knew that."

Serena's face crumpled and she put her arms around her daughter, laughing and sobbing at the same time. They clung together for several moments, then Destiny pulled back. It was unnecessary to add anything more. They both knew they were very different women, with different needs and different goals. They might never be the chums some mothers and daughters were—though that eventuality looked less and less impossible. Yet it was important—no, critical, for each to know that the bond was there and precious to both of them.

Brandon took two tissues from the box on the dresser and handed one to each of the women.

"We'd love to stand up for your wedding," Destiny sniffed. At her mother's expression of shameless gratitude, she felt a twinge of pain. How little it had taken to make her mother happy and how long and selfishly she had withheld it. She turned to Brandon. "I know you're planning to leave this afternoon, but could you put that off a couple of days? After the Janeiros have left, we can make plans for the wedding."

Serena put a hand on her fiancé's arm. "Oh, Brandon. Could we? I'd love that."

"Then we'll do it."

"Good." Destiny squared her shoulders and extended her hand to Brandon. "Friends?" she asked.

For an instant he didn't move. Destiny stretched her hand out a little farther but he pushed it away.

"No," he said, then took her in a bear hug. "Family."

When Rafe hadn't returned ten minutes before the parade was to begin, Destiny sent everyone off and stayed behind to wait for him. Josephina insisted that she and Toby wait with her. Destiny was high on love and drunk with its power. Unable to sit at the table with her in-laws, for whom she had made coffee and spread out the Digby Head Daily News, she stood at the counter and put away the clean contents of the dishwasher.

Toby glanced at his watch and noisily folded the classified. "The genius is going to make us late," he complained.

Benevolence drained to Destiny's toes and she was suddenly filled with a warlike love, the kind that sent men to fight for their country, that made mothers shield their children without thought for themselves, that put wives squarely in the path of whatever would harm their husbands. With temper soaring in her like a flaming rocket, Destiny felt affirmation of what she had discovered last night. She was Rafe's and he was hers—and whoever sought to hurt him would answer to her.

Destiny took the chair that stood at a right angle to Toby's, ignoring Josephina's conciliatory effort to intercede. She tore the newspaper from her father-in-law's hands and tossed it on the floor as he looked at her with astonished brown eyes.

"You listen to me, Toby Janeiro," she snapped, her voice clear and strong. "I am in your son's life to stay, and

I am sick and tired of your condescension. Your son's name is Rafe. Or Rafael...." She gave it the Portuguese pronunciation. "Or you could call him, 'son.' I know he would like to hear you call him that." She glared back into his indignant dark stare and felt stronger yet when she noted the barest flinch. "But you will not call him 'genius' or 'college man' or any of the other condescending nicknames you use to deny his importance to you." She narrowed her eyes. "Or I will make you sorry. And don't think for a moment that I can't or that I won't."

There was a flare of genuine surprise in Toby's eyes. "He knows I...care for him."

Destiny nodded. "That's true, and it's hard for me to understand that kind of generosity. Without any encouragement from you, he's able to understand how you feel and love you back. With no sincere expression of feeling from you, he believes in you and your place as head of his family." She got to her feet and pushed her chair in. "Well, before I believe in you, you'll have to stop blaming Rafe for the fact that you got older and that when he took your place, he was even smarter and stronger than you. He feels that he learned from you and that he is what he is because he had you for a father. All your sons are wonderful, but Rafe is very special." The firmness in her voice began to wilt as emotion overcame her anger. Josephina was wringing her hands and Toby was ashen. Destiny realized for the first time the enormity of what she was doing, challenging the Portuguese patriarch. Had she a right to preach like that when it was a lesson she had only just learned herself? Of course, she did, she told herself, standing a little straighter, when it was in defense of Rafe. She wagged a finger at Toby, but her voice cracked. "If you hurt Rafe one more time, you... you will answer to me!"

Ready to dissolve into tears, she turned away from her father-in-law and marched for the back door, only to find herself halted by a stunned pair of dark eyes. Rafe was home.

Destiny heard him say her name as she stepped over Joe and ran past him toward the car. Not wanting to see the disappointment in his eyes caused by yet another of her shrewish displays, she pulled the car keys out of her pocket and ran.

Head down, all her attention focused on reaching the Mercedes, she couldn't help a perverse surge of disappointment that there were no pursuing footsteps, that Rafe had called her name only once.

She was within several yards of the car when something solid hit her in the small of the back, dropping her in the still-dewy grass as though she'd been tackled. Taking a few seconds to catch her breath, she felt a velvety tongue working over her face while its owner whined persuasively.

"Joe!" she gasped. The dog barked in excitement and anticipation of the promised ride. "You nit!" She pushed him away as she turned, groaning, onto her back. Bracing herself on her hands to sit up, she caught sight of Rafe moving slowly toward her across the lawn. Her heart began to pound. He looked very angry.

Joe kissed her ear, and she suddenly understood why Rafe hadn't chased her. He hadn't had to. Joe had already been in pursuit.

Rafe stopped at her feet, pausing to look down on her with an expression that was difficult for her to read. While it was obvious that he was angry, his expression was also filled with anguish and a hesitation totally foreign to the man she knew. He finally moved around beside her, pulled up on the knees of his jeans and squatted on his heels. His dark eyes went over her flushed and tearstained face with a grim uncertainty, finally settling on her watchful eyes. Despite the quiet of his anger, she felt the tension in him.

Irritated with herself for having lost her temper with his father when she'd had such hopes for the day, she reacted defensively to what she thought was his silent condemnation.

"Well, damn it!" she said angrily, sitting forward to dust

her hands off. "I will not..." She looked into his face so close to hers and repeated emphatically, "Not...let him treat you that way anymore. From now on every time he..."

He interrupted her tirade with the barest pressure of his index finger across her lips. "Where were you going?" he asked softly.

She noted the tensing of his jaw as he awaited her answer and was confused for a moment by his attitude. And then she was cheered by it. Was she to understand that he was more upset by the fact that he had caught her running away than by finding her shouting at his father? Then she remembered that he had arrived home to find her in a temper and running toward the car with the keys with which he had entrusted her. Her heart bled for him as she realized what he must have thought.

Frantically patting the grass around where she sat, she finally located the key ring at the base of a dandelion. She handed it over with a grin. Joe whispered a woof and danced excitedly.

"I was going to take a drive to cool off," she explained hurriedly. "It was either that or slug your father." He studied her another moment, and she reached out to gently stroke his knee, her grin vanishing, her eyes honest and intent. "I could never live without you again, Rafe. I love you and I need you. I'd like us to get married again. Right away."

He sat in the grass, one knee bent, and continued to study her for one interminable moment. Then the tension drained out of him with one joyous bark of laughter and he pulled her to him, tucking her between his knee and his chest.

"You scared the hell out of me, woman!" He kissed her soundly, then crushed her in a bear hug, his arms trembling with the emotion released in him. He pulled her away to look into her face as though hoping to read there what he was afraid to believe. After a brief perusal of her love-bright eyes and flushed cheeks, he shook his head slowly in wonder.

"My God, it's really there. You love me and you want to be with me. Forever." He breathed a broken sigh and asked softly, "Des, are you sure? I couldn't live through losing you and Cara again."

She twined her arms around his neck, loving the way he felt after her long, lonely night. She leaned her forehead against his chin and sighed. "Rafe, you can not only trust in that, you can bet on it. And you'll make a bundle." She looked up into his eyes, hers filled with love. "We're going to make it this time. The world has no freedom to offer that could ever compare with being bound to you forever."

"Oh, Des." He held her close, twining a hand in her hair and tugging gently until her lips were raised to his. "I'll try hard not to be too possessive."

She smiled as his lips came down, knowing his kiss would be possessive, despite his promise.

His lips paused a centimeter from hers. He smiled in response. "You're thinking that I can't do it."

"No. I'm thinking that I don't want you to." She reached up and took his kiss. "I finally understand that you're possessive because you love me and that loving possessively bears no resemblance at all to attempting to own. It's a different concept altogether. And I'm going to spend the rest of our lives being possessive of you, so please don't stop."

Rafe crushed her against him, granting her wish. When he finally pulled away, there was adoration in his eyes. He tucked a wayward strand of hair behind her ear. "I don't think I've ever been championed so eloquently or so bravely."

Destiny was about to express feelings of despair about his father when a voice from above their heads spoke with dry amusement. "Hey, Rafael! We're missing the parade. Or did you two have other plans for this morning?" Destiny looked up in surprise to find Toby standing over them,

Josephina behind him. He appeared to be his usual, cynical self but he reached a hand down to help Destiny to her feet. Then he helped Rafe up, retaining his son's hand, his eyes brooding.

"You know how I feel, Rafe," he said gruffly.

Rafe nodded. "Of course I do."

Toby turned to Destiny with an I-told-you-so expression. She folded her arms, standing firm. "That's only because he can read your mind after living and working with you for so long. I think you should tell him."

The men looked at each other, the gravity of the confrontation softening because the feeling, if not its outward expression, was there—had always been there.

Toby turned to Destiny, the barest nod of his head acknowledging her place in his life with budding respect. He turned and slapped Rafe's shoulder with that swing that could fell a tree. "I love you, son," he said.

Epilogue

"What do you think, Des?" Faye asked.

In the basement of the Trading Post, Destiny held up the
sample of toddlers' bibbed "short-alls" she would be delivering to Havilland House that afternoon. She inspected
the cuddly brown bear peeking out at her from a small
backpack she had designed in a coordinating fabric and
attached to the back straps with Velcro. The bear was
Faye's contribution to what had been a fun and rewarding
collaboration.

"I think Bear-Backs are going to be the hit of holiday
market," Destiny said, laughing. "And if my nephew
Mikie is a good indicater of the toddler consumer, we'll
make our fortune."

"Great. You don't think the pattern for the bear has to
be changed?"

"He's perfect. All we have to do is hope Havilland
House likes the finished product as much as they liked the
design."

Faye smiled at her friend as she put the sample back on
its hanger and covered it with plastic. "They seem to be
convinced that you're a genius. They loved your winter line
of leisure wear, and all your designs sold out at spring
market in November. Apparently you were ready to make
the change to fashion."

"Mom!" Cara shouted from the top of the stairs.

"Down here!" Destiny called up.

In a lavender wool coat and hat Destiny had designed, Cara came running down the stairs, flushed and excited. "Daddy says you have to hurry if we're gonna make it to the plane."

"All right. I'm coming." Destiny tossed the garment over her arm and hugged Faye. "Have a wonderful holiday," she ordered. "Then get back into bear production. I'll see you right after the first."

"Right." Faye followed the two upstairs to the door. "If you have time between your mother's wedding and Christmas with Rafe's family, let me know what Havilland says about it."

"I will, I promise. Bye!" Destiny and Cara ran out to the curb where the Mercedes idled as Faye waved from the shop window. It was bitterly cold, the sky muddy and threatening. But as Destiny slipped into the front seat beside Rafe, the bleak cold outside did nothing but intensify the cozy warmth and intimacy of the car.

"Sorry." She apologized for keeping him waiting. "We always get to talking and planning and forget what time it is." Destiny pulled the plastic up over the top of the hanger and held the short-all out for Rafe's inspection. "Here it is. What do you think?" She turned it over to show the backpack and Faye's charming bear. He laughed and leaned over to kiss her.

"I think you're brilliant. Are you two planning other projects together?"

"As soon as we come home." Destiny settled into her seat as Rafe pulled out onto the road. She cuddled close to him, resting her hand on this thigh. "Can you believe two whole weeks together without your work or mine interfering? Won't that be fun?"

Rafe thought about that. "Two weeks of noisy children, occupied bathrooms, ending with indigestion that'll last until February." He nodded grimly. Lots of fun."

Destiny elbowed his ribs. "You love it and you know it."

Laughing in agreement, he pulled onto the interstate highway. "I suppose I do. Are you buckled in, Cara?" He glanced into the rearview mirror.

"Yup." She tapped the metal buckle at her side. "Where did you say Grandma Fleming and Bran are going on their honeymoon?"

"Monaco," Destiny replied. "Brandon has friends there."

"And Grandma and Grandpa Janeiro are coming to Newport for the wedding?"

"Yes. And we'll drive back to New Bedford with them."

Cara squealed, overcome with excitement. "This is going to be so great. But how do we get from New York tonight to Rhode Island. Isn't the wedding day after tomorrow?"

"We're going to stay overnight in New York," Rafe explained, "See a Broadway show, then fly to Newport tomorrow."

"We're gonna see a Broadway show?" Cara asked in awe. Only the granddaughter of Serena Fleming, Destiny thought, would react to that news with the reverence it deserved.

Having heard the tenor of her voice, Rafe smiled at the road, thinking with ever-growing pride what a special child his daughter was.

Accurately reading his expression, Destiny patted his thigh, silently sharing his feelings.

"You know, I'm really glad you guys got married again," Cara said.

Rafe found Cara again in the mirror. "Oh?"

"Yeah. Have you noticed that everything's different? Not just big things, like the fact that we moved and that I go to a different school and that Mom's got a different job. But even the little stuff is different."

"How so?" Destiny asked gently.

There was silence a moment while Cara thought. "Well, there's a lot of laughing now. I mean, I always had fun, whether I was with you, Mom, or with Daddy. But now I hear you guys laughing and it makes me feel good, even if I don't know what you're laughing about. I like Saturdays 'cause we always do something, the three of us. I like going to the market with Mom pushing the basket and Dad throwing junk stuff in, like Twinkies and potato chips. And thunderstorms aren't so bad anymore. And we have Jenny, and there's Joe." Another moment's pause, then she asked suspiciously, "Are you sure he's gonna be okay while we're gone?"

"I'm sure." Rafe tried to make his voice emphatic but Destiny heard the emotion in it. "Frances wanted to have some time to herself. She'll take good care of him."

"I know. It's just that I'll miss him. But we'll all be together." Cara sighed, turning philosophical again. "I guess that's what I like best. Even when we're with Dad's family and there's a million people all over the place, we're still the three of us, and I'm always so glad to look up and see you guys there, even when I'm having fun with Josie. Oh, look!"

Cara pointed to a particularly beautiful snowy meadow and was soon making notes in her diary, a new compulsion since she turned ten a month earlier.

Destiny took the opportunity to speak softly to Rafe.

"That's what I like best, too," she said, stroking the taut thigh under her hand. "Just being us—even when you're across the room, or out of town on business, you fill my thoughts and my love for you affects everything I do." She snuggled a little closer, resting her head on his shoulder. "Of course, when you're right beside me, that's best of all."

Rafe put a hand across her knees and pulled her closer still, nearly overpowered by what he felt for her. If Cara was not in the back seat, he was sure they'd do something shocking at the first available rest stop.

Cara's diary closed with a decisive snap. "Now, can we talk about you guys having a baby?" she asked candidly.

Destiny's head snapped up in surprise, but Rafe looked down at her with a broad grin as he changed lanes to follow the highway to Portland and the airport. "Funny. That was my very thought."

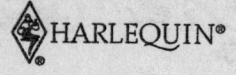

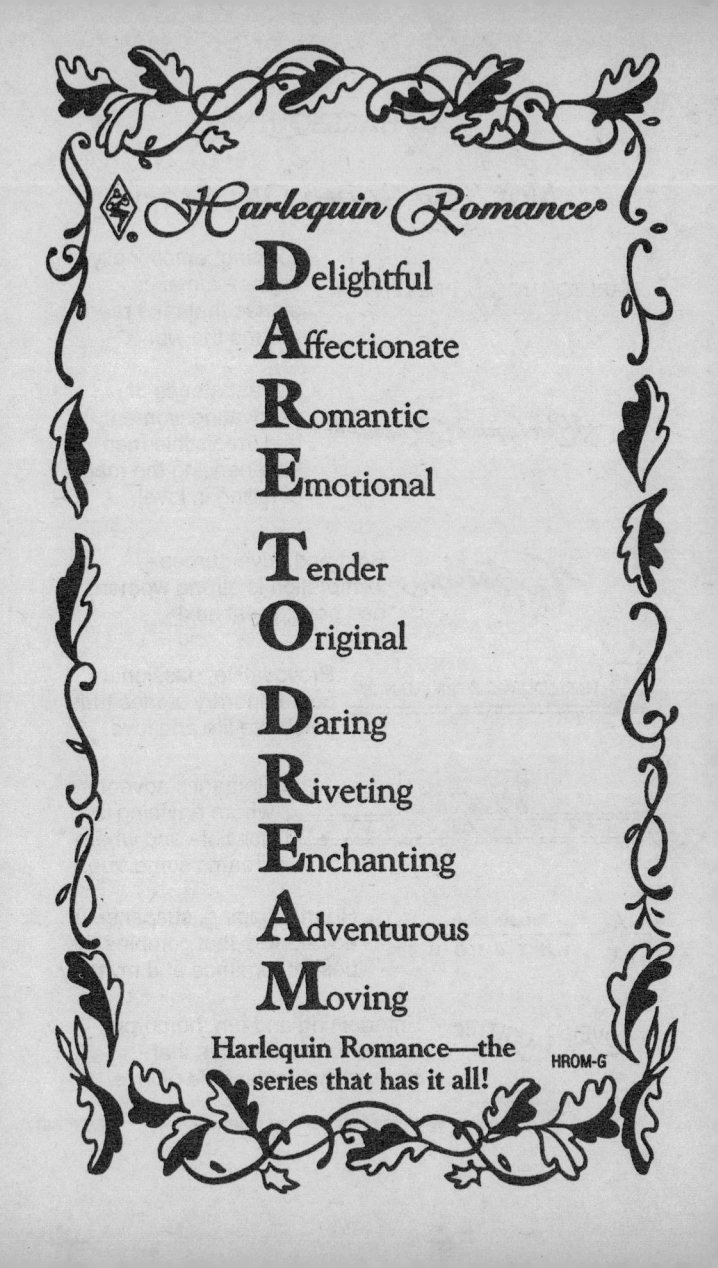

Harlequin Romance®

Delightful
Affectionate
Romantic
Emotional

Tender
Original

Daring
Riveting
Enchanting
Adventurous
Moving

Harlequin Romance—the
series that has it all!

HROM-G

HARLEQUIN  PRESENTS®

HARLEQUIN PRESENTS
men you won't be able to resist falling in love with...

HARLEQUIN PRESENTS
women who have feelings just like your own...

HARLEQUIN PRESENTS
powerful passion in exotic international settings...

HARLEQUIN PRESENTS
intense, dramatic stories that will keep you turning
to the very last page...

HARLEQUIN PRESENTS
The world's bestselling romance series!

HARLEQUIN®

I N T R I G U E®

THAT'S INTRIGUE—DYNAMIC ROMANCE AT ITS BEST!

Harlequin Intrigue is now bringing you more—more men and mystery, more desire and danger. If you've been looking for thrilling tales of contemporary passion and sensuous love stories with taut, edge-of-the-seat suspense—then you'll *love* Harlequin Intrigue!

Every month, you'll meet four new heroes who are guaranteed to make your spine tingle and your pulse pound. With them you'll enter into the exciting world of Harlequin Intrigue—where your life is on the line and so is your heart!

Harlequin Intrigue—we'll leave you breathless!

HARLEQUIN SUPERROMANCE®

...there's more to the story!

Superromance. A *big* satisfying read about unforgettable
characters. Each month we offer *four* very different
stories that range from family drama to adventure and
mystery, from highly emotional stories to romantic
comedies—and much more! Stories about people
you'll believe in and care about. Stories too
compelling to put down....

Our authors are among today's *best* romance writers.
You'll find familiar names and talented newcomers.
Many of them are award winners—and you'll see why!

If you want the biggest and best in romance fiction,
you'll get it from Superromance!
Available wherever Harlequin books are sold.

LOOK FOR OUR FOUR FABULOUS MEN!

Each month some of today's bestselling authors bring four new fabulous men to Harlequin American Romance. Whether they're rebel ranchers, millionaire power brokers or sexy single dads, they're all gallant princes—and they're all ready to sweep you into lighthearted fantasies and contemporary fairy tales where anything is possible and where all your dreams come true!

You don't even have to make a wish...Harlequin American Romance will grant your every desire!

Look for Harlequin American Romance wherever Harlequin books are sold!

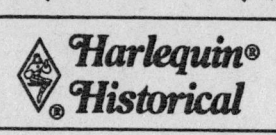

Harlequin® Historical

If you're a serious fan of historical romance,
then you're in luck!

Harlequin Historicals brings you
stories by bestselling authors, rising new stars
and talented first-timers.

Ruth Langan & Theresa Michaels
Mary McBride & Cheryl St.John
Margaret Moore & Merline Lovelace
Julie Tetel & Nina Beaumont
Susan Amarillas & Ana Seymour
Deborah Simmons & Linda Castle
Cassandra Austin & Emily French
Miranda Jarrett & Suzanne Barclay
DeLoras Scott & Laurie Grant...

You'll never run out of favorites.

Harlequin Historicals...they're too good to miss!